IF THE
SHOE
FITS

IF THE SHOE FITS

A **MEANT TO BE** NOVEL

JULIE MURPHY

HYPERION AVENUE

Los Angeles   New York

First Edition, August 2021
10 9 8 7 6 5 4 3 2 1
FAC-020093-21169
Printed in the United States of America

This book is set in Adobe Caslon Pro
Designed by Marci Senders

Library of Congress Cataloging-in-Publication Data

Names: Murphy, Julie, 1985- author.
Title: If the shoe fits / by Julie Murphy.
Description: First edition. • Los Angeles : Hyperion Avenue, 2021. •
Series: Meant to be ; 1 • Summary: "In this modern retelling of
Cinderella, plus-size Cindy dreams of becoming a shoe designer. But when
a spot opens up on her stepmother's famous reality dating TV
competition, Cindy is thrust into the spotlight in ways she never
thought possible"—Provided by publisher.
Identifiers: LCCN 2020043723 • ISBN 9781368050388 (hardcover) •
ISBN 9781368070140 (ebook)
Subjects: GSAFD: Love stories.
Classification: LCC PS3613.U7428 I34 2021 • DDC 813/.6—dc23
LC record available at https://lccn.loc.gov/2020043723

Reinforced binding

To Ian, mon petit chou

PROLOGUE

"Once upon a time . . ." a plump ten-year-old Cindy with golden hair pulled into a bumpy ponytail and cheeks flush with warmth said quietly to herself as she waited on the front porch, her chin resting on her kneecap with a poop-emoji Band-Aid stretched across an especially nasty scab. "A girl waited for her Prince Charming carrying the most precious cargo, hoping that if he showed up late, it would at least be late enough that her pizza would be free thanks to Marco's Speedy Delivery Guarantee."

Cindy dreamed of many things, but at the top of that list was the hope that someday she would cash in on that guarantee and finally get a free pizza. She'd come close many times, but victory had always escaped her.

A white Toyota Yaris covered in bumper stickers that said things like JESUS IS COMING, LOOK BUSY, and MY OTHER CAR IS A TARDIS pulled up short, breaks wheezing to a halt, as a lean teenage boy in a faded Marco's T-shirt stumbled out with a pizza in hand.

"It's about time!" Cindy said as she hopped to her feet. "You were this close to owing me a free pizza, Blake!"

At the sound of his name, Blake tripped on the curb, the pizza box nearly flying into the air.

Cindy couldn't help but cringe a little at the thought of her pizza landing facedown on the sidewalk.

"Did I make it?" Blake asked between panting breaths.

She checked her cell phone and then held it up for him to

1

see the time. "Barely," she said as she handed over her dad's crisp twenty-dollar bill.

Blake shook his head. "You'll get that free pizza one of these days, Cindy."

Cindy's cheeks flushed with heat. He remembered her name. The cute, much older teenage boy knew *her* name. And the free pizza? Well, that would happen eventually. It was fate, after all. Pizza was always fated.

She stood there with the warm box in her arms as he drove off down the street, and the moment his car disappeared into the hazy Burbank horizon, she ran back into her house. "Dad! Pizza's here!"

Cindy and her father, whose only religion was Thursday Pizza Night, sat in the living room, where they ate directly from the box. Their thirteen-year-old Pomeranian, Mac, circled the coffee table, chuffing in the hopes of a loose pepperoni.

Mac was three years Cindy's senior, and he'd miraculously outlived every possible medical complication to the extent that Cindy's father, Simon, joked that the dog might outlive him. Mac had been a peace offering from Cindy's father to her mother after a disagreement about wanting children. Cindy's mother, Ilene, was ready and her father was not. A dog, it turned out, was not the best thing to offer your wife when her biological clock was ticking. Simon saw the error of his ways the next morning when he found that Mac had not only torn through his favorite loafers but would also need a pricey procedure to excavate chunks of the shoes from his intestines. At least a child was unlikely to eat his shoes.

It took two miscarriages and three years of trying, but eventually, they got their miracle. Cindy Eleanor Woods. Even King Mac welcomed her with open paws. *It was meant to be*, Simon swore as Ilene held Cindy for the first time. And despite the years of disappointment and pain, Ilene couldn't help but agree.

Cindy loved hearing this story. She knew it was probably painful for her dad in many ways, but she adored hearing any memory about her mother that wasn't her own—whether because she was too young to remember it or it was simply before her time. They were surprise gems for Cindy to unearth. It was as though her mother were still alive in some reality, creating new memories to be treasured.

"Cindy, baby," her father said as he handed her a napkin. "I-I've got something important to talk to you about."

"Okay," she said with hesitation. Adults always said *important* when they meant *sad*.

"First, I need you to know that I love you very much." He shook his head and laughed to himself. "If your mother were here, she'd say I sound like an after-school special."

Cindy wriggled uncomfortably, a sad but encouraging smile begging him to get it over with already.

"I love us," he said. "I love the life we've made together, even if it's not how I'd always imagined it would be. And I don't want you to think that this has anything to do with me trying to replace our life . . . or your mother. No one could replace her. I know that all too well."

"Dad, just say it. It's okay. Just say it, please," she pleaded, remembering the fear she felt when her dad was so upset about her mother that he could barely get the words out. She knew her mother was gone, and all she wanted was for the news to come fast. To rip it off like a bandage.

"I met someone. Someone I really like."

Cindy nodded as she snuck Mac a piece of crust, though he promptly spat it out after realizing it wasn't pepperoni. "What do you mean? You've met someone? Like, at the store?"

"I've— I'm dating someone. And it's quite serious, actually." Simon chuckled, as though that surprised even him. "She has two daughters around your age. I think the three of you might really hit it off. If . . . If things work out, you'd have the sisters you always wanted."

Discomfort bubbled in Cindy's stomach. She *had* always wanted a sister or two, but that was back when her mom was alive to make that dream come true.

"I was thinking maybe we could all get together for dinner soon," he said.

"Here?" Cindy asked, glancing over to the kitchen, where she could so easily remember her mother and father cooking and fighting and dancing and doing all the things that made this little house feel like home.

"Well, no," he said, watching Cindy's gaze. "Not if you don't want to. Maybe we could start out on neutral ground. Maybe that mini golf place down the road with the great taco truck?"

Cindy nodded. Through all of this, her father had been her pillar. She knew he deserved to have someone to lean on too, but the thought of him with someone else . . . hugging, kissing, laughing, moving on . . . All of it meant one thing: Her mother really was gone.

"We'll take it slow," he said, seeing all the hesitation and anxiety furrowing in her brow. "And no matter what, we'll always have each other. Anyone else who comes into our life is just the cherry on top."

Cindy grinned. "I like that. The cherry on top." She couldn't help but wonder about her new potential sisters. Were they pretty? Smart? Thin? Funny? Mean? Cindy looked down at her round tummy and her mismatched pajamas. Would they like her? Cindy was a little bit of a loner. It was part of her only-child DNA.

Simon leaned back in his armchair with a worn paperback in hand and Mac in his lap, leaving the remote to Cindy. She flipped through the channels until a lineup of glittering women caught her eye. It looked like a beauty pageant, but these women weren't onstage. They were in front of huge white château that looked more like a castle than a house, with a stunning staircase leading to the massive front door and two turrets on either side.

Each woman wore a dramatic evening gown paired with the perfect high heels that made their legs look like they went on forever. There were ruffling hems and studded shoes, some with straps that went up around ankles like pointe shoes and others that were sleek and quiet in the same way a sports car could be.

A man with rippling black hair in a crisp tuxedo stepped out in front of the women and faced the camera. "Good evening, and welcome to the series premiere of *Before Midnight*. I'm your host, Chad Winkle. Tonight, I'm proud to bring you a groundbreaking social experiment from groundbreaking producer Erica Tremaine."

Simon looked up as Chad continued. "Twenty-four women and one very eligible suitor. Will they find love before the clock strikes midnight? Stay tuned."

The camera swept down the line of women, showcasing their rainbow of dresses and shoes once more, and Cindy, who was absolutely bewitched, let out a gasp. "All those shoes."

Simon put his book down, perplexed. "How do they balance in those things? Some of them look like they've got knives strapped to their feet."

"They're beautiful."

Simon chuckled. "Not as beautiful as you."

Her jaw dropped in feigned disgust, but her blushing cheeks couldn't lie. "Gross, Dad. I was talking about their shoes."

"When I met her, your mother had a closet full of shoes she never wore," he said. "She said she liked the idea of them."

"What?" Cindy asked. "What are you talking about? The only fancy shoes Mom ever had were those blue ones from your wedding."

The satin pointy-toe heels had been dyed the perfect shade of blue for their wedding day, but after a few years, they'd faded into a soft bluish white. Cindy kept them tucked under her bed in the box they'd come in, along with her mother's locket, hidden in the toe for safekeeping.

"She wore those shoes down the aisle and then kicked them off as soon as the ceremony began." Simon smiled widely. "Your grandmother was not happy."

Cindy didn't know much about her grandparents except that on her Mom's side they were pretty stuffy and thought that Simon was stealing her away from the comfortable lifestyle she deserved.

"But she also had a bunch of fancy work shoes squirreled away."

Cindy swiveled back to face the television. "If I were allowed to wear high heels, I'd put them on every day even it meant wearing them on my hands."

Simon snorted. "Good thing you're not allowed to wear high heels."

"Someday," Cindy said, her attention drifting from her dad back to the dazzling women lined up on the television screen. "Someday."

CHAPTER ONE

"Okay, wait," I say. "This time I'll sit on the suitcase and you try to latch it. Besides, I'm bigger than you by a lot."

Sierra holds an arm out to me with a sigh, and I pull her to her feet. "Cin, we've already made three trips to the post office to ship shoes home. Don't shoot the messenger here, but . . . you might have to part with some of—"

"Don't! Don't even say it, S!" I plop down onto the trunk with a defeated pout. "Is it such a crime to love shoes this much?" I ask. It sounds materialistic, I know, but each one of these shoes represents a moment in time for me. A pair I saved up for. A pair I bought for a date. For a wedding. A funeral . . . And even a few pairs I've crafted myself. Shoes aren't just an obsession for me. They're my life's work. Or they were, at least.

Sierra squats down and makes another attempt on the latches before looking up to me, her thick black brows furrowed.

"Give it to me straight, doc," I say.

"Three pairs," she says. "If you can part with three pairs, you might actually make it to the airport on time and not miss your flight. And before I hear even a squeak about getting on the next flight, you can't afford the change fees."

The words *afford* and *fees* turn my spine into a rod. "Okay, okay, okay." I stand up and flip the case open, running my fingers over each stiletto, sneaker, and wedge. Every last strap, ribbon, stud, and stone. Each of these shoes holds a story for me. It's not like I just walked into a Saks and bought my first pair of Manolo Blahniks full price. This is years of scouring clearance basements, eBay, Poshmark, and even craigslist for everything from Steve Madden to LuMac to Gucci. And some of these are even more precious than that. Some of these are one of a kind. Cindy originals.

I hand Sierra my red patent leather Kate Spade kitten heels. "You always liked them best," I tell her. "And really, I should have gone up a half size."

She holds them to her chest, her eyes beginning to glisten. "I couldn't," she says. "But I will."

I laugh and maybe even cry a little. When Dad died during my senior year of high school, I couldn't imagine what my future might hold or if I would even have any future worth imagining at all. I nearly passed on coming to New York and just planned to take some community college classes until I could figure out my next move. All I wanted was anything that felt familiar or reminded me of Dad, but the only family I had back home was my stepmom and stepsisters. And then I met Sierra—this effortlessly cool girl from a huge Greek family who can find common ground with just about anyone. If it wasn't for Sierra, I would have never made it in NYC. I don't believe in fate, but if I did, having Sierra as my freshman roommate would be the closest thing to fate that I could imagine. Now, with graduation just last week, Sierra is family, and she's the kind I chose. According to my dad, the family you choose is just as meaningful as the one you're born with. If, after four years at Parsons School of Design, Sierra is the best thing I walk away with, it will have been worth it. (And after the disaster that was my last semester, that just might be the case.)

I stuff my Balenciaga slides and my favorite loafers from Target into my purse and latch the trunk. (Hey, I'm not all highbrow.)

My phone vibrates with an alert. "My Lyft is here." Inhaling deeply, I try sucking back every brimming tear. "Okay, this is it," I tell Sierra.

I pull her close to me in a tight hug. "I love you, I love you, I love you," we both say over and over again.

"FaceTime every day," she says.

"Twice a day," I promise.

"And this isn't a forever thing, okay?" Sierra demands desperately.

Sierra is staying here in New York. Her internship turned into a part-time gig as an assistant to the assistant of the head women's sportswear buyer at Macy's. When she's not doing that she's pulling barista shifts to make ends meet. It may not sound like much, but it's bigger plans than I managed to piece together while I completely crashed and burned, barely making it to graduation.

I nod into her shoulder, unable to say anything without crying.

"We just gotta figure out our next steps. This nannying thing is only to get you on your feet. Temporary."

"Temporary."

We say one more tearful goodbye after loading my trunk, two suitcases, and carry-on into the car, and then I'm off.

"JFK?" the driver confirms as he taps the screen of his cell phone with another phone wedged into the crook of his shoulder.

I give him a thumbs-up, and we're off. I want to beg him to slow down so I can say a proper goodbye to this city and all my places. The 1 train stop on Twenty-Eighth Street. My bodega. My bodega cat. My favorite Peruvian chicken place. The jumbo screen outside of Madison Square Garden, always flashing. My favorite Korean beauty shop with all the best face masks. But, much like the past four years, it all passes in a blur, and before I know it, I'm waiting to board my flight with thirty minutes to spare.

I run to the newsstand in front of my gate to grab a few magazines, but the only offerings are various Kardashians and Sabrina Parker, so I grab three mini snow globes for the triplets and a bottle of water. Hovering around the gate is a cluster of men in slacks and sport coats, like someone might try to steal their business-class seats if they don't claim them first. My stepmom, Erica, sent me enough money to upgrade to first class. It was supposed to be a graduation gift, but I used the cash to ship most of my shoe collection across the country instead. Erica probably would've just paid for that too, but there's no handbook on cultivating a relationship with your stepmother and asking her for money after the sudden death of your father.

After Dad died, I spent six months living with my stepmom and stepsisters. Even though we'd moved in with Erica back when she and Dad got married the summer before ninth grade, those six months after he died felt like I'd been dropped in someone else's life. Erica and her daughters, Anna and Drew, knew how to exist without Dad. I . . . didn't. After I left for college, Erica began to build a new house that she finally finished last year. The only place that feels like home anymore is the apartment I just packed up.

My phone rings, and I expect it to be Sierra already checking in on me, but it's not. "Hey," I say.

"Darling," Erica croons. "Did you make it through security okay? We've got to get you signed up for CLEAR. TSA pre-check is almost always more crowded than the actual TSA line these days."

"I really don't fly that much," I say.

"The triplets are chomping at the bit, waiting for you. Can you believe they're turning four this summer? I'm sending my driver to fetch you."

"I can just take a Lyft," I say as I tiptoe through a clump of teenagers on a high school trip. "Excuse—" I teeter before losing my balance and catching myself on a random person's armrest.

A hand braces my arm, steadying me, and when I look up, I'm practically in the lap of a guy who could double as Prince Charming. Dark hair and deep brown eyes with flecks of amber and a hint of olive in his complexion. Our gazes lock, frozen for a moment.

"A Lyft!" Erica shudders. "The new rideshare pickup at LAX is an absolute disaster. An actual regression in evolution. I insist—"

"Hey, Erica? Sorry. I gotta go."

I push myself back up as the heat in my cheeks flares. "I'm so, so sorry," I tell Prince Charming.

He grins back at me, and his teeth are so white they could be photoshopped, except this is real life. "Ahhh!" he quietly fake screams. "Don't step on the lava!"

My brow furrows as I try to make sense of what he's talking about.

His smile droops. "You know lava? Like when you were little? The floor is made of lava! Jump from cushion to cushion!"

"Ohhhhh! Right, yeah, I was more of a reader, I guess?"

"I read," he says immediately.

"No, no, I didn't mean that you don't," I say, trying to recover.

"Now boarding Group A," says the gate agent through the static of the intercom.

Prince Charming stands, and of course he's tall too. "That's me. Uh, excuse me."

I double back. "Watch out for the lava!" I call as he circles around the row of seats to where the rest of the first-class passengers are lined up.

"Watch out for the lava?" I say back to myself.

Below me a group of teenagers chuckle. "Real smooth," says a white girl with thick brown curls slicked back into a ponytail.

"Could you not?" I snap back at her as I shuffle down the aisle and wait for my boarding group. I feel immediately bad for being a grumpy spinster. Mean teenage girls and awkward interactions with living, breathing Prince Charmings. Some things never change.

CHAPTER TWO

The minute I get on the plane, I immediately regret my decision to forgo business class. I shimmy down the aisle sideways so that my hips don't hit any of the business-class passengers while they enjoy their mimosas and Bloody Marys. When I make it to my row, a small, elderly women gets up from the aisle seat as I hoist my bag into the overhead compartment with a grunt.

Sitting in my window seat is the king of all bros—a white guy in a polo shirt with the collar popped and sunglasses with lenses so reflective, I can see my own disappointment staring back at me. Delightful.

"Excuse me," I say to King Bro, "but I think you're in my seat." I hold my phone out so he can see my digital ticket.

He doesn't budge. "Oh, we're going to the same place, sweetheart."

I can feel the crowd behind me losing their patience, and so am I. "That's right," I say in my best kindergarten teacher voice. "We are. In our assigned seats."

The guy grumbles and yanks the armrest up as he slides into his rightful middle seat. I'm forced to contort my body over his, which is no small feat for anyone, much less a plus-size girl in a flying tuna can.

I sit down and say a prayer that the seat belt will fit. You never know on planes. Sometimes the seat belts are just fine, other times I swear that the only people the manufacturers had in mind were children. Luckily, though, this time I'm able to safely buckle up without having to ask the flight attendant for a seat-belt extender.

I close my eyes and press my body into the wall of the plane. Either I'm going to sleep for the next six hours or I'm going to pretend to, because I'm not talking to this man-spreader any more than I have to.

Call it exhaustion or determination, but I pass out for the first two hours, and when I finally look out the window, we're somewhere over the sprawling plains of the Midwest. What wakes me, however, is my King Bro seatmate standing up to go to the bathroom.

The woman in the aisle seat looks over to me as he wiggles past her, and we share a knowing look.

I take the moment of freedom to reach into my bag for headphones and see what the airline has to offer in regard to entertainment.

"Excuse me? Miss?" a familiar voice asks.

I look up to find Prince Charming holding my Balenciaga slide out to me from the aisle. He looks down to the woman in the aisle seat. "Pardon my reach." And then back to me. "I think you might have lost this in our . . . kerfuffle."

I let out a snort. "Is that what you call it?"

He smiles. "I watch a lot of *Masterpiece Theatre*, okay?"

"Oh, really? Are you more of a *Downton Abbey* fan, or does *Poldark* really scratch that itch for you?"

"Well, since you asked, I'm ride or die for *Death Comes to Pemberley*."

"Okay, you really are an old woman."

The woman in the aisle seat eyes me.

"And there's nothing wrong with that!" I say too loudly, and find myself very grateful for the roar of the jet.

Just then King Bro is back. He looks to Prince Charming and squares his shoulders, nostrils flaring. Men like him are a species I have no interest in acquainting myself with.

"Hey, man," says Prince Charming.

King Bro tilts his chin upward. "Sup."

Prince Charming points to the middle seat. "That your seat?"

King Bro nods once, and I'm surprised he doesn't beat his chest to claim his territory.

"You interested in switching?" Prince Charming points back, a few aisles up. "I'm right there on the aisle. Extra legroom."

King Bro looks to me. "This guy bothering you?"

I can't help but let out a chuckle. "Uh, no."

King Bro eyes Prince Charming.

And then Prince Charming gives him a grin—the kind that works on every living thing. "Just wanting to catch up with an old friend."

King Bro laughs. "Well, bro, don't let me stop you! Exsqueeze me," he says as he stretches over the woman in the aisle. He lifts his head to me briefly. "Sorry, babe. Legroom calls!"

You know, the *exsqueeze me* had almost endeared him to me, but then he had to go and call me babe.

After a quick bag switch, Prince Charming is settling in next to me, and my mind begins to sputter about all the ways my heavyset hips might encroach on his space.

"I can put the armrest back down if you want," I tell him, already picturing the bruise it will leave on my thigh.

"Nah, I'm good." He reaches down between his legs and under his own seat, feeling around with a thoughtful expression on his face.

"Everything good down there?"

A sheepish expression passes over his face. "I . . . was checking for a life jacket."

I lean a little closer and whisper, "You know we're flying over an uninterrupted continent, right?"

"We could go down over a lake," he says very seriously. "Or a river. An exceptionally wide river. You don't know."

I hold my hands up. "Fair."

14

"It's not that neurotic," he says defensively. "I just want to be prepared."

I check under my seat quickly. "Tip-top shape here."

"Oh, if you think this is dramatic on my part, you should see me on a helicopter. I would rather lie naked in a pit of scorpions."

"That's . . . a visual," I say, unable to ignore the warmth in my cheeks at the thought of him naked.

"Who would even want to fly on a helicopter? If that propeller goes, you're done."

"They're like the motorcycles of the sky," I say, egging him on a little.

"Yes! Thank you. Well, now that you know my deepest fear, I can officially trust you to help me with my drop-down mask when the time comes."

"I swear to properly apply mine and then help all the surrounding children, yourself included."

"Thanks." His grin sparkles.

I feel that eager twitch in my chest like when your sense of humor perfectly aligns with someone else's. It's like scrolling through radio stations. Static, static, static, and then suddenly—*click!*—they're on the right wavelength.

We sit there for a few moments, completely silent, staring blankly into the screens on the seat backs in front of us. Finally, the woman on the aisle snorts before putting her headphones back in and returning to her crossword.

"Extra legroom? Is that all?" I ask. "You look like a first-class kind of guy." And he really does in his crisp white T-shirt, fitted dark jeans, olive-green bomber, and a pair of sneakers from a small brand out of Australia that is about to explode.

"Well, since you mention it, I was in business, but missed my first flight, so I took what I could get."

I groan. "There's nothing good about missing a flight."

He shrugs. "This isn't so bad."

I have to press my lips downward to stop myself from smiling like a total goober. "So what was it? Traffic? TV show filming on your street? Trekking to JFK is like a real-life hero's journey."

He laughs. "I was just second-guessing my trip. Thinking about putting it off or just canceling altogether."

I sigh, leaning back into my seat. "I didn't want to leave either, but I didn't really have any other options at the moment."

He taps around on his screen absentmindedly before pointing at the logo for *Before Midnight*. "You ever seen this show?"

"Once or twice, I guess," I lie through my teeth.

"You know, I heard that the single guys on that show are more well vetted than vice presidential candidates." He scrolls back a couple seasons until he lands on Tyler Buchanan's season. "And I know for a fact that this guy left the girl he chose for one of the producers on the show."

I have to grit my teeth to stop myself from mimicking exactly what Erica would say to this. *I cannot confirm or deny those allegations.* What Prince Charming doesn't know is that the producer Tyler fell for was a he, not a she.

"Is that true?" I ask. "Well, I don't know what kind of person thinks they could actually find true love on a show like that, but at least their foolishness makes for some good entertainment for the rest of us."

He cracks a stiff half smile and sighs. "At least it's good for something."

The flight attendant strolls down the aisle with a drink cart, and Prince Charming orders himself a whiskey. "And whatever she wants," he tells her.

The flight attendant practically preens in his direction.

I throw a hand up. "Oh, I'm fine with just ginger ale."

"Oh, come on," he says.

"Um, okay, just a champagne, then."

The flight attendant fills my plastic cup to the top, and it might be crappy champagne, but at least they're not skimping on it.

Once she moves on to the next row, he holds up his glass. "To missed flights and a transcontinental trip we might soon regret!"

I laugh and clink my cup against his. "To . . . that!"

For the rest of the flight, we both have our headphones in. I settle on old episodes of *The Office*, and he watches *Terminator 2*. (It doesn't count as stalking if you're sitting butt to butt with someone in economy, okay?)

When we land, almost everyone stands up the moment the fasten-seat-belt sign is turned off.

"There are two kinds of people in this world," he says as he shoves his headphones into his bag. "The kind of person who stands up immediately no matter how close they are to the exit door and the kind of person who waits in their seat like a civilized human being."

"Yes! Thank you!" I say. "This is my pet peeve."

I peer over the row ahead of me to see King Bro elbowing his way into the aisle.

"Looks like we know what kind of guy your old pal is," he says, nodding his head toward King Bro.

When it's our turn to go, Prince Charming stands up and helps as many people who need it with their suitcases. He takes one look at my luggage tag shaped like a stiletto. "I'm guessing this one is yours."

I laugh. "I've got a thing for shoes."

I work my way out into the aisle, but when I turn back to see where my new Prince Charming friend is, I see that he's stuck where I left him, still helping people with their bags. On the one hand, I find this very endearing, and on the other, I wonder how bad he is at setting boundaries in his everyday life.

Once I make it up the jet bridge, I race to the bathroom, because that champagne is going straight through me whether I like it or not.

When I make it out of the restroom, I wait for a few minutes, hoping to catch him. I didn't even get his name. After I give up on finding him, I hoof it to baggage claim, where a row of drivers in full suits is waiting with iPads on display reading their passengers' last names.

A tall bald white man in a black suit and sunglasses is waiting for me with a sign that reads TREMAINE.

I walk right up to him before he notices me. "Tremaine?"

"Oh yes, Ms. Tremaine?" he asks.

"Woods, actually, but Cindy is fine," I tell him. "And you are?"

"Bruce Anthony Colombo the Third, but you can call me Bruce."

"Good to meet you, Bruce. Are you new to Erica's team?"

"I wouldn't say new, but newly exclusive."

Erica's success has skyrocketed in the last four years, so it shouldn't surprise me that she now has a private driver.

"I've got a luggage cart." Bruce motions to the baggage claim. "Shall we?"

I smile sheepishly. "Um, you might need two of those."

We stand there waiting for ages. (Tip for LAX first-timers: Never—I repeat—never check a bag. Sadly, I had no choice.)

"Stuck in baggage claim inferno, huh?"

I turn around to find Prince Charming, a little wrinkled from the long flight and hair rumpled from fingers running through it.

"You too?" I ask.

He points to his carry-on. "Just here to meet my driver."

"Excuse me," Bruce says, "Ms. Cindy, it seems that a piece of your luggage was damaged in travel. It appears to be duct-taped together, and I think we might need to speak with the airline. All these airlines are the same. Can't even get a bag to the place it's supposed to be in one piece."

Damn it. I hope I didn't lose a shoe. There's nothing worse than an unmatched pair. "Oh, okay, yes, I'll be right there."

Prince Charming chuckles. "So that's your name. Cindy."

"I meant to introduce myself," I tell him.

"Well, I'm Henry," he says.

Bruce clears his throat. "It appears another bag—"

"You better take care of that," Henry says.

I nod. "Yeah, well, nice to meet you, Prin—Henry. Thanks for saving me from the lava and the world's worst seatmate."

He nods. "And don't forget the lost-and-found shoe service."

"Never!" I call over my shoulder as I follow Bruce to the customer service desk.

CHAPTER THREE

E rica Tremaine is a household name in this town. When I was in tenth grade, the *Hollywood Reporter* dubbed her the new reigning queen of reality TV. Her specific flavor and real moneymaker is reality dating shows. She started out on a late-night MTV dating show in the early '90s where one person drove a taxi around a major city while they went on a speed date with the person in the back. They picked up and dropped off multiple passengers, and at the end they picked the person they wanted to date. Things really took off for her when I was in middle school and she pitched a show called *Before Midnight*. Now she pilots an entire franchise, including *Before Midnight* and its various spinoffs.

She's not what I would call warm or even maternal, but my dad loved Erica and her two daughters, Drew and Anna, so I love them too. Not for what we have, necessarily, because they still feel like strangers to me in many ways, but for what our relationship symbolizes—my last living connection to Dad.

When Bruce pulls into the half-circle driveway in front of Erica's sprawling and completely renovated midcentury modern home in Silverlake, I see one of the triplets peeking through the curtain of the large picture window before someone yanks them back.

"Uhhh, just a minute . . ." Bruce mutters as he fumbles with his phone.

I peer over his shoulder and see him type in all caps: *THE BIRD IS IN THE NEST.*

My eyes well with tears as I put two and two together. I might be devastated to be leaving New York and my chosen family, but being home—even if home is a guest room in Erica's swanky new house that I only stayed in for a few days over Christmas break—makes me emotional.

Bruce catches my gaze in the rearview mirror. "Ms. Cindy, I'll, uh, bring your bags in if you'd like to go ahead."

I take my carry-on and leave the others for him. (I'd hate to ruin everyone's surprise or make them wait any longer than they already have.)

As I check the knob, I find the front door unlocked. "Hello?" I call, my voice echoing into the sitting room. "Anyone home?"

A tiny giggle comes from behind one of the armchairs.

"Helloooooooo?" I call again playfully.

"Surprise!" the triplets scream as they jump out from behind furniture with homemade signs clutched in their tiny fists.

"Cindy!" Drew and Anna screech in unison. They both prance out from the hallway in the trendiest yoga outfits I've ever seen. Drew in an all-white set with mesh up the leg, and Anna in a strappy taupe set that is just slightly darker than her actual skin. Both of them gazelle-like with perfectly sun-kissed light brown hair and their normally alabaster complexions tanned a few shades darker thanks to the DIY home spray-tan video they just filmed.

"Nice outfits!" I say as the two of them sandwich me on either side and the triplets go for my knees.

"You likey?" Drew asks.

"Thanks, babe," Anna says. "We were shooting a sponsored post earlier today."

"We could totally get you a set," Drew tells me.

Anna gasps. "Oh my God, the three of us should totally colab. Ahhhh! It's so good to have you home."

If Instagram were a living, breathing thing (and sometimes I think that perhaps it is), it would be Drew and Anna. They're often mistaken for twins, but they're nine months apart. Honestly their only distinguishing feature is Anna's birthmark on her shoulder and Drew's fuller lips. (Though last Christmas Anna got lip injections, and even Erica kept calling her Drew.) They both graduated the year before I did. For the first few months after high school, they tried school and a couple of different odd jobs, but eventually they started a joint YouTube channel called VeryNearlyTwins, and since then they've become full-time influencers.

"How was your flight?" Drew asks. "Was it warm nuts or room temperature?"

"Did you ask the pilot for wings?" asks Gus, his arms wrapped around my leg and a thin line of chocolate ringing his mouth.

"Oh, I totally forgot," I tell him.

"Did you bring us souvenirs from New York?" sweet little Mary asks.

"I might have a surprise or two in my bag," I say, thankful that I had the foresight to snag three mini snow globes from the newspaper stand next to my gate at JFK.

Jack does a dance and pumps a fist into the air. "Yes!"

My heart swells at their wild excitement. The triplets were born via a surrogate Erica and Dad had both picked out before he suddenly died. After some consideration, Erica decided to go through with it, and at first, I was so deeply angry . . . but then they were born, and it was like I got three little pieces of Dad back. It was like we all did.

"No, you see—" Erica walks in from the kitchen with her phone wedged between her ear and shoulder. My stepmother is the kind of woman who looks like a tall glass of water in anything, but most often opts for wide-leg pantsuits that nip in at the waist. Her silver hair is cut into a severe angular bob that perfectly highlights her sharp cheekbones. If Anna Wintour and Katharine Hepburn had a baby, her name would be Erica Tremaine. "Darn it! Did I miss the surprise?" She sighs, and says into the phone, "Let's put a pin in this."

"It's okay, Erica!" I say. I honestly wasn't expecting anything.

She beckons me to her with both arms, and I limp toward her with Gus still wrapped around my leg.

"My darling!" she says, pulling me close to her, and it's easy to lean into her affection, letting my body slump against hers. "Did you put on a sheet mask for the last thirty minutes of your flight like I told you to? Plane air just wreaks havoc on my skin."

"No, but I'll be sure to moisturize tonight," I tell her.

She lets go and takes a step back to get a good look at me, and I can see the way her eyes shift a little. And I see it too every time I look in the mirror: Dad. His jaw. His nose. His eyes. He said Mom was always so jealous of how much we looked alike.

"I'm so glad you're home," she finally whispers. "Okay, let's order sushi tonight! Anna? Drew? You girls better not have any plans. Family night."

Anna whimpers a little, and I think I hear her say something about a date, but Drew kicks her in the shin.

I'm so used to being here for holidays for just a few days at a time that I'm not sure what to expect from everyday life here. Is family night a regular thing? It wasn't when we were all in high school. In fact, there were a lot of nights when it was Dad cooking for the three of us kids and leaving a plate for Erica in the fridge. He never seemed to mind much. He knew what he was getting into with Erica, and family nights were not a regularly scheduled event.

After Bruce brings in my bags, Erica has a meeting to run to and ropes Anna and Drew into watching the triplets before demanding I take a nap and shower.

To my surprise, Erica has me set up in the little pool house off the backyard. She says I need my space (which I do, though this is way

more than I ever had in the city) and that it gave her a reason to reno-
vate the pool house sooner than later. It's definitely a step up from the
guest room next to the triplets.

After a long hot shower, I plop down on the bed to FaceTime Sierra.
The phone rings and rings, and just when I'm about to give up, Sierra's
face lights up the screen. It seems somehow impossible that I saw her
just earlier today. That moment feels so far away. The time difference
between NYC and LA makes for a very long day.

"C!" she shouts over blaring house music. "We're at Graham's! I
wish you were here!"

"I wish I were too," I tell her.

"What?" The speaker crackles. "I can't hear you!"

"Text me later," I shout in my otherwise-quiet room.

"Sierra! Get back here!" someone calls from behind her.

"C, I can't hear you, but I love you! I'm glad you made it okay. I'll
text you later!"

I nod and wave. The phone goes black, and I put it on my bedside
table before curling up on my side. This was supposed to be my big
year. I was going to graduate with an epic portfolio and get a handful of
incredible job offers. But that's not how my senior year at Parsons went.

Instead, all the grief I'd ignored and shoved off after Dad died hit
me all at once. Dad died. Erica went ahead with the surrogacy. And
I went off to New York to run away from my feelings about all of it.
Everything was fine. People were so surprised to see how well I'd dealt
with it all. But then Erica bought this new house last summer and I
came home over Labor Day to pack up my room and go through a few
of Dad's things Erica had saved for me. And it hit me all over again,
except then it was three years' worth of pain all bottled up just waiting
to be felt. Fresh waves of grief, not only for Dad, but Mom too, because
not only was it Dad's stuff, but also some of hers. Small pieces of

jewelry he'd saved for special occasions like graduation or my wedding. Everything I'd never have with them settled like a weight in my chest.

And ever since then, I can barely bring myself to even sketch. All the joy is gone. It's not an escape anymore, because there's no hiding from this kind of grief. But maybe someday it will quiet just enough for me to find my way back to design. Maybe . . . My thoughts slow just long enough for me to drift off to sleep.

CHAPTER FOUR

Anna squeals with excitement as she unpacks dinner, and Drew and I help the triplets set the table.

"That smells so good," Drew groans.

"Fork on the left, Jackie," I remind him as I come up behind him. "Mary, can you grab some napkins?"

"What about me?" Gus asks, his little glasses sliding down his nose.

"Gus, how about you take drink orders?"

He nods with a hop and runs straight for Anna.

Erica floats in from her office, inhaling deeply. "I need a gin and tonic."

"Gus, did you hear that?" I ask

He studies the little notepad he's begun to take orders on. "How do you spell that?"

Drew and I laugh. "I better go help him," I tell her.

I take over the adult drinks while Gus rounds up juice boxes for himself, Mary, and Jack.

After a few mixed-drink trial and errors (I'm no cocktail genius), the seven of us finally sit down at Erica's long dining table.

With Erica at the head, and me seated beside her, Erica takes out her Bluetooth earbuds and puts them on the table. "No more calls at the dinner table," she tells me.

"Wow," I say. "You've come a long way."

She laughs dryly. "It's a daily struggle. But my parenting coach says it's essential." She raises her glass.

"Parenting coach?" I ask.

"Yeah," says Drew. "Our dear mother has hired some kind of parenting guru to shepherd her through motherhood."

"Where was this guru when *we* were kids?" Anna asks with a snort.

Erica smiles and rolls her eyes. "The chaos of your childhood bonded the three of us together. How many other women could say they were raised in a production trailer?"

Drew shrugs. "A third of LA at least." She turns to me. "Erica's parenting coach has her doing dinner without interruptions, biweekly family nights, and get this—no more on-site production duties. She's passed the torch."

"Wow." This version of Erica—or really just the fact that she's here and not at work—is completely foreign to me.

Erica sighs. "It's true. They've tamed me. I miss the adrenaline of being on location, but a full night's sleep is a luxury I never knew I was missing." She clears her throat. "Okay, brood."

All around me, my stepsiblings raise their glasses and juice boxes.

Erica glows as all our attention turns to her. "Our sweet Cindy is finally home with us again. Cindy, my darling, we love you. I know you're figuring out your next steps, but whatever you do, your future is bright."

"To Cindy!" Anna says, clinking her glass with mine.

"You guys!" I say. It's no wild night with Sierra, but maybe being here with my family . . . for a season . . . won't be so bad after all.

I reach across the table and cheers with their wineglasses and juice boxes.

The triplets eat fried rice, while Anna, Drew, Erica, and I tear into the sushi. After the initial quiet that comes with the start of a good meal, Erica turns to Anna. "Is Victor coming by tonight?"

"They broke up," Drew says before Anna even has a chance to answer.

"Drew!" Anna says.

"If Mom knows you broke up with him, it'll be harder for you to take him back when he comes groveling."

"Well, that was a truth bomb," I say.

Erica reaches over Drew and takes Anna's hand. "I'm sorry, dear, but I know you'll find someone who truly deserves you. And can also hold down a job."

Anna huffs. "Victor had a job."

"Poorly managing your Poshmark closet doesn't count," Drew tells her.

"Ouch." I suck in a breath through my teeth. "You're better off, Anna."

It honestly blows my mind that Anna or Drew would ever put up with trash guys like Victor.

Erica's phone rings from inside her pocket, and we all look to her.

"Mom," says Anna, "you can answer. You don't have anything to prove by not answering your phone. It's no biggie."

"No biggie!" chirps Mary followed by Jack and Gus.

Erica pulls the phone out of her pocket and resolutely sends the call to voicemail. "Whatever it is, it'll be there for me to resolve after dinner," she says, like she's trying to convince herself. "Now, Cindy, tell me all about your senior project."

I open my mouth to tell her that my adviser cut me a last-minute break and let me exhibit some handcrafted shoes from my semester abroad junior year, that in actuality I could only bring myself to do the bare minimum for the last nine months, and that it's a miracle anyone even let me graduate. But Drew interjects herself. "It was balls-to-the-wall amazing!"

"Balls to the wall!" Jack shouts.

Drew bites her lip and whispers, "Sorry."

"Jackie," Erica says, "that's not something we say outside of this house, understand?"

He salutes her. "Balls to the walls!"

Erica rolls her eyes. "Can't wait to explain that one to Coach Geneva. Cin, I wish I could have been there for your senior project and for graduation."

"But you sent the next-best thing," I tell her.

Erica couldn't make it across the country—in the peak of casting season for *Before Midnight*—with the triplets in tow. She sent Anna and Drew in her place, who showed up to my graduation with literal cowbells and made enough noise when I crossed the stage to rival the large Italian family behind them.

"And then—oh my God," Anna says, "Cindy took us to this epic graduation party one of her classmates' parents threw on the rooftop of the Standard, and, like, I had a moment—cross my heart—where I thought maybe I could be a New Yorker."

Drew laughs. "That moment passed very quickly."

"It was brief but real!" Anna leans her head on my shoulder. "Cindy would have shown me the ropes, right, Cin?"

"Anna, my sweet sister," I say, the word still feeling a little weird in my mouth after all these years, "I don't know how to say this, but I just don't think you're cut out for public transportation."

Erica laughs so hard she's gasping for air, and the triplets look from one to another in confusion.

"Adult jokes," Gus says with a sigh.

Erica's phone rings again, cutting through our laughter. She glances at the caller ID and says, "Oh, shoot. This will only take a sec." She swivels to the side in her chair and speaks into her earpiece.

"I'm telling Coach Geneva!" Mary says in a singsong voice.

Erica inhales deeply, giving Mary a pointed look, and says, "Beck, you've got ten seconds. I'm in the middle of family dinner."

We all watch while she listens intently.

"You're here? At my house?" Erica sighs and turns to us. "Any chance we could set an extra plate?"

"On it," Drew says.

Erica stands and heads for the door. "All right, I'll buzz you in."

Moments later, Erica returns with a stout white woman with half-shaved black hair wearing combat boots and jeans rolled at the cuff with a white tank top and thick red suspenders—which it seems are more of a necessity than a style statement.

"You all know Beck," Erica says. "Cindy, you might remember Beck from the wedding years ago. She's sort of my—"

Beck plays at flipping her nonexistent hair. "Protégée!" Then her eyes widen as she notices me. "Wait. This is Cindy? Simon's Cindy? You're—you're a woman!" She turns to Erica. "She's a woman!"

Erica smiles, guiding Beck to an empty chair. "Our little Cindy is all grown-up."

Without a moment of hesitation, Beck reaches across the table to help herself to sushi, and with her mouth full, she says, "Big problem. Who blurbs dropped out!"

"Who?" asks Erica.

"Who!" says Beck, pointing at her mouth. "Who!" Finally, she waves two fingers in the air, and swallows the remains of her sushi with a gulp of water. "Two! Two girls!"

Erica groans. "There's always one or two. Who do we have in the wings?"

30

I watch with fascination as their conversation ping-pongs back and forth.

Beck takes another bite of tuna, and her eyes practically cross with satisfaction. "You know, I can't remember the last time I ate a meal at a table." She finishes off her bite and points her chopsticks at the triplets. "You enjoy this while it lasts, because one day you're thirty-two years old and eating a romantic dinner by yourself over your trash can so that it will catch the crumbs and save you the three minutes it would take to clean up after your damn self."

The triplets blink, staring blankly back at this strange creature who has very suddenly infiltrated their home.

I let out a low whistle. "That went bleak fast."

Beck grins. "And that's why reality television is never real." She holds up a finger to count. "We lost the virgin from Kentucky. Something about her grandma being upset or— I don't know. And then turns out the swimsuit model from Miami isn't bisexual. She's monosexual . . . for women."

"Oh," says Erica with a laugh in her voice. "Well, I guess that one worked out for the best. Though that would have made for some *delicious* television."

"I want to eat your brain," Beck says with complete sincerity.

"Mommy!" Jack screams, instant tears running down his cheeks as he darts around the table to Erica. "Don't let Beck eat your brain!"

Mary crosses her arms over her chest and says, "Jack, you baby, she's not going to actually eat Mommy's brain."

"You're right." Beck grins. "Because I only eat little children's BRAAAAAAAAAINS!" She gives her best zombie growl, and Mary and Gus both squeal with delight while Jack curls into Erica's lap.

Erica sighs. "We don't really have the time to vet any new contestants. Not fully, but . . ." She taps her index finger against her closed lips as she loses herself deep in thought.

31

All of us—even the twins—are completely silent so as to not interrupt any possible genius idea she might be sprouting.

"I've got it," she finally says. "Drew and Anna."

"What?" they both say in unison.

Beck gasps. "Twins."

"We're not twins," they both say.

"According to who?" asks Beck. "This is perfect. Twins? Twins! Our viewership will lose their minds!"

Erica turns to Anna and Drew, and I can't help but notice how absolutely perfect they are, even with their messy ponytails and work-out clothes. "What do you think, girls? Are you up for it? You've both been begging me for years. Besides, I think you'd both have fun . . . and now that you're a little older, I think you've got a better grasp on how to handle something like this."

I think what she means is that sending her eighteen-year-old daughters on the show just a month after high school graduation would have been a disaster, but now that they're older and have had some real-life heartbreaks at the ripe old age of twenty-three, they might not be so surprised to learn that the suitor didn't fall for them at first sight.

"Wait," says Anna, trying her best to temper her excitement. "Is this for real–for real?"

Drew gasps. "Who's the suitor?"

Erica clicks her tongue. "I can't even divulge that information to my daughters. But listen, if you do this, we need to keep our family connection on the down low."

"And hell!" says Beck. "We might as well throw in Cindy while we're at it!"

Anna and Drew both go wide-eyed and shriek. "Yes! The trio back together!"

They both wiggle and dance in their seats, and I can't help but smile at the thought of being included with them.

32

"Oh, we're only down two girls. Let's not mess with our numbers," Erica says in a no-nonsense tone that not even Beck crosses.

I'm so used to recusing myself. To pulling back before I can be pushed out, that my response comes naturally. "Yeah," I say. "I don't think I'm the right fit for something like that."

The idea of me joining the cast of contestants is quickly forgotten as my stepsisters obsess over every detail, like what they'll pack and who will dog-sit their Morkie, Gigi. While they talk logistics with Erica and Beck, I sneak off with the triplets and help them get ready for bed, including a bedtime story about how to save your mom from getting her brains eaten by her junior producer.

After the kids are in bed, I find Erica at the kitchen table having another drink.

I search the fridge and find a spiked pomegranate seltzer. "Do you mind?" I ask.

"Oh, honey," she says, "this is your house. Is the guesthouse to your liking?"

"It's gorgeous," I say. "In fact, I think I might just sit outside by the pool and enjoy this before bed if you don't mind."

"How about some company?" Erica offers.

"Sure."

I walk out through the massive sliding glass doors that Erica seems to leave open for the most part, and settle onto a teak lounger with black-and-white-striped cushions.

"Here. Bundle up. It's chilly." Erica sets her drink down and hands me a blush chenille blanket before she wraps a matching one around her shoulders and leans back on the lounger beside me.

We sit there in silence for a moment, searching for stars we know

33

are there if we could only see past the light pollution. After growing up in LA and spending the last four years in NYC, stars are some kind of elusive thing to me. I'm so used to not seeing them that when I finally do, they're breathtaking. Alas, no stars for me. At least not tonight.

"Thanks for putting the kids down," Erica says. "I meant to read to them tonight, but time just got away from me. Happens more often than I would like to admit."

"They were exhausted anyway. Besides, it sounds like you're really trying with this coach."

Her eyes search the hills above us as she shakes her head. "I wasn't supposed to do this without him. Anna, Drew, and I got by just barely. Some days I would call in sick for them because I couldn't get them to school that day. And then . . . in high school, but with Simon . . . things fell in place, sort of. The girls didn't need as much from me, and they had Simon too. But . . . he was a much better parent than I ever could be, so here I am, trying my best. For the triplets, but for him too."

With Erica, Dad was the one to beg for more kids. He wanted to be the stay-at-home dad to rule all stay-at-home dads. He wasn't shy about hinting at it, and of course Anna, Drew, and I were always encouraging him. Finally, Erica caved. It wasn't that she didn't want another kid with my dad. It was that she didn't want to be pregnant. So when Erica suggested they use a surrogate, Dad happily agreed.

The surrogate was a hippie from West Hollywood named Petra. Just days before she was set to be inseminated, Dad was struck by another car on the 405 as it was changing lanes. He was in their blind spot.

Eventually, Erica decided to go through with the surrogacy. She said it was her way of healing, and even though it was excruciating, I'll always be grateful that she made the decision to honor Dad by going through with his dream of having a baby. Even if they couldn't do it together. The surprise, though, was that instead of one baby, Petra carried three.

It was a bumpy ride with Erica trying to find her footing, but their nanny, Roxanne, was her saving grace. Then two months ago Roxanne met a girl and fell in love and decided to travel the world with a backpack and a laptop.

That's where I come in. Even though Erica is trying to be more present, the triplets have had a revolving door of sitters since Roxanne. And with little to no post-college prospects, it felt like the right thing to do was to come home and help out until Erica can find someone to be here full-time. I love the triplets dearly, but I also have to keep reminding myself that this is temporary and that hopefully someday— *one* day—my creativity will come rushing back.

Erica takes a sip of her drink and sets it on the little glass table between us. "You know, I was a wreck over missing your graduation."

"Honestly, it's fine. The day was total chaos, and it's such a long thing to sit through for five measly seconds."

"When the show is done filming, we'll throw you a big party, and I'll see about getting in touch with some fashion industry contacts I may have. I just can't believe someone didn't swoop in and nab you the moment you walked across the stage." She sighs. "Creative businesses are such fickle things. I'll put in some calls, but until then, it just means so much that you'll be here with—"

"Erica, can I ask you something?" Ever since Beck left, something has been festering at the back of my mind.

"Of course," she says, still a little startled that I interrupted her. The list of people who interrupt Erica Tremaine is very short.

"When Beck was here . . . why did you shoot down the idea of me going on the show? It can't just be the number of contestants. That's fluctuated before . . . and I know you need me here with the triplets . . ."

"Oh, darling, it's just a silly show. You wouldn't want to waste your time with that. You've got so much ahead of you. Reality TV is a perfect fit for some people, but for others, it can haunt them for years."

"Is it . . . Is it because I'm fat?"

She gasps and then chuckles nervously. "You're not fat! Don't say that about yourself."

Erica and I have worked through a lot over the years. At first, I thought she was some vicious power-hungry Hollywood big shot who would eat my dad alive. But for as much as we've grown, the one thing she still can't quite seem to make sense of is how to talk about my body.

"Erica," I say firmly. "I know what I am. It's fine. But is that why? Is that why you told Beck no?"

Her lower lip quivers for a moment and then she bites it, holding it in place. "Cin, the moment those girls walk into that château, they become internet fodder. I know you're beautiful and perfect, but others might not be so kind. I can't guarantee you any kind of special treatment once you're at the château. Cameras start rolling and that's it. I don't think I could live with myself knowing that your father left me to take care of you, and I let you become just another thread on Reddit about why some loser hates . . . plus-size people."

Something inside me bucks against that notion and says that I shouldn't have to alter my life because of some internet troll's opinion. But then again, I would never in my life go on this show. I have zero desire to be a part of something like that. One guy dating you plus twenty other women at once? No, thank you. And there's something about Erica being protective of me that makes me feel wanted and safe. Like family. Real family.

"You know I'd never go on a show like that anyway. No one finds the love of their life on a reality TV show." On a plane . . . maybe. Definitely not on a helicopter. I smile to myself and then dip my head down so I don't look like some kind of daydreaming idiot.

Erica laughs, obviously relieved to change the subject. "Such a skeptic, aren't you? What ever happened to magic? Fairy tales? Fate?"

I scoff. "I think fairy tales might be more like cautionary tales than

36

anything else. And fate is just an excuse for people to be inactive participants in their own lives."

We go back and forth like that for a while longer, laughing and talking about true love and statistical probabilities and nightmarish reality TV stars. I almost tell her about my random little meet-cute on the plane, because I know she'd eat that up, but soon I'm yawning so hard that my eyes are watering and I have to go to bed.

We say good night, and Erica gives me a kiss on the forehead as she whispers about how happy she is to have me at home. I can't help but wonder if it's because she loves me so much or the help I'm going to provide with the triplets. Either way, as I walk into the pool house and take a glance at the canopy of twinkling lights over the beautiful backyard, I can't help but feel like this place isn't my own. It's just another stop on a long search for home.

CHAPTER FIVE

"**M**ommy said not to wake her up!" a squeaky voice says.

"It's almost lunchtime," another says. "If we don't wake her up now, she'll sleep until dinner."

"I'm hungry," a third pipes in.

My speech comes out all garbled, so what I mean to say is *I'll be right there*, but what I do say is "Bright bear."

I force my eyes to open, but after sleeping so hard, even that simple act is dizzying. If it's already lunchtime in LA, it might as well be happy hour in New York.

"I think she's awake," Gus whispers.

I smile at the sound of his voice. "I can hear you three." Sitting up in bed, I let out a long stretch. "Is it too late for breakfast? I was really hungry for brain cereal!"

Gus and Jack shriek and run back to the main house with Mary stomping behind them. "Cindy doesn't eat brains!" she tells them.

After I brush my teeth and spray some dry shampoo in my roots, I pop open my trunk to choose a pair of shoes. I don't have many rules, but the first and most important among them is: shoes first.

I settle on my black Comme des Garçons Converse high-tops from the PLAY series with a red heart with eyes creeping up the side, and grab a yellow-checkered sundress from my carry-on that I managed to snag at a little plus-size resale shop in Brooklyn.

My first day as a nanny isn't really a first day since it's Saturday and Erica made me promise to sleep in. (Apparently, I'm a woman of my word.)

What I don't expect when I walk toward the kitchen is to find Anna and Drew frantically planning an epic shopping trip while they guzzle pressed juice. Erica is sitting at the formal dining room table with two laptops and three phones. Beside her is Beck, who looks like she definitely did not sleep since I last saw her.

"Whoa, did I just walk into mission control?"

"Good morning! Good afternoon!" says Erica.

"We brought you a green juice," says Anna, not looking up from her iPad as she and Drew map out their plan of attack.

"Oooh, thank you," I say, though I think I might need something a little more substantial than pressed juice.

I find the triplets with their noses pressed to screens while they play games and watch videos on YouTube of other kids playing with toys—something I'm not sure I can actually wrap my head around. "Okay, who wants some grilled cheese?"

The three of them turn to me, practically drooling.

"I'll take that as a yes."

I head into the kitchen, making sure to crack open my green juice, and start an assembly line of bread, cheese, and mayo. (Mayo is better on grilled cheese than butter. Prove me wrong. I dare you.) Soon, the smell of the sizzling cheese creates an audience, and just like that I'm making eight sandwiches instead of four.

When Beck's sandwich is almost ready, she settles onto a barstool opposite me on the other side of the island. "Erica tells me you're designing shoes now?"

I flip a grilled cheese over and try not to scoff. "I wouldn't say actively. Right this moment, I'm making grilled cheese." I glance up to Erica on the other side of the vast open-concept living/dining room, who has a phone wedged into the crook of her shoulder, a pencil between her teeth, and her fingers hovering above her keyboard.

"And doing a mighty fine job," Beck tells me.

"Glad to hear it." I sigh. "But yeah, I went to school for design. Shoes. And clothes. And handbags. And anything I could fill the pages of my sketch pad with. But shoes were my first love."

"You're a real find, Cindy." Beck leans across the island, and her voice drops a few octaves. "You should know I wasn't kidding about you joining the show."

I shake my head and tuck a stray hair behind my ear. "I'm not cut out for reality television. Besides, you heard Erica."

"Leave Erica to me," she says.

"You sure that's safe?" I ask with a raised brow.

She shrugs. "Who better to convince the master than her apprentice?"

I slide Erica's grilled cheese onto a plate and run it over to her.

"Think about it," Beck says when I return. "Most of the girls that go on this show don't show up for love. They're there for exposure. Their big break. There's nothing wrong with that. You think the suitor's intentions are always pure? This could be huge for you as a designer. Audiences would love you."

"Erica seems to think differently," I say under my breath. Besides, I don't really have much to offer as a designer at the moment.

Beck leans in even closer. "Erica is scared," she says as though she knows exactly what I'm talking about. "She's iconic. I idolize her. But when you're an idol, you don't have to take risks. It's time for America to see women of all shapes and sizes go after their dreams."

"I wouldn't say my dream is some random dude who's looking to up his status with a starring role on a dating show with over twenty other women. . . ."

40

"Can you even fathom what it's like to go to bed one night totally normal and wake up the next morning with your name on the tip of the entire world's tongue? You want the world to see your work? What better way than once a week on primetime television?"

That's enough to make me pause. I've spent the last four years in and out of internships, just praying that someone's assistant would take me seriously or that I'd get two seconds of face time with a brand director who could give me at least an ounce of feedback. And last year felt even more desperate as I secretly hoped that every person I met would be the one to spark that creative flame for me again.

Even if I did have a vision for what I want my career to look like, going on some TV show feels like a shortcut somehow. But plenty of people do it. One of the girls who was disqualified one year went on to be the female suitor the next season, and now she has her own show on the Food Network. Sometimes you just have to take whatever step you can and hope it leads you in the right direction.

"I couldn't leave the kids," I say, forcing myself back to reality.

"I can have Erica a new nanny in three days. She's just been holding the spot for you to get you to finally accept some cash from her, and you know it's true."

I'd suspected as much. If I'm being really honest with myself, I know there are plenty of people for this job—many of whom are much better qualified than I am. My only childcare experience is watching my upstairs neighbor's newborn while she took a shower one time.

"Beck," Erica calls. "Did you ever hear back from Nick on the location scouting for the week-two date? Are we locked in on that yet?"

"Uh, let me check." Beck raps her fist on the marble countertop. "Think about it. Promise?"

"Sure," I say half-heartedly.

I spend the rest of the afternoon with the triplets. We watch a show about baking gone wrong, and I keep an eye on them while they splash around in the shallow end of the pool.

While I'm sitting at the edge, with my legs dangling in the water, my phone rings.

Sierra's face pops up on my screen. "How has it only been twenty-four hours?"

"Oh my god, is that really it?"

"Who is that?" Mary demands.

I flip the camera around so Sierra can see the triplets and they can see her. "This is my best friend, Sierra. Say hi!"

"Hi!" they scream in unison.

"They are so cute!" she says as I turn the phone back on me. "I'm sorry about last night. It was so loud in there, but I have to tell you what happened!" Her cheeks are flushed, and she looks like she might just burst.

"Okay . . ."

"I met someone."

My jaw drops. Sierra is about as interested in romance as she is in learning how to repair lawn mowers. "Who? What?" I lower my voice to a whisper. "Are they there? Like right now? I'm gone for *a day* and you've already got a one-night stand under your belt?"

She laughs. "Slow your roll, perv. I met the head of brand development for Opening Ceremony. She gave me her card, Cin! She told me to call her first thing on Monday morning to set up a lunch date! I just showed her some of my work super fast, like, on my phone, and she was so into it."

One thing you can trust in fashion is that no one is polite just to be polite. If someone is interested in your work, it's genuine. "Whoa, Sierra. That's amazing. You'd be such a good fit there."

"I know, right? Totally my aesthetic. I'm going to spend the weekend beefing up on brand history."

"They're going to love you," I say with a forced smile.

"What about you, California girl? Any life-changing news to share?"

"Just living my best nanny life. I might pursue my big dream of becoming a grilled cheese chef."

She rolls her eyes. "You can still come back. I could probably even float your rent for a month and tell Wendy your room isn't for rent anymore."

Outside of Sierra, our apartment was one of the hardest things to give up. We lucked into it thanks to a lead from an off-campus housing coordinator and an alumni who took a job in Spain and agreed to sublet to us on the cheap-ish while Erica helped fill in the gaps. "No, Erica needs my help and Wendy is moving in on Tuesday, you nut! You can't just bail on her like that. And she can actually afford the rent, so maybe you should try keeping her happy."

She shrugs. "Wendy would live. And so would Erica. She could hire a nanny in a heartbeat. We can totally figure out a way to make this work."

I look past my phone to the triplets. "Gus, Jack, Mary, say byyyyyyyye, Sierra!"

"Byyyyyyyyye, Sierra!" they chirp back chaotically.

"Bye," I tell her. "I love you. Call me on Monday when you hear back from them."

Sierra puffs out a frustrated sigh. "Bye. I love you back."

After a little while longer out by the pool, I get the triplets out and dried off. Each of them takes a turn using the outdoor shower and then letting me wrap them up in big, fluffy towels.

As we file back in the house, Erica stands. "Cin, take a break. I'm going to stretch my legs and make sure my three little mice get dressed. Besides, I might need you to keep an eye on them tonight if you don't mind? You don't have any plans, do you?"

I shake my head. "Not a one."

"I'm choosing my own clothes!" says Mary before she tears off toward the bedrooms.

"This should be good," Erica says as she follows behind Jack and Gus.

I plop down across from Beck. "Where'd Anna and Drew go?"

She doesn't look up from her laptop. "Someplace called Euphora for enough face masks to last them the length of the show."

"You mean Sephora?" I ask.

"Sure, yeah."

I trace a knot in the wood of the kitchen table with my finger, waiting for my mouth to open and just say the words. I've been hoping for inspiration, for something to get me out of my rut. What if it's here, right in front of me? Sierra's getting her shot. What if this is mine, wrapped in a reality-TV-shaped box? "I'm in."

Beck looks up then and closes her laptop. "Say that one more time."

I nod. "I'm in. Let's do this."

Her eyes brighten for a moment and then immediately narrow into business mode. "Leave Erica to me."

"I want to tell her."

Beck grimaces. "You sure about that?"

If I'm going to do this, I need to have a backbone. Might as well start with going up against the will of the fiercest woman I know. "I'm sure."

Erica sweeps back into the room and reaches for a bubble water in the fridge. After a moment, she glances over her shoulder to find both of us staring at her expectantly. "What?"

I clear my throat. "Erica?"

"Yes, dear," she says as she closes the fridge with a carrot stick in her hand.

"I'm going on the show."

She drops her carrot and turns fully to face me with her forehead knotted in confusion.

I stand up from the table. "Beck asked me to be a contestant on *Before Midnight* and I accepted. If you say no now, all you're telling me is that Anna and Drew deserve to have a chance to find love—or hell, at least get five minutes in the spotlight—and I don't." I turn to Beck. "You two can figure out the logistics, but I'm doing it."

"Cindy." Her voice is soft and taken aback. For the first time since I've known her, Erica Tremaine is speechless.

The rigid posture I'd been maintaining loosens as I cross my arms over my chest. "I know everything you said last night came from a place of love. But now I need respect. I want to do this. Please don't be the reason I don't."

Erica reaches down to pick up her carrot and takes a chomp out of it. I don't say anything about the five-second rule, because for as much money as Erica pays to have this place cleaned, she should be able to eat off the floor. With slightly more composure, she turns to Beck. "If this goes south, it's on you."

Beck nods. "Fully aware, Captain."

"Sisters," Erica says. "Sisters vying for the suitor's attention." Her gaze drifts past us into the backyard. "I guess three is better than two."

CHAPTER SIX

"Can I come in?" Drew wraps her knuckle against the fitting-room door. "I couldn't find the next size up."

I open the curtain for her to join me and Anna, who's sitting on a giant beanbag. I told Drew that I had tried on their largest size, but she shook her head and held her phone out to me as proof. "See! It says right there. Now carrying extended sizes."

I explained that stores like these (trendy little places that are suddenly on the body-positive train if they can make a quick buck) usually only offer larger sizes on their website, but she insisted on checking in person.

I plop down on the leather beanbag alongside Anna. "What I really want to know is who actually considers beanbags to be appropriate dressing room seating?"

Anna crosses her arms over her chest. "This is ridiculous. How are you even supposed to know if something fits you if you can only buy it online? Especially if it's a brand you've never shopped!"

I'm too jaded to join in on her outrage, and I'm also having major flashbacks to every trip we made to the mall in high school. Back then, the options were even more limited.

"I can just work with stuff I have at home," I tell them. "I don't need a whole new wardrobe just for a TV show."

"I remember Mom saying there was a wardrobe department for the one-on-one dates and stuff," says Drew, but by the look on her face, I can tell she's thinking what I already know. If we're having this much trouble shopping in this store, the likelihood of the show having my size on hand is basically nonexistent.

"All right, let's go," I say.

I wiggle my way out of the beanbag, and then Drew and I pull Anna to her feet.

We file out of the fitting room full of rejected clothing and make our way to the front door.

"Thanks for coming in, girls!" the shop clerk calls after us. "Sorry you didn't find anything this time."

We're nearly out the door, but Anna whirls back around and stomps up to the counter. "Actually, my stepsister found plenty of things she loved, but for whatever reason, your company doesn't carry her size in store."

The woman steps back, startled by Anna's bravado.

"Um, we know that you, like, have no control over that, but maybe you could pass the message up the chain of command," I offer.

The woman notices me, seemingly for the first time. "Oh, right, of course. I think we might have some of our basics in an extra large if you'd like to try them."

"Does my sister look basic to you?" Anna snaps.

"Anna," I chide. "Come on."

Anna walks back over and loops an arm through both mine and Drew's as we walk out together like an unstoppable Red Rover force.

"Anna," Drew says once we're in the clear, "that was so unlike you."

Anna gasps. "I know!" Her voice returns to its normal levels of sweetness. "But it felt good. A little sexy too. I should talk about this on my Instagram stories."

I lean my head against her shoulder. "Kitty's got claws." I wasn't sure what to expect when I got back to LA, but being back with Anna and Drew feels . . . comfortable. I guess if I'm doing this reality television thing, at least it's with the two of them.

I spend the week with the triplets during the day while Anna and Drew get touched up in every possible way you can imagine. Highlights, facials, waxing, manicures. If it can be polished or shined or stripped of hair, they've got it covered. I join them for a few things as time allows, like a quick manicure and getting my split ends trimmed, but Erica's schedule is busy, which means mine is too. I promised Erica I'd at least spend the week with the triplets, and she promised me she'd find a more permanent solution for them while I'm gone. And every night as I'm falling asleep, I have to remind myself that this is what I wanted, and then I wonder very briefly who the mystery man might be. Too bad Prince Charming won't be able to swoop in and rescue me if the suitor is just another dude bro.

Three days before I'm set to leave Erica's house for the château, a film crew descends upon me. I knew they would be here to do pre-interviews for the season premiere, but I'm still taken by surprise. I keep expecting there to be formal introductions to the crew, but instead they all just buzz round me like I'm a set piece.

Beck told me to show up barefaced and to have several different clothing options ready, so I opted for a white sundress and my mom's old locket with a picture of my dad inside.

The moment I walk out of the pool house, three very distinct women descend upon me. The first one, a petite Black woman, wears her hair in retro pinup curls around her face with the rest swept into a silk scarf. She runs a hand through my hair without even asking and begins to examine my roots. "Huh, not much damage."

Another woman, this one tall and white with wavy long blond hair and the kind of makeup that looks like no makeup but actually takes a ton of skill, holds a blush compact up to my face. "Good cheekbones," she says.

And the third and final woman, with olive-toned complexion and dressed all in black, stands a few feet back with a loose measuring tape clutched in her fist. "Definitely meatier than Beck said she would be," she says in a thick Eastern European accent.

"Meatier?" I ask.

"That's Irina," says the girl with the silk scarf. "She's wardrobe and has no filter, but compared to other wardrobe people I've worked with, she's more bark than bite. I'm Ginger and I do hair. You'll mostly do your own hair during the show—other than for one-on-ones—but I'm around for touch-ups. Same goes for makeup."

The woman with the blush moves to inspecting my brows. "And I'm Ash. I'm technically not supposed to touch your brows, but you've got just . . ." She attacks with a pair of tweezers. "Just one hair out of place."

I let out a low hiss. "Thanks, I think."

The three quickly lead me into the main house, where they have a makeshift station set up for all their prepping and primping.

While Ash applies my foundation, a very fashionable woman around Erica's age steps up to us and says, "Cindy? Hi, my name is Tammy, and I'll be playing your stepmom today. Maybe we could run lines when you're done?"

"Um, what?" I look to Ash for an answer, but she's busy at work on my face. The woman is ushered away before I can ask for more details. "Beck?"

"Coming!" her voice calls from across the room. "Cindy!" she says as she approaches me from the side. "You look radiant! Isn't Ash the best?"

"The best," I say quickly, even though I'm not yet qualified on the topic. "But could you please explain to me why some random woman named Tammy just came up and told me that she would be playing the role of my stepmother? And apparently I have lines? I thought reality TV was supposed to be real . . . ish."

"It is. Totally. But sometimes, we have to fill in the blanks a

49

little. And Erica can't play your stepmom for obvious reasons. Do you know how many questions that would raise? It'd be a PR nightmare. Everyone would think you only got on the show because of nepotism and connections."

"Well," I say, "that *is* how I got on the show."

"The American people don't need to know that. Sometimes we have to go above and beyond to keep the magic alive. This isn't really a *lie*. It's just an *alternate truth*."

"Um, that sounds like a lie."

"Lips relaxed and parted," Ash demands.

I let out a groan through my relaxed and parted lips as she applies a sticky gloss.

"And you don't have lines," Beck assures me. "We just had to give Tammy some parameters to work in so she'll have some ground rules and then improvise a little. It'll be so natural, I promise. You won't even know the cameras are here."

I look around at the crew running cords and staging lights all over Erica's living room. "Not likely," I say through my still relaxed and parted lips.

"Oh, by the way," says Beck, "change of plans. Anna and Drew aren't your sisters anymore. At least not on the show. So make sure the other contestants don't find out you're related, okay? That would just get . . . messy."

"Wait. What? I thought the whole thing was that we were three sisters vying for the suitor."

Beck shrugs. "We're taking a different angle with you and—"

"Beck!" someone calls for her.

"Gotta go!" she says as she disappears into the tangle of crew members.

"Angle? I have an angle? What's my angle?"

But no one answers. My stomach flips at the thought of going at this alone. Anna and Drew will still be there, but any shot I had at hiding behind them is gone.

When I'm done with hair and makeup, I'm guided to the couch, where some random person shoves a pillow behind my back so I'm forced to perch on my ass.

Beck sits down on an ottoman across from me and behind the camera. "Okay, we're just going to have a conversation. I'll ask questions and you answer. If something else comes up, just keep talking. We might have to pause every once in a while, for noise. When that happens, Ash, Ginger, or Irina might swoop in and fix your hair or whatever. Cool?"

"Uh, sure. There are . . . a lot of people here." I force myself to breathe evenly before I hyperventilate.

Beck comes to sit down next to me on the couch. "Listen, if we were doing your pre-interview weeks ago like we did for the other girls, we'd be able to ease you into this a little bit more. But as it stands, we're running against the clock with little time to be precious. I want you to be comfortable, so I can send everyone who doesn't need to be in here right now outside, and we can do this with a skeleton crew. You also need to know, though, that when you get to the house, it's going to be this but on steroids. I'm talking vein-busting, ball-shrinking steroids."

I nod. I hear what she's saying. There's no time to ease me into this, and maybe that's what I need—to just be immersed in something so fully that I can't even think too hard about it. "They can stay. But, um, could I have a glass of water or something?"

Beck nods and snaps her fingers. "K! Water."

Within seconds, a gangly-looking white boy is holding a bottle of water with a straw in front of my face. "Sip," he says.

"I don't need a straw," I tell him.

"Yes, she does," Ash, Irina, and Ginger say in unison.

"It's paper," he tells me, obviously bored. "Save the turtles."

51

I oblige and take my sip while he holds the bottle for me, and the moment I'm done, I say, "Well, that was awkward."

Beck waves me off. "That kid just got paid to serve you water. He's fine. You're hydrated. We're all good." She stands and heads back to her ottoman. "How's our light? How do we look?"

Irina rushes in. "Lose the necklace."

I hold my hand over it and instinctively say, "No."

"It ruins the shot," Irina says with defiance.

We both look to Beck for a tiebreaker, and I think if Irina takes this necklace off me, I might cry, which is ludicrous, but I'm about as high-strung as an extreme couponer waiting for her grand total right now. "Necklace stays. It's . . . approachable-looking."

Irina mutters under her breath, and I think she and I might go toe-to-toe before all this is said and done.

"Quiet on set!" a South Asian girl with two long braids and a clipboard covered in band stickers calls out.

"Thank you, Mallory," Beck says.

The whole room goes completely silent. So silent, in fact, that I'm scared I might be breathing too heavily, and what if they can hear it on the mic dangling above my head just out of frame?

Beck nods to the guy behind the camera.

"Rolling!" the girl with the clipboard shouts.

On and off for the next hour, Beck pretty much does a post-mortem of my life leading up to this moment. The only exclusion is any specific details about Erica. Other than that, she asks about everything. My dad's death. The triplets. Fashion school. Moving back home to California. Eventually Erica enters, stepping in and out periodically, giving her nod of approval, and I try not to let my eyes stray. We pause a few times for planes overhead or car alarms, and sometimes I say something that I'm asked to repeat, but with more "emphasis"—whatever that means.

When we're done, the whole room collectively sighs, and within seconds, the volume of the crew has exploded again.

Beck pats my knee. "You did great."

"You didn't tell me you were basically going to neatly display my guts for the whole world to see."

She laughs. "It feels like a lot, but we need options. Different angles. And don't worry about all these people. A lot of them just check out while the cameras are rolling until it's time to do their job again. And anyway, all this is going to get cut down to, like, two minutes of actual footage." She holds a finger up and listens to something in her headset before running off.

I think all that is supposed to be comforting, but going through the labor of putting my whole life on display is a little bit painful in a different kind of way.

Erica plops down on the couch beside me, and crew members skitter away like little ants fleeing a destroyed anthill. "They could have at least cast someone who looks like me," she says, motioning to the woman in the kitchen, where Beck is setting up a shot. "Sorry that I can't actually play your mom," she tells me.

"It must have been really weird for Drew and Anna."

She lets out a dry chuckle. "Their fake mom's name was Natalie. They were very into it, actually."

"How am I not surprised?"

"I wish I could have been here this morning. Our suitor was having a . . . situation."

I nudge her with my elbow. "Wow, talk about vague."

"You're lucky I even said that."

I swivel, turning into her. "Just tell me one thing. Do you think I'll even like him?"

I expect her to brush me off, but instead she presses her finger to her lips and thinks for a long moment. "You know, up until last

53

week, I would have said no way . . . but people have ways of surprising you . . . and the two of you—" She stops suddenly, returning to her poker face, like she's just realized she accidentally traded producer hat for stepmom hat. "Come on. Let's get you touched up." She stands. "We need touch-ups!"

Within seconds, we're swarmed.

Erica squeezes my hand before leaving me with Ash, Irina, and Ginger.

For the rest of the afternoon, my fake stepmom, Tammy, and I bake fake cookies and do fake dishes and have fake conversations and have fake fun. The whole time, from behind the camera, Beck urges, "Smile! Act natural!"

Those three words spin circles in my head for the rest of the day and well into the night as I pack my bags and tuck the triplets into bed once more. *Smile. Act natural.*

CHAPTER SEVEN

The next morning, I do a quick run through my room to make sure I didn't miss anything. Dropping down to one knee, I check under the bed, but I don't find a stray shoe or eyeliner. Instead, all I see is a large cardboard box. I reach forward and drag it out. Scrawled across the top in Erica's quick handwriting it says, *Simon's for C.* A soft gasp escapes me.

Last summer, when I tried sorting through some of Dad's things, I asked Erica if she could just save some of them for me. I'd already taken one of his threadbare flannels, his favorite slippers, and a few of his Clive Cussler novels just after he died, so I felt okay leaving it to her to decide what was worth keeping. Especially when the alternative was me facing all the pain I'd been hiding from for years.

I let my fingers dance along his name for a moment. A part of me feels sick to know that I slept here all week with his remaining belongings just hovering beneath me, like a ghost. I wasn't ready last summer, and I'm definitely not ready now. I slide the box back where I found it and take my luggage across the yard and into the main house.

Inside, Erica is rushing around with a woman slightly older than her in a floral Oxford shirt, khaki Bermuda shorts, and thick-soled walking shoes. "And this is where I keep their favorite cups. They'll use the other cups, but these are their favorites. Gus hates celery. Mary will tell you she can swim without her puddle jumper, but she's lying. In fact, it's best to assume Mary is lying more often than not. She's not malicious. Just creative. And Jack is a bigger softy than he lets on and—"

The sound of my two large suitcases rolling over the tile interrupts Erica's rapid-fire info dump on this poor woman.

"Oh, Cindy!" she says. "You're ready! Let's get Bruce to take you to the Marriott to meet the rest of the girls."

"Maybe I should take a Lyft or something? Less conspicuous?"

Her eyes light up. "Yes!" She turns to the woman beside her, who is surprisingly unfrazzled. "This is Jana. She'll be taking over with the triplets for the summer."

Jana smiles. "Nice to meet you."

"Jana was the behind-the-scenes nanny for that *Nicole + Joel + More* show. You know, the one with the young couple who were having fertility trouble and then ended up with quintuplets."

"Oh, yeah," I say. "Didn't he cheat on her with . . ."

Jana smirks. "With their new nanny. After I moved back to Los Angeles."

I nod. "Well, I guess triplets will be a breeze for you."

"That's what I was trying to explain to Ms. Tremaine," she says gently but firmly.

Erica sighs. "Sorry, mom anxiety is at an all-time high today."

I nod and stand there for a moment. I hate saying goodbye, especially to Erica. Do we hug? Say I love you? The two of us weave awkwardly back and forth for a moment before opting for a side hug. Nothing says *You're my only living almost parent* like a goodbye side hug.

I leave my phone in the drawer in the kitchen, but before I power it down, I shoot off one text to Sierra. *I'm disappearing for a little while, but if you tune in to Channel Eight next Tuesday night, you'll see why. I love you.*

***

When I arrive at the hotel, I find that the show has taken over the unopened hotel bar.

There's a small check-in table with some junior assistant producers, including Mallory from yesterday with the braids and the band sticker clipboard. I line up, get a name tag, and am instructed to leave my luggage and go mingle with other cast members.

"Cin!"

My heart swells at the sound of Drew's voice.

Her head bounces above the crowd of women—all of them tall and thin in very chic, low-maintenance looks.

My hips and I part through the crowd until I see Anna and Drew. "Thank God," I whisper.

"It's so good to see you!" Anna says loudly, sounding more like an acquaintance than a sister.

A woman who could potentially be a long-lost Kardashian with smooth straight black hair stretching nearly to her waist crosses her arms over her busty chest. Pointy nude nails make her fingers look endless. "And how do you three know one another?"

Anna's expression goes blank, but Drew swoops in to the rescue. "We went to high school with Cindy. She was a year behind us, right, Cin?"

I nod. The best lie is always the truth. "Yep, high school."

"Isn't that cute?" the woman says.

Anna beams. "Addison, this is Cindy. Cindy, this is Addison." And then like she's the mayor of HottieMcLegville, Anna introduces me to the rest of the girls in their little circle. Zoe, Claudia, Jen S., Jen B., Jen K., Gen with a *G*, Jenny, Olivia, Trina . . . The names keep coming. There are a few lawyers, one doctor, and a teacher, but most simply say they're in social media consultation, which seems to be code for Instagram model.

"Okay, ladies! Please take a seat," Beck calls through cupped hands from where she sits on top of the bar. "Orientation time, people!"

We crowd around little round tables, and I find myself safely tucked between Anna and Drew. I wave at Beck, but her gaze coasts right over me, and I'm guessing it's because she's trying not to play favorites. Then again, that assumes I'm her favorite. I shake the thought from my head. She's probably that friendly with all the contestants so they warm up faster. *Get it together, Cindy. This isn't real life. This is reality television.*

I felt good this morning. I put on a pair of pointy coral patent leather loafers I made for my final during my study abroad in Italy and a crisp white T-shirt tucked into my favorite cuffed mom jeans. But every single woman here is shiny and glossy and polished in a way I've never been. I am definitely out of my depth here.

"All right, class, listen up," Beck says. "Most of you know me, but for those who don't, I'm Beck. Back at that table are Zeke, Mallory, and Thomas. They are your assistant producers. And this is Wes." She motions to the tall guy with light brown skin beside her with his hair shaved close on the sides, leaving a pile of curls atop his head. "Think of Wes and me as co-captains. We are your junior executive producers. We are your people. If something happens, you talk to us. If something that is supposed to happen doesn't happen, you talk to us. Think of us as your mothers, your sisters, your therapists, your fairy godmothers, but also your dad who sometimes has to lay down the law."

"Tell us a dad joke!" someone shouts.

Without missing a beat, Beck says, "I'm reading a book about anti-gravity. It's impossible to put down."

Half of the room laughs dryly, while the other half makes a confused tittering noise.

"And of course, the renowned Erica Tremaine is your show creator and executive producer. She will be in and out during production.

We're about to load you all up on a fancy bus," she continues. "At which time we will distribute a welcome packet with some house rules, a map of the château, a brief bio of our mystery suitor—"

The women, including Anna and Drew, whistle and squeal.

"I heard he's a pilot," someone behind me says.

Beck clears her throat. "And you will also find your room numbers along with the names of your roommates. We have about four girls to a room, but that will change as many of you are eliminated. Tonight, we go from twenty-five to eighteen, so some of you won't even have a full room by the time you close your eyes."

The women groan, and even I feel a sinking pit in my stomach.

"This is when I should give you a lecture about sisterhood and playing nice and yada, yada, yada, but let's be real: When has that ever made for good TV?"

The room goes sharply quiet except for the producers chuckling at the back of the room.

"I'm kidding," Beck says. "Sort of. In all seriousness, we want you all to get along, of course, but don't forget that this is a competition with true love on the line."

Around me, several women nod with fervor. Not Addison, though. She sits with her legs crossed once at the knee and again at the ankle— is the woman a contortionist? Maybe a contortionist influencer? Is there an audience for that?

"And of course," Beck continues, "a hundred thousand dollars."

Everyone lets out an excited whoop! Even me! I could do so much with that money. I've been aimless for the last year, but I can't ignore the little burst of excitement I feel when I think about what I could do if I won. That money, even after taxes, could be a real start to something huge for me and what might someday be my brand. I wiggle my toes inside my shoes, the worn leather insoles perfectly formed to the shape of my feet, and for a moment I imagine what it might be like to see these babies on shelves everywhere in all kinds of sizes and colors. And a very small part of me even aches for my sketch pad. Not because I have any huge ideas just bubbling at the surface, but because I miss the feel of it in my hands.

"For a lot of you, this will be a life-changing experience, and we truly do hope you bond with one another, but don't forget what you came here for. Or *who* you came here for." Beck claps her hands together. "File up in a line outside the buses waiting for you in the carport. Please make sure your luggage is clearly marked . . . and with that, we're off to the château!"

We all cheer, and Anna squeezes my hand. "I can't believe we're actually doing this!"

On the bus, Drew and Anna sit together and I sit behind them. Several women walk past me in search of other contestants, but a petite white woman with light brown hair wearing a pink-and-white-striped shirt dress and matching espadrilles stops at my row. "Is this seat taken?" she asks in a Southern drawl.

"All yours," I tell her.

She holds a hand out to me, and I'm honestly surprised she's not wearing matching lace gloves too.

"I'm Sara Claire," she tells me.

I shake her hand and try to wedge myself against the wall to give her a little more space. "Cindy," I tell her. "Just the one name."

She giggles, and then pats my thigh. "I've got plenty of room, Cindy. No need for shrinkin' yourself up into a ball."

"Th-thanks," I say, feeling a little self-conscious that she noticed, but then again, I've heard that Southern women have a way of being both polite and direct.

We sit in silence as we begin to read through our welcome packets.

MIDNIGHT CHÂTEAU RULES

1. No glass containers—none whatsoever!—in the hot tub.
2. Lights-out rules enforced. (Time varies by night.)
3. No cell phones. No emails. No texts. No communication with the outside world.
4. Violence will not be tolerated. Any violence will result in immediate elimination and potential law enforcement involvement.
5. Smile! You're on camera.

A chill runs down my spine. Creepy.

Beside me, Sara Claire gasps. "We're roomies!"

I look over at her packet and then quickly flip to the third page to catch up.

ROOM 6:
Sara Claire
Cindy
Addison
Stacy

"I hope Addison and Stacy are nice," Sara Claire says.

I peer over my shoulder to where Addison sits a few rows back, whispering to another woman.

"That might be asking for too much," I mutter.

I flip back a page to find it labeled **SUITOR BIO**.

This season's suitor hails from an iconic family known for their fashion empire.

What? The possible heir to a fashion empire? "Did you see this?" I ask, pointing to the bio.

Sara Claire peers over my shoulder. "I wonder what brand it is?"

"I don't know, but the fashion industry is a smaller world than you'd expect, especially for the big luxury names." I continue to read, searching for a hint.

> *The suitor is known for his sharp-witted humor and business savvy. He might be vicious in the boardroom, but he's a total softy with the ladies. His hobbies include sailing, water polo, high-stakes Scrabble, and returning his mother's phone calls. He's ready to upgrade from his single lifestyle and finally settle down with a woman who will challenge him and help represent the family brand.*

Sara Claire taps her pink nail against the page. "Playboy reputation rehab."

"Huh?"

She turns to me and in a low voice says, "These guys are always some kind of archetype. Country boy with family values looking to settle down? He's really a right-wing nut with mommy issues. Free-spirited adventure seeker looking for his soul mate to plant roots with? Immature daredevil who thinks he's more special than everyone else. You gotta read between the lines."

I tilt my head, looking at the bio once more.

She points to the second line. "*Sharp-witted humor* means 'sarcastic jerk.' *High-stakes Scrabble?* More like a gambling addiction. *Single lifestyle?* Sounds like he's got a thing for one-night stands."

I look at her once again, trying to size her up. Sara Claire is not what I expected. "How do you know all this?"

"I'm in the business of business. Hedge funds. Family business in Texas. Daddy calls me his BS radar. I go to meetings and look pretty. Everyone underestimates me, and I hear all the things their mouths aren't sayin'."

"Whoa," I say. "That job sounds wild. What are you even doing here?"

She shrugs with a smile. "Would you believe me if I said true love?"

"Wait. You mean you actually buy into all this stuff?"

"Listen, I'm thirty-two. In Southern years, that's ancient. I've tried every app. Every church singles group. Every website. Every friend of a friend." She shakes her head, thinking of something to herself. "When the casting scouts approached me, I figured I couldn't tell my mama I tried everything to give her grandbabies until I really had tried everything."

She must notice how wide my eyes are at that statement, and she swats at my leg. "You're young still, but one day you'll wake up and wonder where the time went." She laughs. "Or maybe you won't."

"But you really want to fall for some playboy looking to rehabilitate his reputation?"

She waves. "I've worked with all kinds of scum, and what I can tell you is that one thing we all have in common is skeletons in the closet."

We drive for another hour, but the whole time, Sara Claire's words sink in. I don't know what my skeletons would be, but I'm sure they're there.

I feel fidgety and anxious without my phone, so I guess it turns out I'm more addicted to that little brick of technology than I thought. Eventually I just press my head against the glass and watch as Los Angeles slips by us as we drive deeper into the mountains.

A few girls complain of motion sickness, and I hear someone behind me whisper, "I always thought the château was on a studio lot."

Another voice replies, "I heard it's on an old compound some cult used to own before they had a big shootout with the FBI. Supposedly no one would buy it, so the network got a great deal on it."

I chuckle to myself, knowing that both of those stories are a little bit true. The show started out on a studio lot but quickly moved out to the mountains when they got a steal on the property formerly owned by Vince Pugh, a '90s teen movie star who turned out to be an actual serial killer in real life. He'd bought the property from a studio exec whose wife wanted to bring the French countryside to Southern California.

When we pull through the gate of the château, there's a lot that looks familiar and more that doesn't. Just on the other side of a stretch of tall hedges are rows of trailers and trucks full of equipment strategically tucked away. On the other side of the hedges, a long driveway with elaborate landscaping on either side leads to the front entrance, which welcomes us with its marble staircase and stately turrets. It's a little dingier and much smaller than it appears on television, but that doesn't stop just about everyone from gasping. And I have to admit, something about the dramatic roofline speaks to me.

As the bus door wheezes open, Beck jumps on board. "Okay, ladies, you are responsible for getting your bags to your room. This might be the notorious château, but it is not a hotel. There is no valet. Pay close attention to your house map. If a door is locked, it is locked for a reason. If it's not on the map, you don't need to know what it is. And honestly, if you find a locked door, I can nearly guarantee you that the only thing behind it is old camera equipment. And before you ask, yes, the suitor is staying on the property. And no, I won't tell you where."

A few women shriek, and then Beck steps back, clearing a path for us.

We all pause for a second, then make a run for it. It reminds me of exiting the plane when I first landed at LAX, and Prince Charming—I mean, Henry—and I bonded over our annoyance with the chaos before he kindly helped a whole slew of people with their bags.

I let the others go ahead of me until it's just Beck and me on the bus. When I walk past her, I wait for her to give me some kind of sign that I'm not just another contestant to her. She scrolls through her phone as I make my approach, and I feel a sudden pang of jealousy at the sight of someone with a phone.

Whoa, maybe I do need a technology detox.

Beck looks up just as I walk past her and gives me a big wink. "Sara Claire is a good egg. Stick with her."

"Well, she *is* my roommate."

She smirks knowingly. "And you think that was an accident? Very few things on this show happen by chance. You'll like Stacy too."

"Thank you," I tell her, before jogging down the steps and dragging my two hulking bags up to the château. I can't expect Beck to play favorites, but at least it's nice to know that I've got a friend in this place.

All the rooms are upstairs in a long corridor with two large dorm-style bathrooms.

If I wasn't so busy with my own luggage, I would find it highly entertaining to watch all these women dragging huge overstuffed suitcases up the expansive spiral staircase. In fact, one contestant loses a grip on one of her suitcases and it comes barreling down the stairs, nearly taking me and one other girl out.

At the end of the hallway, I find room six, where Sara Claire is already hanging up her suitcaseful of colorful dresses. "There she is!" She turns to Addison. "This is Cindy!"

"Oh, we've met," says Addison dryly. "Cindy seems to know everyone."

I smile tightly. "Hi, Addison."

Perched on the bed across from her is a Black girl with springy curls dressed in an adorable floral crop top with matching skirt and a pair of white Air Jordans. Her skin is perfectly dewy with just the right amount of highlighter, and her black liquid eyeliner is the most precise cat-eye I've ever seen.

"And this is Stacy!" Sara Claire tells me.

"Hey," Stacy says nonchalantly. And I immediately know that Stacy is the exact kind of girl I gravitate toward. She'd totally fit right in with Sierra back in the city. They're both the kind of girls whose confidence and calm energy make them the coolest people at every party.

"Hi! I love your shoes. Where are you from?" I ask.

"Thanks. I'm a total sneakerhead. Chicago. Born and raised. Librarian by day. Makeup artist by night." She pulls a small oil diffuser from her bag. "Will this bother anyone if I use it?"

"Oh Lord, no," says Sara Claire. "I welcome it!"

Addison wrinkles her nose. "I guess not, as long you don't use any patchouli. Bleh."

I turn my back to Addison and give Stacy a wide-eyed look. "Doesn't bother me at all."

Stacy chuckles at my expression as she continues to unpack her bag. "So, Addison, what is it that you do?"

"I'm an actress and model."

Sara Claire gasps. "Would you have been in anything we'd know?"

"Oh my God!" Stacy says. "I knew I recognized you!"

"I've done lots of things," Addison says quickly. "I'm going down—"

"He got me a FitBike. It's all I've ever wanted,'" Stacy says in a robotic voice, quoting the now-infamous FitBike commercial that released last Christmas. In it, a woman receives a FitBike for Christmas, and with a glazed-over expression, she drones on about how all she's ever wanted is a FitBike. Pretty soon #RobotWife was trending and the internet had its holiday-season meme.

"I've also been on *CSI: New Orleans* before, and I did a few Target swimwear campaigns, so that dumb commercial is, like, the bottom of my résumé, just for your information." And with that, Addison turns on her stiletto heel and stomps off down the hallway.

The three of us are quiet for a second after the door closes before bursting with laughter.

"In my professional opinion," Sara Claire says, "she should embrace her meme status. Fame like that rarely strikes twice."

"Right!" Stacy agrees.

I kneel down in front of my suitcase to unzip it. "Honestly, that GIF of her creepy robot smile was one of my favorite reaction GIFs last year. Too bad she's so snotty."

Stacy plops down on my bed. "Ho-ly . . . is that your shoe collection?" She reaches in for a pointed powder-blue satin Stuart Weitzman stiletto with a crystal brooch. A total dupe of the shoe my mom wore on her wedding day, which was actually from Payless.

"I guess you could say I have a thing for shoes?"

"I thought I was obsessed," Stacy says as she turns the shoe over. "We wear the same size!"

I smile. This is what I love about shoes. I love that I could potentially be wearing the same size as this gazelle-like goddess sitting before me. There may not be much we can bond over in the clothing department, but shoes are an exception. In middle school and high school, I would spend hours shopping with friends, and I'd always end up browsing the accessories and shoes, because there was no chance any of those stores carried my clothing size. But shoes? I could make shoes from just about anywhere work. Shoes aren't perfect. A lot of brands don't carry wide widths or go above a size ten, but for me, they've always been comforting.

"They might be a little stretched out, because my foot is on the wide side, but you're welcome to borrow any pair you want," I tell her.

"As long as you can help me make my eye makeup half as gorgeous as yours."

"Deal," she says.

There's an abrupt knock on the door, and Mallory, with thick, wavy hair bunched into two pigtails, sticks her head in the room.

"Hey there, Mallory," says Sara Claire.

"Ladies, we need everyone ready for introductions in an hour and a half."

"Introductions?" I ask.

"To the suitor," Mallory calls as she shuts the door behind her.

I look to Sara Claire and then Stacy. "Is this really happening?"

"You bet your tush it is," Sara Claire shouts as she jumps up onto her bed and begins to use it as a trampoline. "Y'all ready to meet my future husband or what?"

Stacy smiles slowly, like a cat. "Let the games begin."

CHAPTER EIGHT

S tacy was kind enough to do my makeup, which I appreciate, because that's one thing I've never gotten into. Give me a tinted moisturizer and I'm good. However, I did come here with a clear vision of what I would wear to the first ball, and tonight is all about the shoes.

My shoes, Cindy originals from sophomore year, are a pair of strappy turquoise heels with matching feathers shooting up from the ankle strap and curving around the back of my ankle. It took me weeks to find the perfect feather and days to figure out the best way to attach each feather, but when the design finally matched the vision I'd dreamed up on my tablet, I wanted to strut around in these babies everywhere. They're my ultimate confidence-boosting shoes, and tonight, I'm going to need every bit of confidence I can get.

For my dress, I'm in a Sierra original, an ivory midi gown she made last fall that hugs me all the way down to my mid-calves and has a high slit up the back. It doesn't hide an inch and definitely makes it very clear what I'm working with. I figure if this guy is going to give me the boot on the first night, it's probably because of my size, and if that's the case, the sooner the better. The neckline is a deep square cut that gives me what Sierra always refers to as bar-wench cleavage, and the sleeves are a sheer mesh. The whole look is more "woman with an agenda" than "pageant contestant."

"Whoa," Stacy says as she zips me up, both of our reflections beaming back at us in the mirror. "This is like bombshell chic."

Stacy wears a mustard-yellow silk gown with a high neck and

deep V-cut back. It's the exact right amount of sexy. And Sara Claire stuns in a jewel-encrusted hot-pink strapless gown with a sweetheart neckline.

"We're hot and we're ready for this dang ball!" Sara Claire says as she swings the door open.

The ball is another *Before Midnight* franchise staple. It's basically a cocktail party held on the first night and then again before every elimination. On television, it appears to be elegant, with champagne fountains and ice sculptures. It's also every contestant's last chance to catch the suitor's attention.

We step out into the hallway, and as we're following the herd of women down the stairs, I think to ask, "Where's Addison?"

A woman with a narrow nose that just barely lifts at its point says, "Oh, the producers came and got her and a few other girls to have their hair and makeup done by the crew."

"What? I thought that was only for one-on-one dates," someone else says.

The woman shrugs. "I guess the producers are already playing favorites."

Sara Claire nudges me. "They're just trying to get in our heads."

"Who is?" I ask.

"The producers," she says simply.

And it's then that I'm reminded of the fact that no one here knows just how closely I'm tied to the brains behind this machine.

"The crazier we are, the more entertaining we are, and the more entertaining we are, the higher the ratings," Sara Claire says as we walk out the front door and board golf carts that look like tiny minivans that take us past the front gates to where lines of tents are set up with rows of chairs.

I know everything she's saying to be true in a theoretical way. I've heard Erica say countless things just like this on phone calls, but seeing the reality of it is . . . unsettling. It's a side of Erica and her job that I knew existed but never thought I'd have to interact with.

"Ladies!" Beck says through a bullhorn. "Your seats are labeled. This is the order you will be going in. You'll get in the white Rolls-Royce, and yes, she is our baby. A 1950 original. The car will take you through the gates, you'll meet the suitor, and then head into the house, where the bar will be open to you. When we're done filming out front, the suitor will come and mingle out in the courtyard. This is your time to get to know him before this evening's elimination ceremony. Reminder: Some of you will be going home before lights-out tonight."

Beside her, Wes crosses his arms and smirks. "Go big or go home," he yells. "Literally!"

I glance around nervously, searching for Anna and Drew. I see them both sitting together in the second and third chairs beside Addison, who is wearing a gold lamé gown with a front and back so low it makes me nervous. Still, she looks like an actual goddess.

I wave to them, but they're both nodding intently as Beck talks to them.

I find my seat down near the end, next to a woman with red curly hair and three oranges in her lap.

"I'm Judith," she says as I sit down. "I juggle."

"Cool," I say, unsure what to make of that.

From years of watching this show and living with Erica, I know that intro night is a beloved fan favorite. There's Twitter discourse, message boards, and even drinking games! (Drink every time a contestant introduces themselves with a pun the suitor doesn't get!)

But the point is that the most memorable women on the first night receive the most camera time when they get the public talking. Of course, the decisions are always left to the suitor, though I can't help but wonder how many of his decisions are influenced by producers pulling strings behind the scenes.

The question is what can I do or say in ten seconds that will make me stand out among the crowd? (The very beautiful and glamorous crowd.)

Between Juggling Judith and Meme Icon Addison, I don't really have much to offer in such a short span of time.

"Twins!" someone shouts. "You're up."

Anna and Drew stand up, and I nearly shout, *They're not twins!* But they're gone and in the Rolls-Royce before I can even give them a good-luck wave.

"Twins," says Judith. "Now that's a good shtick. They haven't had that before."

The line moves more quickly than I expect, and with every girl that leaves, the rest of us move down a chair until it's just Judith and me.

"Good luck!" I call to her as she slides into the back of the limo, the oranges gathered in her arms.

"I don't need luck," she says seriously. "I've got skills."

"We saved the best for last," Beck says as she slams the door.

I scoff at that. "Yeah, right. More like this guy is gonna be a total zombie from meeting twenty-five women back-to-back."

Wes tilts his head, listening in on his headset. "Move it!" he shouts as he runs past someone from craft services balancing a tray of sandwiches. "We've got a breakdown happening by the pool." He holds the walkie-talkie up to his mouth. "No, let her spiral! I need those tears!"

I don't know if it's his gross reaction to some woman in crisis or if it's just my nerves, but I feel sick to my stomach.

"Whoa there," says Beck, steadying me. "Ignore him."

I shake my head. "I don't think I can do this. I need to go home. There's still time. Erica would only be a little bit annoyed if I left now. I haven't even really been on camera. And I can apologize to the whole crew that came out to the house the other day for wasting—"

"Stop." Her voice is stern. "You can do this, Cindy. You look incredible and you're smart and funny and talented. The suitor is going to love you. The audience is going to love you. And most importantly, they're going to die over those shoes."

I look down at the feathers framing my ankles. My shoes. My beautiful shoes. Even if all I do is walk out there and introduce myself, millions of people will at least know my name and see my shoes. Even if I never design another shoe again, I'll always have that moment.

I take a deep breath. I can do anything in these shoes.

"Wait!" Ash yells, sprinting up the hill from the trailers down below. "Wait!"

When she reaches us, her chest is heaving, but she's holding a high-lighter and brush in her hands. "Sorry Wes had us so busy all night, but I wanted to get up here to check on you."

"Me?" I ask.

Ash smiles with a laugh. "Yes, you, Cindy." She winks. "We all have our favorites, you know."

And that little piece of information steadies me even more. "Thank you," I whisper.

She dusts my cheekbones and the tip of my nose with rose gold. "Perfect."

The Rolls-Royce is straight out of a fairy tale—a glistening white against the swirling sunset sky, and welded to the grille is the sparkling *Before Midnight* logo, a ticking Roman-numeral clock. This is really happening.

The car drives me the short distance up the rest of the hill and through the gate of the château as though this were my first time arriving here.

The car stops, and the driver in the front calls, "That's your cue!" through the crack in the divider.

I open the door and step out, imagining the camera zooming in for a close-up of my shoes. (Hey, a girl can dream.)

As I stand, I take a deep breath and a quick moment to smooth out my dress, and for just a millisecond, I think, *What if... What if this random guy really is the love of my life? What if fate is actually real and the two of us are meant for this moment?*

I look up and am briefly shocked by all the lights and cameras and crew quietly stepping around us.

My vision focuses, and my gasp cuts through the humid night air.

Tall, dark hair, impeccable suit.

Henry.

Prince Charming himself.

CHAPTER NINE

By the way his jaw drops, he's as shocked as I am. Or maybe he doesn't recognize me. After all this glam, I look like an entirely different person.

"Uhhh, w-wow." I can't stop stuttering. "It's y—"

"So nice to meet you," he says, his expression perfectly retracting back to completely even-toned coolness. "I won't bite."

Blood rushes to my chest and up my neck. Him. Biting. *Get your mind out of the gutter, girl!* "I'm Cindy," I blurt. "I love shoes." *I love shoes?*

He looks down, and then with admiration, he says, "And I can see you put your best foot forward. Aren't those striking?" he asks. "Just like you."

At my side, a crew member waves me forward.

Oh. Right. Walking. I should do that.

I step forward as Henry holds his arms out, and I lean in for a hug.

"Henry," he says, his breath tickling my neck. "I'm Henry."

I step back and instinctively bite down on my lip, nerves getting the best of me. "I better get to the ball. See you in there?"

"I plan on it," he says.

I walk into the château, trying to do my best supermodel strut without looking like a wounded animal. (What they don't tell you in the pamphlets is that half of fashion school is pretending you're a runway model. Sierra's walk is honestly *America's Next Top Model* level of fierce.)

75

I open the door, and from the other side I hear a pained groan.

"What the . . ."

Anna reaches out and yanks me into the foyer.

"Shhhh." Drew holds a finger over her lips.

"We're not supposed to be here," Anna whispers. "But we couldn't miss your entrance."

"You look incredible," Drew tells me.

My stepsisters pull me in for a three-way hug, and it feels so good to be alone with them for even a brief moment.

"Did they really make you two introduce yourselves as twins?"

Anna rolls her eyes. "They're making a bit of it. People keep calling us twins, and then we correct them and say that we're almost twins."

Drew shrugs. "It's annoying, but hopefully it will help us stand out."

"Honestly, it's a little creepy," I say.

"You little awkward weirdo!" Anna says. "Stop trying to change the subject. What was going on out there?"

I know that I should keep my secret about Henry to myself. But I can't help it. Not with Anna and Drew. "I sat next to him on the plane," I say quickly.

Their jaws drop in unison.

"You. Sat next to *the suitor* on the flight from New York?" Drew asks, spelling it out slowly and quietly.

I nod.

Anna sighs with delight. "I think he's super cute, and please know that I definitely want him for myself, but oh my gosh, if that isn't fate, I don't know what is."

"There's no such thing as fate," I tell her.

"Anna, stop pretending he's your type," Drew tells her. "You like them a little dirty and underemployed."

Anna pouts for a second, but then nods thoughtfully.

"Stop it," I say. "Both of you. It wasn't fate. It was just a coincidence."

I don't believe in fate. I can't. I refuse to believe that first Mom and then Dad dying was part of some grand scheme. If that's true, whatever's at the end of my rainbow isn't worth what it will have cost me.

Anna sniffs the air.

"What?" Drew asks. "What is it?"

Anna crosses her arms. "Smells like fate. Looks like fate. Must be fate."

Zeke peeks his head in from the courtyard outside. "Ladiessssss," he says. "Your presence is required outside. Ya know, where the cameras are?"

"Take a chill pill, Zeke," Drew says in a you-work-for-my-mom voice.

Anna swats at her. "Be right there, Zeke dear."

Both Drew and I eyeball her as the door shuts behind him.

"What?" Anna asks.

Drew narrows her gaze. "Don't think I don't see you flirting with a crew member. Mom would kill you."

I laugh as we head outside, thankful to not be the center of attention for a moment.

Meeting the suitor in advance of the show isn't expressly against the rules, but I'm also pretty sure it's frowned upon. A few seasons ago, one contestant had a one-night stand with the suitor at a mutual friend's wedding weeks before filming, and the rest of the contestants would not let it go. She was constantly accused of having an unfair advantage, and they made her life in the house a living hell. So if Henry wants to keep our transatlantic flight a secret, I'm on board. Besides, we're only acquaintances. I don't even know him.

Which is why, when he joins us in the courtyard, I don't make any attempt to swarm him like most of the other women. I glance around to find Addison and Sara Claire hanging back as well.

Sara Claire smiles at me, but she seems guarded in a way she didn't just hours ago. Addison, however, is sending out her usual don't-even-look-at-me vibes.

The courtyard is as decked out as I remember it being on television. Sadly, it turns out that both the ice sculptures and champagne fountain are fake. Still beautiful if you don't stand too close, though. There's a small bar set up off camera with a guy in a bow tie, black vest, and black jeans lazily pouring bottle after bottle. I can see how this all makes for great TV magic, but in person, it just feels like a wedding reception you'd try to leave early.

Over the course of the night, the house staff comes around with trays of drinks, and soon everyone is talking louder, like we're in the middle of a concert. One white woman (who has the longest extensions I've ever seen and can't stop talking about how she drinks mimosas with every meal) falls into the pool, and Henry has a heroic moment as he helps her out and wraps her in a towel. He's met with a chorus of bitter fawning. Another contestant named Brenda, a white Spanish teacher from Nebraska with Shirley Temple curls and clawlike red fingernails, bursts into tears when someone interrupts her attempts at salsa dancing with Henry.

To say emotions are running high would be an understatement. It's almost too much for me to take.

I find Stacy by the outdoor fireplace sitting next to a sobbing East Asian woman in a forest-green satin gown.

"Is everything okay?" I ask as I approach.

Stacy rubs circles on the other woman's back and nods. "We're going to be fine, right, Jenny?" She turns to me and quietly adds, "I thought it was just the white ladies losing it, but I guess none of us are immune."

The crying woman looks up to me and says, "I fell." Another sob hits her, and she begins to hiccup as cameras begin to swarm, her cries their siren call.

"Water," I say. "Let me get you some water."

I manage to track down a bottle of water from the guy behind the bar, and when I return, a small crowd has gathered to hear Jenny's recount.

"I just stepped out of the car, and then my heel got caught in the train of my dress." She sniffs. "And I bit it. Big-time. It wasn't some cute romantic-comedy fall where I, like, tripped into Mr. Perfect's arms. I landed face-first and—and there was so much blood. They had to call the mediiiiiiiiiic," she tells us, her words devolving into another sob.

Around us, I can see the crew eating this up as Wes whispers to one of the camera operators to tighten his zoom.

"At least you didn't break your nose," Addison deadpans.

"Not helpful!" I snap at her.

She practically snarls, making it even clearer she's not here to make friends.

Jenny wipes her tears away. "No, she's right." She smiles up at Addison in a familiar way, like she's very used to playing beta to some other girl's alpha.

Addison looks to me. "And, Cindy, I've been meaning to tell you, I just think you're so brave."

My brow furrows into a knot. "For what?"

"That dress. It's so stunning, of course, but I would just be so self-conscious. It's just really nice to see a big girl rocking her curves, ya know? So body positive of you."

Jenny nods and so do most of the other girls. "So brave."

My blood turns to lava, and I think I might just explode. Being called *brave* is one of my biggest pet peeves. When someone calls me *brave* for going out or wearing a fitted dress or for some other normal thing that every other girl does, what it really means is: *I would be mortified to look like you, but good for you for merely existing even if all I can think about is how fat you are and how I'm terrified I'll one day look like you.* So brave.

Addison places a hand on my shoulder. "I just want you to know that no matter what happens tonight at elimination and no matter who finds true love, the truest love is the love we give ourselves."

Everyone except Stacy lets out a giant *awwwwww.* Our eyes meet for a moment, and it's a small relief to know that someone else is seeing Addison for who she really is.

"I love girl bonding," says Anna, her hands clutched to her chest.

I nearly vault myself across the crowd to shake her shoulders and scream, *Don't you see how belittling this is! I'm not brave for wearing a dress. I'm just living!*

But instead, I clear my throat and say, "Thanks, girl."

"Ladies."

We all spin around to see Henry returning to the group after a brief one-on-one with Sara Claire, who is beaming.

"Hi, Henry," a few girls say in singsong voices.

"Jenny, are you okay?" he asks.

She nods pitifully.

"Took a real spill, there. I think you might be tougher than some of the guys on my college lacrosse team," he says.

"We've been taking very good care of our sweet Jenny," Addison says. She moves to stand right next to Jenny, practically elbowing Stacy out of the way. "Girls gotta look out for each other."

Henry nods. "I couldn't agree more." He laughs quietly. "You know, I've got to be honest with you. The whole concept of this show is a little bizarre to me."

I notice a cameraman look over to Mallory, but she waves him on to keep filming.

"And I know that the risk is on you ladies. You're all here, putting yourselves out there with no guarantees," Henry continues. "And it's just really nice to see you all helping one another out. I know this is technically a competition, but for me, it's more about finding the right connection. That's not some kind of sport. So thank you, Addison. I really appreciate seeing you be kind to the other women."

My blood boils and my lip curls. What kind of patronizing crap speech was that? There was some truth to what he said, sure, but playing right into Addison's deceitful games? Could he be more clueless?

Addison smiles and shrugs innocently. "You think I could steal you away for just a few?"

Henry holds his arm out to her. "Gladly."

She drapes her arm through his, and we all watch them walk off together to the gazebo a few yards past the pool.

A petite brunette with freckles sprinkling the bridge of her nose sighs. "It's not fair how good they look together."

Jenny sighs in agreement. "It's totally criminal."

"Bless her heart," Sara Claire mutters.

I turn to her and find her frowning, shoulders slumped. "You look like you could use a drink," I say.

She holds a hand out for me, and we stomp to the bar. "Bless *you*," she says.

We each get a glass of rosé, and I ask, "How was your one-on-one?"

She eyes me, her lip twitching with uncertainty. I guess in some sort of primal sense we're all competing for love in the real world, but this show is much more direct than people just trying to meet at a bar or on an app. Figuring out how to communicate with the other women and even befriend them is confusing, and there's no rule book for how to navigate it.

"I think I like him," she finally says. "I know that the cameras want to see me swooning and losing it for him. He's the one who decides who goes home, but I need to know if I want to stay here and fight for a chance with him too, ya know? I have a whole career back home."

"That's a lot to leave behind," I say, suddenly feeling like I have nothing to offer—no career, no real family, and not even a home, technically.

"Look at Addison. One thing goes on the internet or TV and no matter how hard you work, it's all you're known for. I don't want to make that same mistake here."

I nod feverishly, because this is a concern I'm familiar with. The decision to be here at all is a gamble.

"He seems like a sort of normal guy, though."

Thinking back to the guy I met on the plane, it's hard to imagine that he would ever sign up for something like this show, but I'm sure he thinks the same about me.

"He's got to know that any woman who's saying he's the one for her after just one night is totally full of it. Surely he has that much—"

She's interrupted by a loud boom and then everything goes black, and the only sound echoing through the mountains is the shrieking of twenty-five women and the curses of a handful of crew members.

CHAPTER TEN

"**W**e're dark!" someone shouts.

"What about the backup generators?" another person yells back.

"Sara Claire?" I ask, trying my best not to sound like I'm scared of the dark. I'm not, but it's also really unsettling to not even be able to see your own hand in front of you, especially in a place you don't know that well to begin with.

I gasp as fingers wrap around my wrist and tug.

"Who is that?" I whisper as I trip over my feet, barely able to keep up in my heels. "Anna? Drew?"

I falter as I accidentally veer off the pathway into the grass, my heel immediately sinking.

The hand pats up my arm, steadying me. "Careful," says a voice. But this voice is deeper than I was expecting.

"Henry?" I ask.

"We only have a few minutes," he says as we take a few more careful steps.

I can hear him fumbling with something and then the clicking of a doorknob.

"Where are we?" I ask.

"Watch your step," he says, grasping my forearm now.

My eyes have begun to adjust, and there's just enough moonlight that I can make out a bed or a couch and his silhouette.

"What are you doing here?" he asks, which is not what I expected to come out of his mouth. "I'm sorry. I didn't mean for that . . . I'm just shocked to see you. That's all."

"Shocked in a bad way?" I dare to ask as I look up to him, searching for the reflection of his eyes. "I guess the better question is what are *you* doing here?"

"Well," he says, "I guess I'm here to meet my future fiancée."

I cover my mouth to stop myself from spitting on him as I sputter with laughter.

"I'm serious," he says with a lilt in his voice. "I, um, meant to ask for your number, though, so I guess this is convenient."

"So you came here to find your wife, but you meant to get my number at the airport?" I can't tell if he's just not taking this show seriously or if he's actually a total playboy, and then I remember what Sara Claire said about him likely trying to rehab his image. He can be as charming as he wants, but I have no plans to be a pawn in his publicity stunt.

He shakes his head. "Honestly, I don't know why I came here. I almost didn't." He sighs, and I can smell the sweet wine on his breath. "I'm just trying to do right by my mom."

"Your mom?" I ask. "What are you talking about?"

The lights flicker back on and off and then on again. We both blink wildly as our eyes adjust to the light cascading from the ornate chandelier overhead.

I can see now that he appears a little more distraught than he sounded. His forehead is creased with worry, and his bee-stung lower lip is turned downward into a frown. But then I remember from the plane how his almost relaxed, eternal expression seemed to be a slight frown, and I can't help but find that to be just a little bit sexy. I've got a soft spot for the sad ones. The thoughtful ones.

"Your mom," I finally manage to say after spending way too much time staring at him. "What does this have to do with your mom?"

He throws his arms up a little. "It's a long story. I just . . . We need a win—the whole company needs a win."

Faraway voices carry down the pathway to—

"Where are we?" I ask, looking around to see a half-made bed and a suitcase on a luggage stand. "Is this your room?" I have so many more important questions. "Your bed is, like, huge. Did you know they have us four to a room up there in the château? What kind of château requires four grown women to sleep in twin beds in the same room?"

That gets a chuckle out of him. "Yes, I know. I'm very lucky. But we've got to get out of here before they find us."

My eyes widen. "Oh yeah." I can only imagine what kind of drama it might cause if on the first night the suitor went missing with one of the contestants during a blackout.

He moves to open the door but stops. "Wait. We have to decide what we're going to do."

"What do you mean?" I ask.

"We're going to keep quiet, right? About knowing each other. I think that would be best," he says.

I press my lips together in a thin line as I think for a moment. I know that logically that is the absolute best choice, but a very small wiggling familiarity in the pit of my stomach is reminded of the one or two times when some jerk has convinced me to be his secret for whatever reason, usually because he didn't want to be the guy dating the fat girl. I shake the thought from my mind. That's not the case here. I'm on live TV, practically courting this guy for the whole world to see, but old habits die hard, especially when you're a fat girl who will forever be untangling her body-image issues no matter how okay she is with herself.

I should tell him that I told Anna and Drew, but then that might uncover my other and perhaps even bigger secret. Stepmom, sisters, and the whole shebang.

"Okay. It's going into the vault. As far I'm concerned we've never met."

He turns, like he's just remembered something, and begins to dig through the hulking wardrobe in the corner of the room.

"Is . . . Is everything okay?" I ask, like I've interrupted something.

He glances over his shoulder. "Yes, just give me a sec. . . . You look great tonight, by the way. I mean, you did on the flight too, but . . . you know what I mean."

My cheeks flush immediately. That's not something I ever expected the Prince Charming from the plane to say.

"Follow thirty seconds behind me," he says. "If people ask if we snuck off, play coy. Keep it innocent." He spins on his heel and walks back to me with something clutched to his chest.

I nod.

"Better for us to fess up to this than . . . well, you know." He smiles, his gaze lingering on my lips. "Here," he says, handing me a slim walkie-talkie with an antenna.

"What? Did you bring this straight from your tree house? Breaker, breaker one nine, this is Cabbage Patch, do you copy?"

He shakes his head impatiently, but he's still smiling. "I swiped them from one of the trailers when no one was looking. I don't even really know why, or how much battery they have, but I guess if we're going to keep a secret, we should at least have some sort of secret form of communication. But, uh, Cabbage Patch, huh?"

"Henry!" a woman's voice calls.

Startled, I drop the walkie-talkie and we both reach for it at once, knocking heads. "Ow, sorry," I say.

"I got it," he says as he rubs his forehead. He stands upright and hands me the walkie-talkie again, but this time his hand holds on for a beat or two and his thumb grazes my wrist, leaving a trail of goose bumps that travel up my arm as I suck in a breath.

His gaze holds mine for a moment before the voice calls his name again, and he snaps out of it with a chuckle. "Shit. Okay, I gotta go."

"Go," I tell him. "I'll follow after. See you later, stranger."

"Try to avoid the lava." He winks and dashes out the door before I can say another word.

I plop down on his bed and begin to count. One Mississippi, two Mississippi, three Mississippi . . .

I try shoving the walkie-talkie down my bra, but the antenna isn't helping anything. Finally, I manage to maneuver it, and thank goodness it's a flexible antenna.

With a few more seconds to burn, I begin to nose around a little. I can't help myself. On his nightstand is a small Moleskine notebook. I reach for it and find the front page to be speckled with numbers and doodles. Flipping through the pages, I don't find much else except for a few funny stick figure drawings and one page that says *JAY, GET ME OUT OF THIS MEETING* in huge caps. I laugh. Subtle.

Doubling back to the first page, I find a clear space and press my lips to the paper, leaving the impression of my red lips for him to find later. It's a secret, untraceable message from me to him. And I instantly regret it. I'm about to swipe my thumb across the page when I realize that it'll just create a smudge, which might actually be creepier. No, no, no. This is way more stalker energy than I meant to give off.

Nice, Cabbage Patch, real nice.

CHAPTER ELEVEN

Elimination takes place around three in the morning. We're all bleary-eyed and yawning, but that doesn't stop the nervous shifting as we wait for Henry to make his entrance. In the row behind mine, a girl yawns loudly, and I find Allison, who fell in the pool, wearing a matching track suit with her still-damp hair swept into a ponytail. At least I can say I didn't have her night.

The crew staggers all of us on the steps of the château. This is the big elimination that will send home seven girls, and despite the moment Henry and I shared in the guesthouse and the walkie-talkie stuffed down my bra, I think I stand a fifty-fifty chance of going home. Maybe he thinks it would just be easier for us both if he sent me home and we didn't have to pretend like we've never met. Or maybe he doesn't care, and he's really just here for his mom—whatever that means. Regardless, I know exactly what I'm here for, and if I stand any shot of taking home that prize money or at the very least making a big enough splash that might end in a job offer or two, I have to last beyond tonight.

"Look alive, ladies!" Beck shouts.

"Roll camera!" someone calls.

"Rolling," the camerawoman calls back.

"Roll audio!"

"Rolling!"

Behind us the doors of the château open with a creak good enough to be a sound effect, and I can't help but turn around. This could be the last time I see Henry.

But it's not Henry. Instead, Chad Winkle, the longtime host of *Before Midnight*, steps out in his signature tux with sparkling deep navy lapels and a matching bow tie. He's a little more salt-and-pepper than I remember, but in general, Chad has aged well thanks to modern science. He lets out a chuckle as he waves to the contestants, and my stomach flip-flops as I recall the last time I saw him—a New Year's Eve party hosted by Erica when I was just a freshman in high school. It was my first semifamous-people party after she and Dad got married. (Unless you count the wedding.) Surely, Chad doesn't remember Anna, Drew, or me, and even if he does, I remind myself that he's a professional television show host and is totally capable of keeping his cool.

"Good evening, ladies," he says as he takes his place in front of the line of Rolls-Royces prepared to whisk away the disqualified contestants. Beside him is a column that you'd normally expect to display a sculpture or flower arrangement, but instead there's a perfectly stacked pyramid of scrolls. "It seems that some of you had some very real connections with Henry this evening. What a lucky man. Let's bring Henry out!"

Henry steps through the doors of the château, and as he makes his way down the steps, a ripple of giggles follows. He shakes hands with Chad and gives us all a smirk and a nod. "Ladies."

"You had some tough decisions to make tonight," says Chad.

"I did. I met a lot of really special people."

"Well, let's get to it."

My stomach clenches into a knot. This is it.

Henry clears his throat to call a name, but Wes shouts, "Cut! Hold your places!"

Irina, Ginger, and Ash run out to Henry and quickly primp, tugging on his suit, tousling his hair, and powdering his forehead.

"Talk about ruining the moment," Stacy whispers behind me, and I snicker.

After Ash, Irina, and Ginger scatter, we're back and rolling.

"Addison," calls Henry, making her the first name to be called.

Predictable. I try not to roll my eyes in case the camera is on me.

He calls a few other names, including Jenny, which is a good look for him, because who wants to be the guy to send the girl who crash-landed on her face home? One by one, they each take a scroll and excitedly unroll it.

"Anna," he says.

My stepsister squeals, but then doubles back to squeeze Drew's hand.

Anna gives Henry a hug and thanks him for the scroll.

As she takes her place back on the steps, Henry calls Drew's name, and I see the tension in her shoulders immediately melt.

Name after name. Sara Claire. Stacy. Allison. Jen K. And then some I don't know. Amelia. Genevieve. Felicity. Morgan.

And then finally—"Cindy."

My sinking heart floats back up my chest like a drifting balloon. I make my way down the marble staircase, breath held. *Don't fall, don't fall, don't fall, don't fall.*

"Will you accept this scroll?" asks Henry as he hands me the final one.

I nod so hard my head could fall off, and then I lean in for a hug, reaching up and sliding an arm around his neck as I casually kiss his cheek, feeling stupidly brave even though my heart is pounding so hard I'm scared he can hear it. "Thank you," I whisper into his ear.

When I turn back, I find Anna and Drew with wide eyes and slack jaws, while nearly everyone else is shooting mental daggers at my face. Including Addison, whose lips are pursed with irritation.

Girls like Addison have never been threatened by girls like me, and I can't help it. I love watching these tables turn.

"Well, ladies," Chad says in his most official host voice. "I'm sorry to say that if you did not receive a scroll tonight, you have been eliminated. Thank you so much for joining us this evening and taking a shot at true love. Please make your way to the front to say your good-byes to Henry."

I clutch my paper scroll in my hand as I watch seven women, including Juggling Judith and Brenda the Spanish teacher, say goodbye to Henry and slide into the back seat of a Rolls-Royce.

Beside me, Jenny frowns. "I really liked Judith."

Behind me, a tall woman with luscious brown curls who I believe is named Amelia says, "Me too. She was my roommate."

"Well, don't get too sad, Amelia," Addison counters. "The sooner other women go home, the longer we stay. Besides, now you have one less person to share a room with."

Amelia shrugs.

"Okay," Wes says through the bullhorn like we're all cattle again, "let's get all the ladies who are left to make their way down the steps and mingle with Chad and Henry. Music will be playing over your conversation, so no need to be interesting. I know we're all way past due for some sleep."

I stifle a yawn and follow down the steps.

"Read your scrolls! Camera two, get me some over-the-shoulder shots of the scrolls," calls Wes. "Grab a glass of champagne from the trays!"

"Do we have to?" Drew says under her breath. She waits for me at the bottom of the stairs while Anna shimmies her way through the crowd to Henry.

I chuckle, and we make our way to Mallory, who is quickly pouring glass after glass of cheap champagne.

"Maybe I'm still on New York time," I say with a yawn.

"Do you think Mom even realizes how much they try to get people to drink on set?" Drew asks quietly.

"I doubt it." But the truth is, I bet the booze mandate comes straight from Erica. She's the brains behind this whole thing. She's been lubricating reality television contestants with alcohol since Anna and Drew were in diapers. Even the scrolls were her idea. She said in high school a boy asked her out by pretending to read from a scroll like it was an official decree, and ever since then, she'd found the idea of this funny, a little inside joke to herself. In fact, they even sent out scrolls as the invitation to her and Dad's wedding. It was a very elaborate affair.

Drew pours her glass on the pavement and turns to me with a fake laugh, as a camera creeps past us.

I want to just give her a hug and walk arm in arm back into the house with her and Anna. I hate that we're not all in the same room, even though I know it's for the best.

I open my scroll to read.

HEAR YE, HEAR YE!

You have been invited to stay at the château, where you will compete for a chance at true love at the request of Henry Mackenzie. Congratulations, and good luck in your pursuit. Henry asks for the pleasure of your company later this week. More details to come.

I roll up the scroll for safekeeping. I know it's just a silly prop, but I feel weirdly sentimental for it already, like it's the one little souvenir of my time here. At least I'll always be able to say I made it past the first round. Drew reaches up and pushes a wisp of hair out of my face. "Anna's got it bad for this guy."

I cringe a little. "Oof, really?"

Drew laughs. "Anna's got it bad for every guy we've ever met. But don't worry. As soon as she sees how much you like him, she'll back off."

I smile down into my glass of champagne. I'd never admit to having a favorite between the two of my stepsisters, but Drew's always been just a little more intuitive and easier to talk to than Anna. I love Anna, but she's a little airy and just a teensy bit self-involved. Her moods and feelings are as fickle as an afternoon rain shower, but even though she can be a little hard to pin down, she's always been good to me.

I mean, mostly good. Except for those few times back in high school when I was a freshman and Anna and Drew were sophomores. The two of them were busy trying to impress the older popular girls ahead of us. And then one day *they* were the older popular girls and suddenly, when they had no one to answer to but themselves, having their chubby half sister tag along wasn't such a social crime.

"Is it that obvious?" I ask. "That I like him?" It's the first time I'm really admitting it, even to myself.

Drew rolls her eyes. "You were the last to get a scroll and you strutted yourself up there, gave him a long hug, a kiss on the cheek, and whispered in his ear. You basically marked your territory. It was super hot, but trust me—if you didn't have a target on your back, you do now."

CHAPTER TWELVE

T he next morning the house is buzzing with eighteen women doing their very specific morning routines. Smoothies, detox tea, avocado toast, yoga, Pilates, meditation. I settle for eggs with hot sauce, sliced avocado, orange juice, and a patio lounger. Last night, I tried to stay awake and flip through a few channels on the walkie-talkie, but after a marathon of filming, I hid my contraband gadget in one of my shoes and passed out.

As I'm eating my breakfast, I can't help but overhear Addison holding court with a small group of women on the other side of the pool.

"Yeah, his mom was iconic, but the whole brand needs a major facelift," Addison whispers.

What? I run through the mental catalog of designers who I consider iconic for anyone who would have a son around Henry's age. After all the excitement of last night, I completely forgot about Henry's mysterious fashion empire roots.

"I just think it's so precious that he's staying in the family business," a small redhead with corkscrew curls says in a dreamy voice.

Addison rolls her eyes. "I wouldn't say it's precious, Chloe. More like a last-ditch effort to save a sinking ship."

Jenny frowns. "I wore a LuMac dress to homecoming in tenth grade. I still have it. I love that dress."

I gasp loudly. LuMac. Lucy freaking Mackenzie. Oh my God. Henry Mackenzie. How could I possibly have missed this?

From the small patch of grass where a few women are doing

yoga, Anna stretches downward and waves at me from between her spread legs.

I snort. Classy. I beckon her with one hand, and she not-so-discreetly extracts herself from the group.

"Isn't this kind of great?" she asks as she plops down on the lounger next to me and takes a swig of my orange juice. "Is this what college was like? I would have been, like, really good at sorority stuff. Kappa Gamma Boo-Hoo or whatever."

I laugh. "No, definitely not. Especially not design school. Um, did I miss something this morning?"

She taps a finger to her lips and thinks for a moment before letting out a soft gasp. "One of the junior producers dropped off these little packets in the kitchen called the Henry Bible, and it's—"

I stand up quickly and run back into the kitchen, where—sure enough!—there on the second kitchen island is a small stack of papers stapled together—much less ostentatious than last night's scrolls.

I grab a Henry Bible for myself and return to the pool, where I find Anna polishing off the rest of my breakfast. "Anna!"

"What?" she asks with her mouth full of my eggs. "You know I can't cook."

It's true. She's like a little raccoon, always eating everyone else's scraps. "It's fine. I'll make some more in a bit."

She lies back and rubs her now-full belly as I study the Henry Bible. The first page is all about his mom and the business, but I probably could have written a better version myself.

Lucy Mackenzie is a Parsons alumna, so I am plenty familiar with her. The faculty talks about successful alumni on a loop, like it's some kind of infomercial even though we've already agreed to sink an ungodly amount of money into our education. Lucy Mackenzie was a favorite of several of my professors. She's best known for her slip dress, which was a '90s phenomenon where everyone started wearing lingerie as clothing. Everyone always credits Calvin Klein or John Galliano as the creators of the slip dress that started it all. But Lucy Mackenzie (maiden name Mercado), a young, recently married half–Puerto Rican designer from Queens fresh out of design school actually debuted her version of the slip dress at her senior show in 1994, which was actually based off a design in her admissions portfolio from 1989. She worked under Isaac Mizrahi on and off for a little while before striking out on her own, and by 1997, her slip dress was being worn by pop stars and the teens who loved them. She managed to evolve through the early 2000s and expand into streetwear and footwear. Now her dresses have become a staple in department store formal sections, which is not so good for a luxury brand. I think I remember my textiles professor saying the company had recently filed for bankruptcy.

As for Henry, the packet tells us he's just about to take over all of LuMac's business dealings and has high hopes of expanding the brand, but as much as I can't stand Addison, she's not entirely wrong. LuMac is in desperate need of a face-lift.

All I know about Henry is what I've heard around Parsons and read on Page Six. He went to Harvard Business School and has been seen all over town with other children of famous people. Though I never actually committed his name to memory, because he was just another designer's kid. Plenty of celebrity kids went to Parsons, so I know the exact type of crowd he might have hung out with. Half-assing their way through school because they've already got a job or a golden opportunity waiting for them on the other end. And charming as he might be, I'm sure Henry is no different.

When I head back upstairs to toy with my walkie-talkie some more, I find Sara Claire in a towel on her bed. "Did you know that girl Chloe has a whole room to herself now?" she asks. "All of her roomies got sent home last night."

"That's some incredible luck," I say, and then eyeing Addison's bed, I add, "Maybe we'll manage to get just as lucky."

"Fingers crossed!" She points to the papers rolled up under my arm. "Well, I was sort of right," she says. "He's here for redemption. I just didn't think it would be Mommy's company on the line. You're in fashion. You heard anything about him?"

I sink into the armchair in the corner. "His mom went to Parsons, like me, and she's a big deal there. I haven't heard much about him other than the usual Page Six stuff." I shrug. "New arm candy every night. Bad-boy antics in the Hamptons. Et cetera, et cetera."

He was so witty on the plane . . . and then again last night, but now it's hard to imagine him as anything more than just another rich boy.

"Where'd you go last night?" she asks. "During the blackout? I kept meaning to ask you."

"Nowhere," I say too quickly. My throat feels like sandpaper all of a sudden. I hate lying, especially to people I like.

"You were there one minute and gone the next, and then when the lights came up, I didn't see you."

I shrug as nonchalantly as I can. "I guess we just got split up in the dark. What do you think, I'm some Navy SEAL?"

Sara Claire snorts. "Yeah, I can just see you slinking around the château in that super-sexy dress with some serious night vision goggles on. Not at all suspicious."

"Da-dum, da-dum," I sing.

"All right, Pink Panther Elite, I'm going to get dressed and then I guess we just go downstairs and wait around for a group-date invitation."

"Oh, yay, more waiting around for men to do something."

"Cue the confetti cannon," she says.

CHAPTER THIRTEEN

Baaaaaa–maste, ladies!
Please join me for a relaxing afternoon with furry
companions followed by a mimosa bar.
Yours,
Henry

"**T**his place reeks," Addison mumbles.

Sara Claire snickers. "Welcome to a farm, babe."

We all sit on our yoga mats, miked up and ready to go. It's our first group date, and while I'm not opposed to yoga or goats, this isn't exactly my ideal first date. The invitation didn't come for a whole two days. A few of the others were about to go absolutely feral, begging the producers for details and hints. But they held firm while keeping us busy with confessionals and interviews. I took every possible moment I could to sneak away and play with my walkie-talkie radio thing like I was twelve years old, but all I heard was a few crew members asking why there aren't enough gluten-free options for lunch.

The group date invitation came at the exact right time, though, because I thought I was about to witness an all-out war when Stacy discovered Chloe had put a completely empty container of soy milk back in the refrigerator.

"Good afternoon, ladies," Henry says as he emerges from the barn with a tall, thin guy wearing a one-piece Lycra outfit and a slouchy cropped sweater over the top.

"Good afternoon, Henry," we all say back to him in a singsong voice that makes us sound like Charlie's Angels and actually makes me a little bit queasy.

Cameras weave in and out of the group, catching everyone's reactions to Henry's muscled thighs in black athletic shorts and the sight of his bare arms on display thanks to his tank.

"When I was in college, I got injured pretty badly on the lacrosse field, and one thing that really helped me rebound was yoga, so my pal Corbin here is going to lead us all in a class with some help from our little friends."

"Cue the goats!" Zeke calls.

Behind Henry and Corbin, the barn doors open again and a dozen goats trickle out.

Catching myself off guard, I let out a delighted shriek. I don't know if I've just never spent enough quality time with goats or if I'm just caught up in the moment, but these little guys are so damn cute it makes my ovaries hurt.

Henry laughs, and a serenely creepy smile spreads across Corbin's face. Yoga instructor or cult leader? TBD.

Corbin leads us through a few basic poses, and I surprise myself with my ability to balance during tree pose. As he leads us into downward dog, a white goat with the name Chippy on his collar walks up the back of my legs and stands on my butt, like he's conquered the biggest mountain of all. And perhaps he has. If it wasn't so funny, I would probably die at the thought of how likely this is to make it onto national television.

We continue on through a variety of poses, and I'm impressed to see just how fluid Henry is in every single movement.

"He's a real snack," says Sara Claire as she displays her expert flexibility, stretching into upward dog. She catches me eyeing her and adds, "Cheered through middle school, high school, and college. I was a tumbler. My body is basically saltwater taffy at this point."

"Very nice," Corbin says to her as he passes us by.

"Teacher's pet," I whisper.

She grins.

After a few more poses, Corbin sits alongside Henry. "Let's transition into couples yoga. Since we're an odd number, I'm going to choose one of you who impressed me during the first half of our session." He points to Sara Claire. "Join Henry at the front."

Sara Claire's eyes light up as she leaves her mat to be with Henry.

"Now, look to your neighbor and partner up with that person," Corbin instructs.

I groan quietly and turn to find that Addison is also less than pleased with our situation.

Since she makes no effort to move, I scoot over with my mat.

"Don't screw this up for me," she says. "The women who perform well or stand out during the group date usually get guaranteed one-on-one time or the solo date."

"Sit down and face your partner," Corbin says. "With your legs crossed and your wrists resting on your knees, take a moment to ground yourself."

I get situated and close my eyes. If I don't have to see Addison, it's like she's not there. I try to think calming thoughts. Father-daughter trips with Dad to see Muir Woods, but that quickly devolves into a heavy guilt in my chest as I remember the box of Dad's (and Mom's) belongings I left under my bed in Erica's pool house. The last earthly pieces of my parents and I left them to gather dust while I ran off to do goat yoga on a reality TV show.

I take a deep breath and try again for new calming thoughts.

Sleeping in so late on Saturday mornings that my bed is hot with sunshine. Color-coding my shoe collection and micro-organizing by heel height. Going to Coney Island with Sierra in the dead of winter. But all I can see is the silhouette of that box and Erica's handwriting scrawled across the top. None of my happy thoughts are able to set me entirely at ease. I haven't felt fully like myself since this whole thing started. It's like I can remember who I envision myself to be and the person who I think I am, but the reality of who I am in this moment feels like a stranger to me.

"Now open your eyes," Corbin continues. "Look into your partner's eyes."

I open my eyes and see Addison making a side-eye glance at Henry and Sara Claire. The two of them are grinning silly at each other. Henry whispers something to her when Corbin's back is turned, and Sara Claire has to bite her lip to stop herself from laughing. The other night, everyone made such a point of how good Addison and Henry looked together, but Sara Claire and Henry are the ones who seem like a perfect match to me. It doesn't take much imagination at all to picture how their lives might intertwine and play out together. A wedding. A family. Picture-perfect vacations. Grandkids. Hand in hand until the very end.

"Stupid hillbilly," Addison mutters.

"She's from Austin," I say. "That's, like, a huge city."

"Whatever. Just look into my eyes or something."

I take a deep breath and proceed to have the most intense staring contest I've had with anyone since Billy Samples challenged me to one in fifth grade. Winner had to do the loser's vocabulary homework for a week. (I won *and* did my own homework, because I'm terrified of getting in trouble.)

"Now reach out and embrace your partner's forearms," says Corbin. "Very nice," he tells Henry and Sara Claire. "Now, everyone, breathe in and out in sync with your partner. You are a unit. Their breath is your breath."

"You're breathing too fast," I tell Addison.

"You're not breathing fast enough," she says.

Corbin walks us through a few poses, some of which involve Addison's ass way too close to my head. "Now, this next pose I only recommend for the most experienced yogis out there. But I think you and Sara Claire can handle it," he says to Henry.

Henry looks to Sara Claire, his brow arched in question, and she shrugs with a giggle.

"This is called the double plank. Henry, you'll position yourself in a plank on the ground," Corbin continues. "And, Sara Claire, you'll also do a plank, but on Henry's back, facing the opposite direction with your feet on his shoulders."

A quiet groan rolls through the rest of us as Sara Claire and Henry play their little game of Twister as she crawls on top of him.

A row ahead of me, Jenny sighs dramatically as she rests her chin in her hands.

"Is it possible for seventeen people to feel like a third wheel at one time?" I hear someone ask.

Sara Claire's perfect breasts brush the back of Henry's legs, and then voilà! They hit their planking pose for just a few seconds before Sara Claire balances on one arm and touches the bottom of Henry's foot with the other.

Henry kicks wildly, and they both tumble to the ground in a fit of laughter.

"No tickling allowed!" Henry cries.

My stomach flip-flops as I notice the crew eating it all up, pulling in closer to the two of them.

Corbin lets out a stilted laugh—this is definitely breaking the rules of yoga. He leads us through one last breathing exercise. "With your eyes closed, I want you to remember that we are all connected and everything happens for a reason. The universe is a series of reactions. Will you be the *re* or the *action?*"

"I think I'm having a reaction to this bullshit," Stacy whispers behind me.

I snort with laughter and my face turns a deep shade of red. When I open my eyes, the only other person who sees me is Henry. He watches me with one eye open and a faint smile.

"Namaste," says Corbin.

Everyone else opens their eyes, and Henry's gaze stays steady on me.

Warmth sinks from my chest all the way down to my belly, and I almost have to force myself to look away.

"Namaste," we repeat.

Back at the house, we all take turns showering post-yoga and slowly congregate downstairs in the expansive living room. Exploring the château over the last few days has been almost otherworldly. The furniture is ornate and lush, but nothing is actually comfortable. The house is clean, but every room only looks good from certain angles, because there are cords and lights left out for night shooting, or rooms with bad lighting. With no library, television, or internet to keep us busy, we've been left to our own devices when it comes to entertainment. Last night, our attempts devolved into a contest of Chubby Bunny, which resulted in us getting in trouble with Mallory, who had stashed the marshmallows for later so they could get some B-roll of us all making s'mores.

"The first solo date is tonight," Chloe says as she methodically scrunches her wet curls in her hands. "I'd bet money on it."

"Unless your money can buy me five minutes on Twitter, it's no good here," Stacy says.

"Am I right?" Chloe asks Mallory, who is sitting perched on the arm of the sofa alongside one lone camera guy and a sound tech in case we do something interesting, but Mallory just shrugs and continues to type into her phone.

Drew sighs. "Sara Claire is a shoo-in for the solo date."

Jenny's whole body flops in agreement.

Anna studies her hand. "Does anyone know how to read palms? I feel like this one line is really short, and what if that's, like, my life line? I was staring at it last night, and I couldn't stop thinking about it. Honestly, it took me, like, three hours to fall asleep, and I forgot to pack my melatonin, so I just really wish I could get an answer."

Stacy takes her wrist and looks over the lines of Anna's palm. "If I had a stupid phone, I'd be able to look this up and tell you, but until then, all I can say is it's either your life line or your love line. But it does shoot off into a—"

The doorbell rings, a deep chime and then a high one.

"I'll get it!" Drew says before tearing off for the door.

Mallory thumps the camera guy on the leg, and he jolts to attention as Sara Claire joins the rest of us with freshly dried hair.

Drew comes racing back, waving a gold envelope in the air. "Gather round, ladies!"

We all pile up on the couches, and even Addison seems to be eager.

"Well, open it!" Allison demands.

Drew steps onto the coffee table and clears her throat. "'Ladies,'" she reads, "'thank you for spending the afternoon with me. You're all the GOAT.'"

"We're the goat?" Anna asks. "What does that even mean?"

"*G-O-A-T*," Drew spells out. "The greatest of all time."

Stacy shakes her head and looks to Mallory. "Please tell me one of you people is writing these corny-ass messages and not this man we're supposed to be finding attractive."

104

A few other girls giggle, and Mallory just says, "It's a pun! Puns can be sexy."

"Sure, Jan," Stacy says.

I turn to her. "I think I love you."

"Keep reading!" Addison shouts.

"From the top, please," Mallory says. "I'd like to get one clean take."

"Okay, okay," says Drew. "'Ladies,'" she reads, "'thank you for spending the afternoon with me. You're all the GOAT. Tomorrow night I hope you'll all join me for the ball, but tonight I'd like to get a little alone time with a girl who really stood out for me today. Sara Claire, please meet me outside the château at seven o'clock, and wear your dancing shoes.'"

Disappointment weighs me down as all the other girls squeal and pretend to be happy for Sara Claire. I know she got the most one-on-one time with him during yoga, so this makes sense, but I held on to some kind of hope that he might choose me after that look we shared.

Sara Claire bounces a little at my side.

"You're going to have so much fun," I tell her, the words burning on my tongue.

CHAPTER FOURTEEN

While Sara Claire is getting ready in the bathroom and both Stacy and Addison are out by the pool, I take the walkie-talkie out to make sure it still has some battery. I flip through a few channels.

"I need a second camera on the car outside the château in thirty minutes. Will Ben be back from—"

I flip again.

Static.

And again.

More static.

"Is anyone else on this channel?" a voice that sounds like it might belong to Wes asks.

"Hello out there?" Beck's voice calls.

I turn down the volume dial and hold the speaker to my ear.

"Have you hopped on email in the last hour?" asks Wes. "Erica says the network likes my pick for wifey."

Beck is silent for a minute.

"You there?" Wes asks again.

"Yes," Beck says. "I heard you. Look, let's talk about this later. We haven't even cleared it with Henry yet."

"Like he—"

"Wes, I gotta run."

The channel goes silent, so I flip over to the next, expecting to find more sta—

"Hello?" a voice asks softly.

I know that voice. That voice is his voice.

I press down on the button on the side to respond. "Henry?"

Behind me the door swings opens. In a hurry, I flip the power switch as fast as I can.

"Hey," Sara Claire says as I'm stuffing the radio in my shoe with my back to her. "Were you talking to someone?"

I turn around, trying my best not to look guilty. It's not easy. "Oh, uh, maybe just to myself. Sorry, I guess I was thinking out loud."

She smiles and shakes her head. "My daddy does that all the time. It's like his thoughts are too big to just live in his head."

"So relatable," I say. "You look great, by the way."

"Thanks." She twirls in her sequined little black dress. Simple but chic. A little boring, but she's the kind of person who just glows, so she could wear anything and you'd still want to talk to her. "Wish me luck."

I swallow dryly. "Good luck."

I spend most of my night sketching in my bedroom, trying to make my brain work again. Most of the other women play drinking games downstairs, but I don't think my liver can take it. Besides, what they're really doing is waiting up for Sara Claire to come home. I'm already feeling a little miserable, and it's the kind of miserable that doesn't play well with others.

I wish I had my tablet. Switching mediums when I was blocked was a trick I learned early on, but alas, no electronic devices in the *Before Midnight* château. If anyone finds the radio stuffed in my shoe, I'll get kicked out faster than I can even zip my suitcase.

The tip of my pencil snaps against my sketch pad, sending a stray line skidding across the page. Maybe I just have to let it go. Even in school, I knew that not all of us would succeed as designers. For some reason, I thought I was special, and that I would defy all odds. But my well is empty. I have nothing left to give. Deep down I know that I could be happy doing other things. At least, I think. I could find some sort of job in fashion. Maybe I could talk to Sierra's contacts at Macy's. Maybe I don't have to create clothing to work with clothing. The thought of it is a little freeing. And yet, it pains me deeply to think of letting my longtime dream go.

At around one in the morning, Stacy wobbles through the door and plops down on her bed. "I think this might be worse than college," she says, her last word devolving into a loud burp.

"Girl, you're nasty," Addison says as she walks in behind her, strips down to absolutely nothing, and passes out in her bed.

Stacy and I share a look, and she just shrugs. "At least I plan on brushing my teeth," she says loudly.

Soon I'm the only one still awake, so I throw a shirt over my lamp to dim the light. Normally, I'd just go to bed too, but I'm pretty sure they're both too drunk to care if I keep putzing around with my sketch pad. I didn't bring my whole collection of pencils with me—shoes were my priority—but I managed to bring a few of my favorites and a kneaded eraser.

The page is smudged from erasing false starts and bad ideas one right after the next. But finally, after an hour or two, I decide to start with the basics: a shoe. A man's shoe—something I've never really dabbled with. A laceless deep blue suede shoe with a blocked-off square toe. And then it's pants, tailored close to the leg and cropped at the ankle. I add a button-up shirt with a tiny floral pattern. A velvet tux jacket and a matching bow tie. It's less of a design sketch and more of a portrait. . . .

Now I find myself attempting to sketch Henry's face. I've always been awful with faces. Sierra used to make fun of me for just drawing smiley faces on every sketch. With a frustrated sigh, I take my eraser to his jawline over and over again, unable to get it just right. The line of it is too soft and then too harsh. I can't find the right balance.

"You're up," says Sara Claire while she tiptoes through the bedroom door.

"Hi," I whisper as I shove my sketch pad under my pillow. "Couldn't sleep."

She nods, balancing on one foot, taking off her gold sling-back heels.

"How was it?" I dare to ask.

"Nice," she says in too high a voice, like she's finding it hard to believe.

I give her a discerning look, and she caves way too easily.

"It was actually really good and I can't believe I'm even saying that about a date that was recorded for national television." She joins me on my bed, scooting all the way back so she can lean against the wall. "Is—Is Addison buck naked?"

I stifle a laugh. "Uh, yeah, she's toasted."

"Oh Lord." She rolls her eyes. "Queen of the memes over here."

"So dancing, huh?"

Sara Claire sighs. "Yeah, they had us go to some honky-tonk, and Wes had to get Irina to hunt down a pair of cowboy boots for me. I thought we'd be going to a club or something, but I guess they're painting me as the Southern belle and wanted to play it up. They even had me change out of this dress"—she motions down to her black sequined minidress—"and put me in, like, a tiny little denim skirt and a gingham bustier."

"A bustier?" I ask.

"My mother is going to die when she sees me prancing around on television in a bra made out of a tablecloth, but at least I don't have to be there to witness her demise."

"Oh God," I say. "I keep thinking about what's going to happen

109

when all the people who know me—like, really know me—see the show."

"Oh, baby," she says. "They've seen. It's Tuesday. First episode aired tonight."

I gasp. "You're right! I swear, time is a meaningless circle in this place." I wish I could talk to Sierra and all my friends back in New York. They probably think something is legitimately wrong with me or my life has turned into some kind of M. Night Shyamalan movie.

She shivers a little. "I'm trying not to think about it. Honestly, I hope I still have a job when I get home. I might be a daddy's girl, but Daddy takes his business very seriously." She takes a deep breath. "So anyway, we went dancing. And then the producers arranged this elaborate romantic dinner for just the two of us inside this really adorable old barbecue joint. There were rose petals and candles, and I got barbecue sauce all over my face—even though we really only ate for a minute so they could get a few shots of us eating ribs—and he did that whole cute thing where he wiped the sauce off my chin and then, that was it."

My shoulders sink. "That's it?"

She shakes her head. "I'm sorry. . . . It's just that this is so weird. . . . Like, I like you. In any other setting, we'd be friends. Actually, we are friends, but . . . I just don't want to make it weird."

I appreciate how careful she's trying to be of me and my feelings, but this might actually be worse than just knowing. "I don't think there's a right way to do this. I think we just have to be honest and tell each other when it's too much and we won't talk about it anymore, but for now . . . you're leaving me hanging! Give me the goods!"

She drops her chin to her shoulder and smiles. "He is a real good kisser. I was so into it, but I kept having to remind myself that we were being filmed, and that this was still for the cameras and that I couldn't let myself get swept up in it all just yet. I've been through a lot, Cindy. I don't know how much more hurt I can handle." She bites down on her lip and leans in a little closer. "But then, while the crew was packing up and we were waiting for our cars, he leaned in and kissed me on the cheek . . . and I don't know, but somehow it was the hottest thing. No one was looking. And you know how militant they are about leaving us alone with him."

I nod. That's like a *Before Midnight* golden rule.

She touches her fingers to her cheek and smiles faintly. "He's funny too. Genuinely funny."

I almost catch myself verbally agreeing with her as I remember our banter on the plane. "Well, maybe I'll get to find out for myself."

I help Sara Claire with the zipper of her dress, and once she's ready to turn in, I click off my lamp and slide my sketch pad under my bed. I wonder for a brief moment if Henry opened the notebook in his bedroom and saw the imprint of my lips pressed inside.

After a few minutes, I'm unable to fall asleep, so I stand up and creep over to my suitcase to grab the walkie-talkie. It's a long shot, but it's worth a try.

"Are you okay?" Sara Claire whispers.

"Just running to the bathroom," I say with the radio pressed to my chest.

"Do you want me to turn the light on?"

"No, no, no," I sputter. "Go to sleep. I'll be right back."

I tiptoe out of the room and down the hall to where the expansive landing opens up to a balcony overlooking the courtyard and then pool.

I sink down to the ground, tucking my knees into my T-shirt, and hold the walkie-talkie to my mouth. Between railing bars, I can see a small light in the distance—the guesthouse where they're tucking Henry away. Hiding him from us in plain sight. It's a little bit genius, actually. The other women would be shocked to know that he's been right under our noses all along.

"Hello?" I ask, still on the same channel as I was when Sara Claire came in.

I stare so intently at the light in the distance that my vision starts to blur.

When I was a kid, after Mom died, I was scared to sleep alone. I don't know why specifically, but I think that I was scared I would wake up and Dad would be gone too. Over the next few months, Dad eased me back into my own bed. It started with me falling asleep in his bed and then him carrying me across the hall. Then him lying in my bed with me until I fell asleep, the scruff of his beard scratching against my forehead. Finally, as I started to go to bed on my own, Dad and I would leave our bedroom doors wide open so that I could call out to him anytime I needed him or just wanted to make sure he was still there.

"Hello?" I would call out, sometimes in the middle of the night. "Hello?"

Usually, he would answer immediately, or sometimes, if he was asleep, it would take him a few seconds. But he always answered. Always.

I hold the radio up once more, Henry's light still glowing. "Hello?"

The closest thing to an answer I receive is his light flickering off, leaving nothing but darkness.

I go back to my bedroom and tuck away my secret radio before sliding back into bed. When I close my eyes, I hope Dad is there calling back to me, like he always was when I needed him most.

CHAPTER FIFTEEN

"**D**o I look okay?" I ask Beck.

She reaches past the camera and loops a piece of hair behind my ear. "Stretch your mouth. Do, re, mi, et cetera, et cetera. Your smile looks a little serial-killer-ish. Just relax. Ignore everyone else."

Tonight they have us intermittently filming confessionals during this evening's ball, so it's hard not to pay attention to all the little dramas unfolding around me. Samantha is accusing Drew of stealing her eyelash glue. Addison is making the rounds and telling people she thinks Chloe is here for the wrong reasons. Jenny is outraged that craft services is serving shrimp cocktail since she's allergic and thinks someone on the crew has it in for her. This place is a circus. (By design, of course.)

"Now, down to business," Beck says. "Have you had any one-on-one time with Henry yet this evening?"

"No." Even though she already knew the answer.

"Help me out here, Cin. Try elaborating."

"Well, maybe you should ask better open-ended questions."

She laughs. "Excuse you, Ms. Producer."

That gets a real smile out of me, even though I'm still feeling a little irritable after last night and then not hearing from Henry today even though I snuck away with that stupid walkie-talkie every chance I got. It feels like I gave some guy my number and he hasn't called.

Beck nods. "Okay, let's try this again. How do you feel about your chances at the elimination ceremony tonight?"

I pout instinctively. "I haven't really gotten to know Henry yet, and so I guess my chances aren't great? But maybe a bad impression is worse than no impression. Or maybe it's like a credit score. No credit is worse than bad credit. Is that how that works? Did I get that backward?"

"So you think other women have made a bad impression?" she asks, not taking my credit-score-nonsense bait.

I narrow my eyes at her. "I think Henry has a selection to work with."

"And do you have any plans to score some alone time with him at the ball tonight?"

"Of course I hope I get to talk to him, but I'm not going to just barge in and interrupt a conversation."

Beck crosses her legs, her ankle resting atop her knee, and I feel like I'm about to get a talking-to. "Why's that? Don't you think any other girl here would do the same to you? Don't you want to fight for this?"

I can't help but feel like Beck is trying to tell me something here, but I don't like the idea of elbowing in on people and playing some kind of game. But that's the thing, isn't it? This is some kind of game. That's the whole point. Do I want to be the girl who got kicked off on the second episode and is barely even memorable?

"Yes," I finally say. "I do plan on fighting for this." And then quickly, I add, "For Henry."

I feel unsettled and queasy. This isn't real. No one's actually here for love, but the thought of using this opportunity with Henry to forward my own career feels different now. I can't ignore the jealousy I felt last night when Sara Claire left for their date. I didn't mind taking advantage of this situation when it was just some nameless guy who probably wouldn't even take a second look at me. But it's not just some guy. It's Henry, and even though I don't really *know* him, I know him

114

well enough for him to be real and for this to be more than a silly game. Even if he is currently ghosting me via walkie-talkie.

"Am I done now?" I ask.

"I'm trying to make a TV show," Beck reminds me. "But fine. Yes, you can go."

I stand and give Sara Claire a high five, tagging her in as she goes to take my spot.

"Have I mentioned how hot you look tonight?" she asks.

"Thanks." I smooth out the wrinkles in my dress. Tonight I went for a vintage black-and-white polka-dot shift dress with a high scarf neck that ties off to the side into a huge bow. It was originally long and shapeless, but I nipped it in a little around the chest and cut it into a mini, and now with my hair swept into a high bun, I'm a '60s dream come true. Of course, my shoes are the real showstoppers. Authentic 1968 Montgomery Ward coral platform wedge T-strap Mary Janes, straight from eBay to my heart.

When Addison saw me, she actually laughed and said, "You're just so quirky. Like a cute little librarian."

She meant it as a diss, but news flash, Addison: Librarians are hot. Look at Stacy.

On the other side of the courtyard, I see Henry sitting next to Addison as he nods along and she laughs at her own jokes. I throw back a quick glass of chardonnay and march over there. If there's any girl's time I'm comfortable crashing, it's hers, and if Beck is trying to make a TV show, I can at least give her something to work with.

"She's on the move," I hear someone call. "Camera on Cindy."

I don't even have to turn around to feel a whole crew at my back.

"Cindy," Henry says as I approach the gazebo, where another camera and full lights are waiting.

Addison doesn't even look up at me as she does her best to pretend that I don't exist.

"Addison, sweetie, could I steal him for a moment?" I say in my sweetest voice.

"Oh!" She bounces to attention. "Sure. . . . Not for too long, though." She stands, still holding Henry's hand as she wiggles a finger at him with her other hand. "I'll be back before you know it."

He gives her a smarmy grin. "I have no doubt."

"No doubt," I mimic under my breath as she walks off.

He clears his throat. "Excuse me?"

I choke on a laugh as I remember the cameras, the lights, and the fact that Henry and I aren't even supposed to know each other that well and people who don't know each other don't usually tease each other like that.

"Nothing," I say, knowing full well that every mic picked that up. And I'm pretty sure Henry did too.

I sit down beside him, and a junior producer hands me another drink, but I don't think I need any more loosening right now.

Henry clinks his glass to mine. "Cheers."

"Cheers."

"So what made you leave your life behind to come on a show like this?"

I snort. "Starting out with the heavy hitters, huh?" I loop a loose strand of hair behind my ear, taking a moment to regain my composure. "I wouldn't say I was leaving a whole life behind. I guess you could say I'm in between things. At a crossroads."

"What kind of things? Boyfriend-shaped things?"

My cheeks immediately flush with heat as I shake my head. "Um . . . I've actually been single for quite a while." I dated Jared, a poli-sci major from NYU, for half of freshman year and all of sophomore year. He was the kind of guy who always said he was fiscally conservative and was constantly exhausting people by playing devil's advocate. Sierra threw me a party when I broke up with him. "What about you?"

116

"I've . . . dated. But nothing serious for a while. At least no one I'd bring home to Mom just yet."

My eyes light up at the mention of his mom. I have so many questions. "Your mom, huh?"

"Ah, that's right," he says. "The fashion student with a passion for shoes."

"Guilty."

He leans back and stretches an arm out behind me. "What about fashion drew you in?"

The corners of my lips twitch, as I'm unsure how to play this. There are lots of answers to this question, and I'm a little scared to share anything too precious—not just with Henry, but with the whole wide world. My relationship with my work at the moment is fragile at best. I'm not sure it could stand the scrutiny of a television audience. But . . . something about Henry's unmoving, stable gaze compels me.

"Ever since I was a kid, I loved the way that clothing could transform you. I've . . . I've always been fat. *Plump* as my dad used to say. And people are so quick to make up their minds about me before I even open my mouth. My style is a chance for me to express myself and to maybe even make someone rethink their snap judgment. But that's just a small part of it. I love the lines. I love that it's art you can wear. I hate how inaccessible and distant art can feel, but you can walk into Target and walk out dressed as a piece of art. That's something almost anyone can do." I laugh a little to myself. "Sorry, I didn't mean to drone on like that."

"No." He shakes his head as his thumb grazes the back of my neck, sending a wave of chills down my spine. "I . . . I've been around this industry my whole life, and it's easy to feel burned out. Fresh perspective like that can be invigorating."

"What about you?" I ask.

He sighs. "It's the family business. I think I definitely have a sense of style, though my mother might say otherwise. But for me, I appreciate the utilitarianism of it all. Clothing is not only an art but a daily need. Not all industries have that same crossover, and I find it fascinating. Admittedly, I'm more involved on the business side of things, but I guess you could say I do have some design thoughts."

"Oh, do you, now?"

He nods emphatically. "Yes, like who actually decided a button fly was a good idea, and is it actually safe to carry a hammer in the loop on a pair of carpenter jeans?"

"Ah, the hard-hitting questions. Watch out. You might just cause the entire industry to crumble."

He smiles crookedly. "I hated fashion when I was younger."

I throw my head back with a laugh—also hoping it will encourage him to touch my neck again. "Was that the big rebellion of your youth? Did you have a run-in with a bolt of taffeta as a child?"

He smirks. "Really? Going after my childhood now?" But there's something in his voice that tells me I've hit a sensitive spot. "You should've seen me. I only wore black jeans and T-shirts in high school. The best reaction I got out of my mom was some speech about how even then I was making a fashion statement."

I can't help but laugh again. "She's not wrong."

"Your turn," he says. "Tell me about your family."

I'm pretty sure you already know my stepmom, I nearly say. "Well, my mom had ovarian cancer and passed away when I was a kid, so it was just my dad and me until he got remarried while I was in middle school. She already had two daughters, so we went from a family of two to a family of five. And now I have three little siblings too. Triplets, actually."

"Whoa. I've always wondered what it would feel like to be part of a big family. And your mother . . . I'm sure she was wonderful."

I nod, my shoulders sinking. He hasn't even heard the rest of the sob story yet. "Dad passed away while I was in high school. It was sudden. And then just like that, my stepfamily became my only family."

He flinches, and his voice is low and scratchy, almost like he wishes the cameras weren't here anymore. "I'm so sorry. You must miss both of them so much."

When Dad died, I heard so many people tell me they were sorry over and over again to the point that the word doesn't even carry meaning anymore. It's just a cloud of a word. You can hear it. You can see it. You just can't feel it. But the way Henry tells me he's sorry makes me feel like he would sacrifice something real for me to have a magical do-over and a second shot. But there's no magic to be found in this story. No happily-ever-after.

"Thank you," I say as I turn away from the cameras to quickly wipe one stray tear. The last thing I need is to ugly cry on television. I'd be the Girl Who Ugly Cried as quickly as I'm sure Jenny became the Girl Who Ate It Big-Time.

With one arm still behind me, Henry takes my hand in his free one and rubs soft circles into my palm. In this moment, it's as relaxing as a full-body massage. And even though the whole world can see us holding hands, every little circle is a secret from the cameras. A private touch for only us. Now I understand completely what Sara Claire meant about the kiss on the cheek, and I can't help but feel that little shadow of jealousy once again.

"Hey, y'all . . ." a voice softly interrupts.

I have to stop myself from audibly groaning.

Henry clears his throat and leans back. "Sara Claire. How are you?"

She smiles timidly, which is annoying, because Sara Claire is not timid, and what is she even doing? She had a whole date with him.

I can feel the absolutely absurd expression forming on my face as I try to look nice and polite while also sending her some kind of signal that says *not now*.

"Cindy darling, do you mind if I cut in?"

I look to Henry and his smile is stiff. "Sure," I finally say, and stand up, my hand slipping from his. "All yours."

I give Sara Claire what I hope is a meaningful look. I know we're all here for the same reason, but it's hard not to feel betrayed, especially after last night.

She giggles as she settles down beside him, fitting perfectly under his arm, and I hate that I hate her right now. It's a disgusting feeling that goes against everything I thought I've ever believed about women empowering each other and lifting each other up. But maybe this show is too much of a feminist wasteland for anything like that to even be possible.

Closer to the house, I find Anna and Drew with Chloe, Jenny, and Stacy all huddled around an electric fire pit.

"She really swooped right in, didn't she?" asks Chloe as the circle widens for me to squeeze in between Anna and Drew.

"I don't think I like that girl," says Anna.

"You don't even know her," I spit back at her.

Anna jerks away a little, and Drew eyes me in a way that says, *And you do?*

"Sorry." I nudge Anna and she eases a bit. "I'm just on edge."

Stacy shrugs. "Besides, you can't get mad because someone is doing the things we all came here to do. Aren't we all here to win?"

A gust of wind blows through the courtyard and a shiver rolls through me. "Yeah. It would have been nice if she hadn't just barged in like that. And it was so unlike her—"

"I don't buy that whole Southern-manners act," Jenny says.

"It doesn't matter if you buy it or not," Addison says from outside the circle. "It only matters if Henry does."

"Good evening, ladies," says Chad as he steps out into the center of the courtyard. "If you'll follow me to the front of the house, it's time for elimination."

"What?" asks Jenny. "We've barely even seen Henry tonight."

"Henry has made his decision. He's ready for the elimination ceremony."

As we walk through the house to the front, where lights and cameras are already set, Drew takes my hand. "Something's up with Anna," she whispers. "Doesn't she seem off to you?"

"What? No. I haven't noticed." But then again, I wouldn't notice after being so wrapped up in myself. "If anything, I'm the one who's off."

Drew shakes her head. "I can't put my finger on it."

As we step out onto the marble staircase, we're directed in opposite directions.

Our hands drift, but Drew links her pinkie to mine. "Good luck, babe."

My relationship with Anna and Drew was so difficult to navigate in high school. Imagine living with the older, most popular girls in school and trying to just be yourself around them. Things shifted their senior year when they became the ultimate queen bees, but I was still always their oddball stepsister whose fashion sense was a little offbeat and who found her solace in the drama costuming department. But after Dad died, they were there for me in a way any other friend just couldn't be, because they loved Dad like he was their own father. The pain I felt was different from theirs, but it was a pain we bonded over. Just getting to see their warm smiles while I'm here in isolation with seventeen other women and a television crew is a comfort I don't take for granted.

Tonight, Mallory lines me up in the front row between Chloe and Addison with Anna directly behind me.

"Welcome to the Midnight Ceremony. This evening is our last big elimination," Chad announces with a line of Rolls-Royces at his back and the huge *Before Midnight* clock towering over us all. "Tonight this group will go from seventeen to ten. As the group grows smaller, it will be more important to make an impression on Henry. True love

121

is on the line. And the clock is ticking." He turns to Henry. "Let's get to it."

Henry's stance is broad with his hands clasped in front of him. For someone who thinks clothing only serves a utilitarian purpose, he looks painfully handsome in a flawlessly cut deep blue suit. His dark eyes flit up toward us. "I've had a great few days getting to know each of you, and it's given me the chance to decide who I need to spend more time with and whose journey here ends tonight." He pauses for a beat. "Sara Claire, will you accept this scroll?"

I glance behind me and watch as she floats down the stairs, her cheeks flushed. "Of course," she says, and when she reaches him, she stands there as they share a silent moment together. "Thank you," she whispers.

I get a sick feeling in my stomach as it hits me. She's really falling for him. She really is. And I want to hate her for it, but isn't that what we're all here to do? Fall for this guy. I remember when we first got here and how she said this felt like her last chance. I know that can't be true . . . but what if it is? And what if I'm just standing in the way?

Addison, Jenny, Chloe, Anna, Gretchen, Samantha, Stacy, Valerie . . . Until only one scroll remains.

"Cindy," he says.

I bite down on my lip to stop my smile from turning goofy. "Thank you." I hold the scroll to my chest as I stand off to the side.

Chad steps forward. "If Henry didn't call your name, then that means you'll be leaving us tonight."

I look up to see Drew still standing there without a scroll, and suddenly, it feels like the rug's been pulled out from under me.

"No!" Anna says. "What about Drew?"

Henry looks up to where my statuesque stepsister in her beautiful lavender silk gown stands, her expression hollow. I knew this would happen and that one of us would have to be the first to go home, but I was absolutely certain it would be me and that I wouldn't have to watch one of my sisters go.

Drew glances to Anna and then me, and shakes her head, trying to smile through her disappointment.

The rejected girls make their way down the steps to say good-bye to Henry, and Drew bypasses him altogether, heading straight for Anna.

"One less girl in your way," she says to Anna with a wink as she pulls her in for a hug.

My chest tightens, and I can feel tears brimming for the second time tonight.

A cameraman pulls in tight on the two of them, and I have to remind myself that we're technically not supposed to be sisters. "We'll miss you," I say quietly, my voice cracking.

Drew pulls me into their hug. "Watch out for her," she whispers into my ear.

"Hug Mom for us," Anna begs her just quietly enough for only us to hear. "And Gus, Jack, and Mary."

Our tearful goodbye triggers more tears from the other women, like it's contagious. I guess we're all tired and a little bit drunk.

After the cars with the eliminated women pull away, Beck emerges from the cluster of crew members and yanks me aside as all the other women trickle back into the house.

"Follow me," she grunts. "Stay quiet."

I follow Beck around the side of the house. "Where are you going?" I whisper.

She doesn't turn around but just waves me up a metal ramp into an eighteen-wheeler full of sound equipment.

She peers out the trailer once more before grinning maniacally and shaking me by the shoulders. "Cindy! They freaking love you!"

"They? Who's they?"

"The audience! The American people! You're a hit! And what you said tonight to Henry about your love for fashion—pure gold!"

Slowly, it dawns on me. It's impossible to forget the cameras, but being so secluded, all the way up here, it is somehow possible to forget about the rest of the world. "I—I— How?" is all I can manage to stutter.

"And thank goodness you weaseled in on some Henry time tonight. You were on the maybe list, and we pull most of the strings here, but Henry has the final say on eliminations. Sort of."

My heart sinks. "What? The maybe list?"

She waves her hand. "Forget that. He kept you! That's all that matters. Well, that and the fact that you're a damn American sweetheart!"

"But there's a list? And I wasn't on the right one?"

She sighs loudly before rattling off a response. "Before each elimination, the suitor starts making a list—sometimes even before the group date—and the production staff has a girl or two they're really championing, and we might have a teensy bit of sway. But really, it's his choice, so all we can do is control the things that might help him decide."

I lean back against the inside of the trailer, remembering the conversation I heard between her and Wes about "wifey." I want to ask her, but I also don't want to lose my walkie-talkie privileges. "And that's why you were asking me those questions during my interview?"

She nods. "Exactly. After seeing the response to you online, I couldn't risk you going home so soon."

"Online? What response? Wait. Go back. You called me an American sweetheart?" Thanks to the no-phone rule, my brain is receiving a higher influx of information than it has in days, and I'm already feeling a little overwhelmed.

She grits her teeth, thinking for a moment. "Oh, screw it." She pulls her phone out of her back pocket. "Erica would actually kill me if she knew I was doing this."

It's been barely a week since I last held a cell phone, and when she hands it to me, I almost don't know what to do with it, so she reaches over and starts scrolling through screenshots for me.

@melodydiaz648
Yes, honey! Finally, a plus-size queen on this show! #BeforeMidnight

@notyourgirlfriend202
Is it just me or is the curvy girl the most interesting one this season? I'm calling it! I've found wifey! #BeforeMidnight

@messyfeminist359
This Cindy girl is FIERCE! Where can I get those shoes? And that dress? #BeforeMidnight

@RealMelanieGoodwin
Who do I get in touch with about these feather dream shoes? I NEED THEM. #BeforeMidnight

@THEalexismartin
Honestly, I was about to tune out of this season of #BeforeMidnight and then Cindy showed up.

I keep scrolling. There is an endless supply of screenshots. "Some of these people are f-famous," I manage to stutter. "Like blue-checkmark famous. Melanie Goodwin is tweeting about me?" Every single one of the famous model's tweets becomes an instant viral sensation. Seeing my name next to hers is surreal.

"Uh, yeah," says Beck. "Everyone is hyped on you! There are GIFs, hashtags, and *People* even published a piece with their picks for the top five and you're in it, baby!"

My jaw drops and my eyes widen as I slide down the wall, no mind for my dress. "*People*? As in the magazine?"

Beck sits down next to me. "Yes! They even called you an up-and-coming designer with an eye for exquisite footwear!"

My heart pounds frantically. An up-and-coming designer? I'm flattered, and yet I feel like a fraud. "What! How did they—"

She nudges me with her elbow. "I might have fed them a quote or two."

I lean my head on her shoulder. "Thank you." After a moment I add, "I feel bad about Drew."

She pats my head. "Drew is going to be just fine. She'll wake up tomorrow morning with an extra hundred thousand Instagram followers and some brand deals in waiting."

"Really?" I ask.

"The magic of television."

Her walkie-talkie beeps. "Beck? Does anyone have eyes on Beck?" Wes asks.

I sit up, and she talks into her walkie-talkie. "Beck here."

"Oh good," he says. "I was about to put an AMBER Alert out on you."

"I'm coming, I'm coming."

Beck stands and then holds out a hand to help me to my feet, which is no easy thing to do in a minidress and platforms.

"Do you think he even likes me?" I ask.

She shrugs. "Enough to keep you. That's what matters."

But is that enough? Is that all I want? For him to like me just enough so that I get my full fifteen minutes in the spotlight?

We walk out of the trailer, and Beck points me to a side entrance where I can easily sneak in.

"Good night, up-and-coming designer!" she quietly calls to me.

CHAPTER SIXTEEN

When I make it back to my room, I'm exhausted, and I guess so was everyone else, because my three roommates are sound asleep. The room is definitely more lived-in than it was when we first got here. Shoes and makeup on every surface and bras hanging from doorknobs and headboards.

After I get out of my dress and put on some shorts and my holey sleep shirt, my hand hovers over the radio hidden in my suitcase. For a moment there tonight, it really felt like Henry and I got lost in each other. The cameras and other women sort of just faded away . . . but in that moment, he didn't even know if he was going to send me home or keep me here.

I grab the radio and sneak out to the balcony after slipping on my hoodie. I have questions. Questions I would like Henry to answer.

When I walk outside, Henry's light is already out. Deflated, I sink down to the ground with my back to the railing.

I hold the walkie-talkie up. "Hello?"

I wait. One Mississippi, two Mississippi, three Mississippi . . .

"Hello?" I ask again.

Nothing.

"Henry?"

Nothing.

"Is this place making you as nuts as it's making me?" I ask into the void. Maybe if I just talk, he'll hear me eventually. "It's . . . It's like being so far away from everyone and then dropped into this social blender . . . It, like, strips everything away, and all that's left is the wors—"

"Cabbage Patch, is that you?" a semigroggy voice asks.

I gasp and hold the walkie-talkie to my chest as I scream in delight with my mouth closed. I press the talk button. "Cabbage Patch, over."

"I guess I should confess that I've never used a walkie-talkie, and so I hadn't really thought through any of the logistics when I handed you one."

I grin as I maneuver around so that I've got a view of his guesthouse. "Ahhhh, yes. There are, apparently, channels."

He chuckles. "Yeah, I've heard way too much about what yogurt does to Wes's intestines."

"Well, that sounds . . . like a personal medical issue."

"Yeah, you and the whole crew would agree."

It's silent for a moment. Left as we are without chaperones, it's hard to know where to start or what to say.

"Where are you?" he asks, his voice raspy, and I can hear the rustle of sheets in the background.

"Out on the balcony at the back of the house . . . I can see you, by the way. Well, I can see your guesthouse."

The light in the distance flicks on, and something shifts—just a slight movement. "That's better," he says. "Now I can see you too. But whoa, you didn't tell me it was cold out here."

I laugh. "You're from New York. This is not cold."

"What do you know about my city?"

"Excuse me, but did you so quickly forget where our flight was departing from when we first met? And, oh my God, you're the worst kind of New Yorker."

"Well, excuse me, but your profile said you were from Los Angeles. There's no such thing as a quintessential New Yorker."

"My profile?" I ask. Of course, they'd give him those little questionnaires we filled out. "What else do you know about me?"

"Well, Cindy Woods, I know that you went to fashion school at my mother's alma mater and that your favorite movie is *Sister Act 2* and you're terrified of ladybugs and that you believe in aliens."

"I'll have you know that ladybugs are very entitled, okay? And there's no way we're alone out here," I tell him. "It's just obnoxious to assume we're the only intelligent life in the universe."

"Honestly, as long as you're not a flat-Earther, I can live with the rest. And I guess when you look at it like that, you sound more logical and less Roswell, New Mexico, gift shop."

"I've always wanted to go to Roswell. Don't tease me."

"We should go," he says, and then quickly adds, "I mean, depending on how . . ."

"Depending on if you pick me?" I ask. It's so hard not to ask him outright why he's here and if he sees himself with any of these other women. Without anyone else around, it's hard not to feel like we're playing by a silly set of made-up rules for no reason.

"Wow, this is weird."

"You're the one who chose to date twenty-plus women on a television show."

"Well, you are one of those twenty-plus women who chose to be here."

"Touché."

"So triplets, huh?" he asks. "Your little siblings. You said they were triplets, right?"

"Yeah . . . you know, I thought seeing my stepmom raise triplets would make me never want to have kids . . . but now I just want a really big family."

"I always wanted siblings," he says. "I was always the one kid in a room full of adults."

"Yes, this! I mean, I wasn't in fancy rooms like you were, I'm sure, but it was always my dad and me for so long, and for a while there, I felt like I was more of a middle-aged man than I was a little girl."

"The rooms weren't always fancy," he says. "Mostly fancy, but not always."

"I knew it."

"So you and your dad were close?"

I nod, even though he can't see me. "We only had each other. We were best friends. Now that I'm older, I miss those days when it was just us. I always remember how quiet it always was with just us, and then after he got married, there was always noise. The house felt full. Quiet was nice, but the noise was . . . comforting in a different way."

"Like white noise," he says softly. "Not in a bad way."

"No, not at all."

"Kind of like New York City."

"Yes, I honestly have a hard time falling asleep if it's not to the sound of sirens."

"God, yes, I need my city noise. Except on my block it's the doorman across the street saying, 'Hey, boss,' on repeat followed by honking horns."

I chuckle. "Well, I didn't have any doormen on my block, but I did have a bodega lady who communicated entirely in grunts. My roommate was fluent."

For a moment there's a lull, but it's enough to remind me that we're almost strangers.

"The family business," I say. "Taking over must be stressful."

"It's . . . It's difficult. Mom's not ready to move on . . . I'm not ready to step in, but I've got a great team in place. There's just . . . a lot."

"Way to be vague," I say with a laugh.

"Sorry," he says knowingly. "I just have to be careful. Certain things get out . . . LuMac loses value, and anyway . . ."

"Is your mom okay? Can I ask that?"

"She's alive," he says tentatively. "I guess just not in a way that brings her joy. She's having to let go of the things that made her . . . her. So, anyway, enough about me."

No, I nearly say, *more about you*. If we were in the real world, I would want to unravel the inner workings of Henry Mackenzie slowly, savoring every layer.

"Shit. I gotta go," he says. "I think I just saw someone up by the trucks. Talk again soon?"

"Promise?" I ask him.

But there's no answer. I sit there for a moment longer, waiting for a response, but nothing. I shove the walkie-talkie in the pocket of my hoodie and stand up. Just as I'm about to walk back inside, Henry's light flickers off and on twice in quick succession, and I can only hope it's his secret way of telling me yes.

I close my eyes, and for just a moment I allow myself to imagine what it might be like to run my fingers along the edge of Henry's jaw and kiss him good night.

CHAPTER SEVENTEEN

Ladies,
Join me today for a match to remember. And if we're
lucky, maybe we'll get in the ring and have a match of our
own, but whatever you do: Don't get your feathers ruffled.
Yours truly,
Henry

T he ten of us are led into a small, crowded boxing gym. The members of the audience are mostly fans of the show who have answered casting calls for extras. It's hard not to see them whisper and point as we all settle into the front row. We've been instructed to dress for a ringside date night. Whatever that means.

Outside of the Rocky movies, I have next to no knowledge of boxing, but I figured I couldn't go wrong in lace-up espadrilles and a black gingham romper.

Beck stands in the middle of the ring on a stepladder, shouting directions through a microphone. "Mallory—wave, Mallory!"

Behind her, Mallory waves limply.

"Mallory," Beck continues, "will be your point of direction. If Mallory motions for you to cheer, you cheer. If she's telling you to be quiet, I don't want to hear you so much as breathe. You hear me?"

Stacy leans over and whispers, "Is it weird that bossy Beck is a turn-on?"

I laugh. "Don't make me ship you two."

On the other side of me, Anna abruptly announces, "I need to pee. Can a producer take me to pee?"

Mallory sighs and dutifully begins to climb under the ropes. On the way here, Wes gave us a very serious lecture about trying to talk to extras or anyone else we saw while we were out, and we were expressly told not to go anywhere alone.

"I got her," says Zeke, jogging toward us. He helps Anna to her feet and guides her toward the restrooms.

Stacy groans. "Man, these people will not give us any breathing room. I feel like we're on a leash."

I nod. "They don't want us finding out what's actually going on in the real world or how we're being portrayed. Do you ever feel like we're a bunch of lab rats?" I ask.

She snorts. "Too real."

After a few minutes, Anna hurries back, out of breath and a little sweaty. "Sorry, they made me go all the way out to the porta-potties. It took forever and it smelled gross."

I sniff her hair. "You still smell like bubble gum, so at least there's that."

A super-ripped announcer dressed like a referee with tattoos running up and down his bulging arms takes the stage.

"That guy looks like a walking advertisement for steroids," I whisper.

From a few feet away, Wes gives me a we-can-all-hear-you look.

"Ladies and gentlemen," the referee/announcer says into a microphone hanging from the rafters, "my name is Tony Danger and I'll be your MC and referee for the evening. Tonight, we've got two fierce competitors. First, though, I'd like to bring up my special guest, Henry Mackenzie, to introduce them."

Mallory throws her arms up in the air, and the whole crowd cheers as Henry jogs up the aisle in a snug pair of jeans, a gray T-shirt, and a leather jacket.

"Good evening, everyone," he says as Tony Danger steps aside. "And thanks, Tony."

"You got it, man."

"I would like to introduce you to two women who could single-handedly kick my ass, Druscilla the Destroyer and Holly GoBiteMe!" Henry steps aside and out of the ring to sit next to Addison at the end of our aisle.

Two women, both covered in tattoos and wearing padded head-pieces, mouth guards, shin guards, tiny metallic spandex shorts, and matching sports bras, race down the aisles to cheers and boos as they bounce into the ring. A whole crew of hype people with water bottles and first-aid kits race behind them.

Anna leans over. "Is that guy rolling out a cart of pillows?"

Behind the women and their posses, there is indeed a scrawny-looking guy with a whole pile of pillows.

On the other side of Stacy, Sara Claire gasps. "Oh my Lord, is this an actual pillow fight?"

"Like a slumber party pillow fight?" I ask.

Stacy leans back and nods. "Some girls on my Roller Derby team do pillow fight matches during the off-season."

"You play Roller Derby?" I ask.

Sara Claire shakes her head in awe. "Yeah, could you be any more badass?"

My eyes flick up to Sara Claire. It's the first time since the elimina-tion two nights ago that she and I have shared a conversation outside of the occasional *excuse me* and *good night*.

Anna's jaw drops. "Is this pillow thing like some kind of weird internet thing?"

I choke on a laugh.

Stacy smiles widely. "I mean, I guess it could be."

"Hell," says Sara Claire, "people will pay for anything these days. You know, I worked with a client who was a state congresswoman, and she had to start cropping her feet out of photos because they kept popping up on websites dedicated to feet."

Anna giggles, and then muses, "I bet there's some good money in that."

We spend the next thirty minutes watching two grown women beat the crap out of each other with pillows. I'm about as subtle as an elephant in a library as I try to catch glimpses of Henry sitting down at the end of the row next to Addison. She laughs way too loudly at everything he says and paws at him shamelessly. At least I'm not alone, though. With our numbers dwindling, every girl in this row is wondering if she'll be next. After this, eliminations will only be one or two people at a time, but it's impossible to feel safe, especially after knowing I was so close to the chopping block the other night.

With every glance in Henry's direction, I hope for some sort of nod or smile—some kind of sign that tells me I didn't make up our late-night/early-morning conversation.

I guess my brush with elimination and talking to Henry made me sure of one thing: I want to be here. And it's not just for the money or the connections. That terrifies me, but it's true.

Feathers fly, drifting slowly down as the two women in the ring absolutely wallop each other. In the end, Holly GoBiteMe lands the final blow and drops down onto Druscilla the Destroyer, pinning her to the mat.

"We've got our winner," Tony Danger calls as he pumps Holly's fist into the air. "Now it's time for a little bit of audience participation." He looks to all of us in the front row. "Ladies, any volunteers? Which of you will fight for Henry's love?"

We all look from one to another, and I get the feeling that no one is too eager to take on this challenge.

Suddenly Addison bolts to her feet.

Maybe it's the adrenaline from just having watched two grown women beat each other senseless with pillows, or maybe it's the memory of what Beck told me last night about how much people are really rallying around me, or maybe it's simply Henry, but whatever it is, I'm on my feet and challenging Addison before any other woman can even raise her hand.

"We've got our challengers!" Tony echoes into the microphone.

"Cut!" someone shouts.

Before I know what's happening, Zeke and Mallory are ushering Addison and me outside to where the trailers are parked. I glance over my shoulder to see Anna holding up two thumbs, and Henry watching us with a furrowed brow.

Irina is waiting for us in a dressing room trailer with a rack of nightgowns and lingerie.

"Really?" I ask.

She shrugs. "If you're going to have a pillow fight, you should at least wear a nightie." Swiping through the rack with discernment, she hands Addison something to try on, and after some frustration and a few grunts, she hands me—

"A housedress?" I ask. "Really?" I'm talking a long floral housedress with snap buttons and pockets on the front. Now, I'm a human girl, so of course I appreciate pockets on a dress, but every other thing on this rack is cute and sexy. I can't walk out there in this muumuu (which I'm pretty sure still has crumbs in the pockets from the last person who wore it) and expect to win against Addison. This isn't just about who can take who out. This is about who can charm the crowd and, subsequently, Henry.

Addison emerges from behind the dressing curtain in a pink silk pajama set with black piping around the legs, arms, and collar. The top is buttoned down low enough to show just a hint of her lace bra, and the shorts show the very bottom of her ass cheek. To be honest, it's more skin than I would want to show, but how is there not any middle ground between sexy silk pajamas that you wouldn't actually want to sleep in and your grandmother's favorite muumuu?

I look down at Irina's offering once more. "This is really all you have?"

She nods.

"You know I'm on the show. You've known since you met me at my house, and you couldn't at least prepare for the possibility that you might have to clothe me?"

She shrugs, her lip curled. "I'll be honest, I didn't think you'd make it this far."

Addison smirks as she pulls her hair into two girlish pigtails at the top of her head. "Just put it on. You'll look fine."

"Easy for you to say," I mutter.

I don the housecoat, and when I emerge, Irina hands me a pair of bunny slippers. "You match," she says, pointing to Addison, who is, yes, wearing bunny slippers, but on her it's cute in a sweet way. Whereas I look like someone's aunt with twelve too many cats.

"I can't wear these," I say as we walk back inside. "I'd rather go barefoot."

Irina shrugs. "Suit yourself."

Then I remember what Sara Claire said about that politician and her feet, and I stop in my tracks to slide the slippers on.

In the ring, Druscilla and Holly help us into headgear and pads.

"Any tips?" I ask Druscilla.

"Go for the legs. Knock her down and then throw your body on

137

top of hers. You look like you've got some muscle. She looks like she could pop an implant, so use that to your favor." She stops herself. "Not that there's anything wrong with implants. My girlfriend has fake boobs and—"

I laugh. "It's okay. I get it." I nod. "Thanks."

"Do you like this girl?" she whispers.

I pause for a second and shake my head. "Not at all."

"Even better," she says. "Think about all the reasons why you can't stand her and let the pillow do the rest."

She leans in. "We had to sign all kinds of waivers about what we can and can't say before they hired us, so I probably shouldn't say this, but I'm a fan." She winks.

I grin, and she shoves a mouthpiece into my mouth. "Kick her ass."

"You got it, coach," I try to say through the plastic in my mouth, but it sounds more like *you got a roach.*

Druscilla crawls through the ropes and grabs me a pillow. "Your weapon, my lady."

In the other corner, Addison bounces, the pigtails dancing around her shoulders as her lips curl into a snarl.

Oh yeah. I can totally do this.

"Ladies," Tony says into his microphone in a smarmy voice. "I want a clean fight. No scratching or hair pulling. I don't want to see fists, elbows, knees, or feet flying. Pillow contact only. First girl to pin for ten seconds wins."

We both nod, and I think Addison actually grunts at me.

Tony steps out of the ring, and the bell barely finishes ringing before Addison lunges toward me and takes the first swing right to my head. I double backward and fall into the ropes. The crowd lets out a low *ohhhh.*

Not exactly how I'd hoped to start this match.

"Geez, Addison," I say through the mouth guard.

She shrugs. "I'm just playing by the ru—"

With the pillow clenched in my fist, I hit her hard, right in the stomach, causing her to stumble out of her bunny slippers. "Me too," I tell her.

She lets out a wild growling, shrieking sound and runs right for me. At the very last second, I jump out of the way, leaving her to bounce against the ropes.

Her face is red and angry. Now I've done it. Now I've really pissed her off.

We circle each other, waiting for the other to make a move or show the slightest sign of vulnerability.

But then I remember what Druscilla told me about using my feelings toward Addison, and it all comes boiling to the surface. The way she called me brave, like I deserved a cookie for having the nerve to be a fat girl in a pretty dress. The way she uses all the girls in the house like chess pieces. The way she acts like this competition was over before it even started.

I let out a guttural Viking-style scream and run at her full force. She ducks a moment too soon, thinking that I'm going for her head, but instead I slide across the mat and take her out at the knees just like Druscilla said I should. Before she has a second to move, I throw my body down on top of her. She wiggles beneath my weight, but Tony is already mid-count.

"Seven, six, five . . ."

"Get off me, you cow!" Addison says just loudly enough for me to hear.

I grin down at her as I take out my mouthpiece. "Just playing by the rules. Moo, bitch. Moo."

"We have a winner!" Tony Danger calls. He pulls me to my feet, and I hold out a hand for Addison, but she ignores me.

I bounce with excitement. I feel like I could punch a hole through the roof.

"What's your name, girly?" he whispers.

"Cindy," I tell him.

"Ladies and gents," he says in his announcer voice, "I give you Cindy *Claw*ford!"

"Cindy, Cindy, Cindy, Cindy!" the crowd begins to chant.

Henry steps up into the ring with a dozen roses in his arms and pulls me in for a hug. "You're quite the wild card," he tells me as he hands me the flowers and presses a kiss to my cheek.

I turn my head so that his lips graze mine. "You like the granny look?" I ask breathlessly. I feel on top of the world, like I've just solved global warming, fixed the health care system, and I still have time to read a good book and put on a face mask before bed. I am invincible.

"Very subversive," he says, his eyes tilted down toward mine and my body still pressed against his.

I'm not a first-move kind of girl. Not because I don't want to be or because I think there's anything wrong with it, but because I've never been courageous enough. The fear of rejection has always pinned me in place, waiting for the guy to go out on a limb first. But I've come all this way, and if I go home tomorrow night without having kissed Henry Mackenzie, I'll wonder for the rest of my life what could have been.

I tilt my head just a millimeter closer, and just like that, our lips are pressed together. His mouth moves effortlessly against mine, and he pulls me in closer to him, wrapping his arm around my waist. My mouth opens for a brief second, and it's just enough for his tongue to dance against mine.

The crowd cheers, and we pull away from each other slowly, our lips touching until the very last second, like we're two intoxicated teenagers drunk on each other.

***

Back at the house, I take a shower while Addison announces that she's moving into Chloe's room.

"I guess she couldn't handle the heat," Sara Claire says when I return wrapped in my towel.

"Guess not."

"Pretty steamy moment there with you and Henry, huh? You know," she says, "it's a competition and I want to stay here for as long I can, but I want us to be friends too."

I nod as I sit down on the edge of my bed. "I want that too."

"We just gotta be real with each other about the fact that we both want the same thing."

"God, this is so weird," I tell her.

She's about to respond, when the doorbell echoes through the house. The date invitation. It's here.

We both run out the door and down the stairs, and I nearly slip on the last step, but I'm still first to the door.

I swing it open and find Mallory waiting there with an envelope. I take it and slam the door in her face, immediately feeling a camera at my back.

"Rude," I hear her say on the other side.

"Sorry!" I call.

Well, I hope being on television straight out of the shower in a tiny towel is on the *Before Midnight* bingo card, because here I am with two cameras on me and a crowd of girls circling me.

I rip past the wax seal in the shape of a scroll to read the invitation.

"Come on," Chloe says. "Read it aloud!"

Addison slinks down the stairs, her hips swiveling with each step.

I pull the card from the envelope and begin to read. My heart sinks. "'Dear Addison . . .'"

CHAPTER EIGHTEEN

"Shit, shit, shit!" I hear someone mumbling as they stomp down the hallway outside of my bedroom as I lie curled in my bed with a fresh blank sketch pad page teasing me.

Although I can see Addison out of the corner of my eye, I refuse to acknowledge her standing there in the frame of my bedroom door.

She clears her throat.

"Hi, Addison," I say without looking up from the page, like I'm actually working on something. "Is there something I can help you with?"

She walks in and hovers above me.

I hold the sketch pad to my chest because it turns out pretending to work on a totally blank page is deeply embarrassing.

"Uh, yeah, actually," she says in the most normal voice I've ever heard her use. "I heard you went to, like, sewing school or whatever."

"I wouldn't call it sewing school, but yes, I know how to sew if that's what you're asking. What's the problem?"

She pouts, and her eyes are a little glassy, like she might actually cry. Pulling her long, perfectly straight hair over her shoulder, she turns around to show me that the zipper of her curve-hugging champagne minidress is split right up the back. "Irina dressed me in this super-expensive dress and I guess the stupid zipper was, like, defective, and now the whole crew is waiting outside and so is Henry and—"

"Why don't you just go ask Irina for help?" I ask.

"She might already be mad at me for . . ." She mumbles the rest, her chin resting on her shoulder.

"I'm sorry. What did you just say?"

"For refusing to wear the first fourteen options."

"Are you serious? This isn't your wedding dress or something."

She turns around, her arms flapping. "Can you help me or not?"

I don't want to. I really, really don't want to, but I'm like a moth to a flame when it comes to a fashion emergency. And even though I truly doubt that karma is real, ditching awful, manipulative Addison in her hour of need is pretty mean. Even for her.

"Take off the dress. I can't promise anything. It could need a whole new zipper. And I only have a travel sewing kit with me."

She obeys and strips down, tossing me her dress as she sits on her old bed in her strapless bra and smoothing undergarments, watching me nervously.

"Watching me won't make me go any faster."

"Just do whatever you have to do. Sew me into it if you have to."

I take a quick look at the zipper, which luckily for Addison is an easy fix. The zipper just got off track, so all I have to do is rip a few stitches, retrack the zipper, and sew it back in place. That, however, doesn't stop me from making some very thoughtful and unsure noises just to keep Addison on her toes.

It's only been a month or so since I last had my hands on a needle, which is an eternity if you look at the last four years of my life, but something about the process of threading it and holding it between my teeth as I use my seam ripper makes me feel at ease. Calmed. Soothed. This was the exact energy I was chasing during our goat yoga class, and it's hard not to feel like a small puzzle piece has clicked into place with the familiar act of simply fixing a stray zipper.

"Done," I finally say.

"What? You mean it's fixed?" She jumps to her feet with grabby hands reaching for the dress.

I pass it back to her and watch her squirm into it. "Be careful. The zipper isn't defective, but it's not as high quality as it should be for a dress that expensive."

She turns around so I can zip her up, and with her gaze steady on the wall ahead of us, she says, "Thanks, by the way."

I'm honestly shocked to hear unadulterated gratitude come out of her mouth. I can't help but assume that not having to make direct eye contact with me made the exchange possible for her.

"I guess this means you owe me," I say.

"I wouldn't go that far."

We all watch from the balcony at the back of the house as a helicopter lands on the helipad painted to look like the *Before Midnight* clock.

"Is it weird that I always assumed the helipad was edited to look like that?" asks Jenny. "Like some kind of TV magic?"

Stacy props her elbow on the railing and cradles her chin in her hand. "Or is it weirder that this show has its own helipad?"

Addison's date is a *Before Midnight* classic, the helicopter date night, and I can't help but take just a sliver of joy thinking about how miserable Henry will be.

Below us, a cluster of crew members escort Henry, dressed in a slick suit with a black tie. He glances up to us, and everyone crams up against the edge of the balcony to get a millisecond of face time, like we're all at a concert and Henry is the headliner we've waited hours for.

"Evening, ladies," he says, tipping his chin to us, his eyes bright with terror—something only I seem to notice.

My eyes widen, and I give him a slight thumbs-up. All I can hear is him telling me he'd rather lie naked in a pit of scorpions than fly on a helicopter.

He inhales deeply, and I can see all the ideas running through his head, trying to figure out how he can get out of this at the last minute. Fall and break an arm? Fake a death in the family?

He's herded off quickly, and I can feel the energy of all the other women ease, like they've all been sucking in for the camera. (Bleh.)

A legion of cameras follows Addison through the wildflower field, her white shawl billowing gracefully behind her. Henry greets her at the helicopter, giving her a kiss on the cheek, and helps her inside as he follows just behind her.

I do feel just a little bit bad for him. RIP, Henry.

Sara Claire lets out a soft sigh. "Am I so silly for admitting I really had my hopes set on the helicopter date?"

"Hell no," says Chloe. "I'm scared of heights, and helicopters are basically flying deathtraps. No, thank you."

Anna yawns. "I'm not feeling great."

I turn to her. "Are you okay?"

Her mouth turns into a frown. "Just a headache. I think I'm going to lie down."

I squeeze her hand. "I'll come check on you later."

"How can it be this depressing to live in an epic château?" Jenny opines.

With the doors closed behind them, Addison and Henry take off, the helicopter hovering for a moment and then circling overhead for the cameras. A few girls wave up at them, and a camera down below focuses in on us, all clustered around this railing in our pajamas like a bunch of sad sacks.

"That's it," Stacy says. "We need pizza and wine."

"Um, I don't think Domino's delivers to the *Before Midnight* château," I tell her.

"To the kitchen, ladies!" Stacy calls, leading the charge.

Downstairs, we all crowd around the island as Stacy pulls together some ingredients for a quick pizza dough. She then portions everything out for us to each make our own mini pizzas, giving us instructions in what I assume is her librarian voice.

"You're like an antidepressant in human form," I tell her.

"I guess it's just the librarian in me taking over. When I'm not at the reference desk answering the same questions over and over again, I'm dreaming up the cheapest programs I can come up with for my kiddos."

"Do you miss them?" I ask.

"I do," she says slowly. "But I don't miss all the bullshit red tape I have to deal with. I just wish I had enough resources to do good by them, but I feel like I'm just writing grants to keep my head above water."

"Have you thought about what you'd do with the prize money?" I ask.

She peers up at me. "Pay off some student loans. Buy my library kids some great stuff we could use like iPads and design programs and as many new books as their hearts desire. What about you?"

"Oh God, nothing as selfless as you," I tell her. "Don't laugh, but I want to start my own line. I'll start with shoes. Move into accessories and then clothing. At least that's the plan. My brain is basically a useless cinder block at the moment, and I haven't come up with a design I love in months."

"You've got writer's block," she says. "Or I guess in your case, it would be designer's block."

"Is there a cure, doc?"

She smiles and pats my shoulder. "I'm not much of a writer, but my ex was. One time I had them in to talk to my kids about writing and they said that you can get a block for a number of reasons. Sometimes you've made a wrong choice and you have to go back and start over.

146

Sometimes you've run out of inspiration and have to rediscover what made you so passionate in the first place. But whatever it is, it helps to take things in bite sizes. Start small. A sentence . . . or maybe for you a line. A color. A fabric. And then go from there."

"You're really smart," I tell her.

"I think you mean my ex was really smart."

I shake my head. "Nope, definitely meant you."

"Well, you'll get past this and then one day you'll wonder how you'll ever have time for all the ideas you have. And when you get that line of your own, I'll be the first person at the store, buying my pair of Cindy originals."

"First pair is on me," I promise her.

We find some spaghetti sauce to use as pizza sauce and scour the fridge for any toppings we can find. I go with banana peppers and extra cheese.

We all take turns cooking pizzas and reminiscing about our lives back home as we go through a few bottles of wine. Back in Wisconsin, Chloe runs social media for her parents' chain of gas stations, Cheese Stop. She also headlines a folk band and plays all over the Midwest on the weekends. Gretchen is a massage therapist from Las Vegas with two moms both named Linda. Valerie is a former dancer for the Miami Heat and a current hairstylist with a son named Carson. Samantha is a nurse with plans to go on to med school after the doctor she was engaged to dumped her for having a job that was too demanding. Jenny is the big surprise—a divorcé and trial lawyer who specializes in malpractice lawsuits.

"Yeah," she says, "I actually met my ex-husband in the courtroom. He was an expert witness in a nose-job-gone-wrong case."

"What a thing to be an expert on," Sara Claire says.

After pizza, we all crash on the couches and play a game of truth or dare, which quickly devolves into just truth until suddenly it's been hours and the camera guys who have hovered around us are calling it a night.

I gasp as we're all cleaning up. "I never went to check on Anna."

"Go ahead," Sara Claire says. "We've got this."

I grab a glass of water and a sleeve of crackers before I head upstairs. "Anna?" I call as I enter her dark room.

She doesn't answer.

"Anna?" I flip the switch and find four perfectly made beds. That's weird.

After leaving the glass and crackers on her nightstand, I check in the bathroom and a few other rooms, but can't seem to find her. All I can think of is Drew telling me to watch out for her. Great job I've done. Sister of the year.

I throw on a pair of Vans and go out the front door to see if I can find her somewhere on the grounds.

"Anna!" I call.

I check around the side of the house where Beck led me to last night so we could talk inside one of the trailers. But it's a ghost town. I walk down the hill to the gate, where the crew is packing it in and heading to their crash pad house just down the road. I almost ask one of them if they've seen Anna, but I'm scared I might somehow get her in trouble.

Back up at the house, I go to open the front door, but it's locked, so I circle all the way around the hedges to where the pool is. The only thing I can see down the path is one single light, which I think is Henry's guest house. I can hear some quiet splashing, but it's too dark to see anything, and I guess it could just be the wind, but . . . I remember seeing some kind of electrical box out here somewhere, so I fumble around looking for the light switch outside the pool cabana when I run into something—no, *someone*. "Anna?"

"Ow! You stepped on my toe!"

"Who is that?" I ask just as I find the switches and flip one of them on. "Addison?" The glow of the interior pool lights illuminates the area just enough for me to see her standing there beside me, still in the champagne minidress she wore on her date with Henry, which I'm surprised is not still happening. "What are you doing here?"

But she doesn't even flinch at the sound of my voice. Instead, her face lights up with delight as she crosses her arms, not tearing her eyes away from the pool. "Oh, I don't think that's the question you should be asking."

My gaze follows hers, and the first thing I notice is a bright yellow triangle bikini top floating along the surface of the pool. But then my jaw drops the moment I see her. "Anna!"

My stepsister is in the pool, her hair piled high into a messy bun, her legs wrapped around Zeke's waist with her arms wound around his neck.

"Uh-oh," her tiny voice squeaks.

"Oh, this is good," Addison says like she's watching the montage part of an Ocean's Eleven movie.

"Shit," says Zeke as he squirms out from under Anna. "It's not what it looks like." He runs a shaky hand through his thick blond curls as he takes the stairs of the pool two at a time.

Anna scrambles for her bikini top with one arm wrapped around her chest.

I race to the edge of the pool and unzip my hoodie, which I drape over her shoulders as soon as she emerges from the water.

"Is this what it looks like?" I ask quietly.

She nods. "I think I fell for the wrong guy. At least this one has a job, though. Right?"

You can't say she's not optimistic.

"*Had* a job," Addison says.

"You can't tell anyone," Zeke begs her. He trips as he tries stepping into his jeans even though he's still soaking wet. "Please."

"You owe me, Addison," I remind her.

Addison touches her hand to her heart, being sarcastically dramatic. "How could I possibly let someone betray Henry like this?"

"Cut the crap," Zeke tells her. "The cameras aren't rolling. What do you want?"

Anna shivers beside me.

"Assurances," Addison demands.

Zeke looks to Anna and then me. "Take her inside, okay? I'll deal with this."

I give Addison a sour look. "Guess you got home early from your date. Must not have gone very well."

Her mouth curls into a grin. "Oh, I think I got here just in time."

CHAPTER NINETEEN

L ast night, I stayed in Anna's room until she fell asleep. I definitely missed out on precious walkie-talkie time, but I couldn't abandon Anna. According to her, she fell hard for Zeke when she and Drew were doing their preshow interviews. She made the first move that day by slipping him her number. They texted day and night for the week leading up to production, and she planned on backing out of the show, but she could never find the right time. She had hoped to get sent home the first night, but instead it was Drew who was sent home before both of us. It wasn't getting sent home that Anna was worried about. It was Zeke losing his job for cozying up to a contestant.

I brushed her hair and rubbed her back, and had every intention of talking to Addison before she went to bed, but by the time I left Anna, every light in the house was off.

In the morning, Anna is crouched beside my bed waiting for me. I gasp at the sight of her chin resting on my mattress just inches from my face.

"I have to tell Henry," she says.

I sit up slowly, propping myself up on my elbows, and look around for Stacy or Sara Claire, but they're both already up and gone. "Wait, wait, shouldn't you talk to Zeke first? At least find out what he promised Addison?"

She shakes her head. "It won't be anything he can actually deliver on. He's a junior producer," she whispers. "He can't even get craft services to remember that he has a nut allergy. Addison will figure that out soon enough and she'll rat him out. If I send myself home, she loses all the power. You have to help me find Henry."

I sit up completely, my head spinning a little from waking up too quickly. "Okay, give me a minute to get dressed, and then we'll figure it out."

She sits there on the floor, her whole body slumped as I put on a pair of frayed denim shorts and a T-shirt that reads I DONUT CARE ABOUT YOUR DIET.

We walk downstairs and manage to sneak out the back door and down the path to where the guesthouse is.

In the light of day, the guesthouse is covered in vines and has a beautiful rose garden just outside the window. I knock on the arched door with a bronze doorknob in the center.

"How do you know where he's staying?" Anna asks as she peers over my shoulder.

"Does that matter?"

"Uh, yeah, actually, it does. I guess I'm not the only sister with secrets."

I roll my eyes. "Trust me. My secrets aren't nearly as salacious as yours."

When I try knocking again and there's no answer, I turn the doorknob, which is unlocked.

"Do we just go in?" Anna asks warily.

"Do you want to beat Addison to the chase or not?"

She nods, and I swing the door open, but it's totally empty. No one. Nothing. The bed has been stripped of all of its sheets, and every sign of Henry from his suitcases to his cologne to his notebook is gone.

"Maybe they moved him," Anna says as we trek back up to the house.

"I guess so," I say.

"There they are!" Jenny calls from the balcony. "Come on! Hurry up! They just announced an elimination ceremony."

"Right now?" I yell back.

"Yes!"

"Aren't we supposed to have another one of those balls?" Anna asks.

I take her hand and we run the rest of the way through the grounds and into the house.

Beck is in the foyer, shuttling girls out to the front of the house. "Move it, move it, move it."

"Where's Zeke?" Anna asks her immediately.

Beck just shakes her head. "Do I look like a lost and found? Come on. Move it."

"That's good," I whisper to Anna. "If Beck doesn't know, then Addison probably hasn't spilled to anyone yet."

Anna looks around nervously, but everyone is already lined up, so I lead her to a spot on the stairs and take the one just behind her. Everyone else has had a chance to change into something sort of cute, but I'm still rocking my just-rolled-out-of-bed hair, cutoffs, and T-shirt.

Once we're all set, a limo drives up the hill and Chad and Henry step out.

"Ladies," Chad says, "I know you were all expecting a ball this evening, but Henry has made his decision and he's got some out-of-town business to attend to, so we're doing things a little out of order today."

"I'm sorry we won't be having our ball this evening," Henry tells us. "But yesterday made my decision very clear." He swallows. "Cindy, will you accept this scroll?"

I nod and take the steps down, squeezing Anna's hand along the way. I'm shocked that Addison wasn't first after their date last night, but I'll take it.

As he places the scroll in the palm of my hand, I say, "Maybe I'll finally score that date."

He gives me an unreadable smile that only makes me feel unsettled.

He calls more names—Sara Claire, Jenny, Stacy, Gretchen, Valerie, Chloe—until all that's left is one scroll and Addison, Anna, and Samantha still standing.

"Well, this is a plot twist I didn't see coming," Sara Claire muses.

Henry plucks the single scroll from the pillar beside him. "I hate this part," he says. "But I think spending time with someone can not only reveal who—"

"Henry," says Addison, her voice more frantic than I thought possible. "I have to tell you something."

I give her an infuriated look, nostrils flared, that I hope says, *I hope every zipper you ever zip breaks.*

Henry looks to Chad, who nods.

"Can we talk privately?" Addison asks.

Anna steps forward. "No. No, you can't. Because I have something to say, and I want to say it right here in front of everyone."

"Anna, no," I whisper.

"I have feelings for someone else," she declares dramatically "I'm sorry, Henry. I know we've only started to get to know each other, but I can't stand the thought of deceiving you."

With all eyes on her, I can't say my stepsister isn't enjoying this.

Valerie lets out a low whistle. "This is like telenovela levels of intense."

Addison crosses her arms with a loud huff, while still trying to appear shocked.

"You have feelings for someone else?" Henry asks.

Anna nods. "I thought it would fade after meeting you . . . but now I miss him . . . and I'm so sorry, Henry, but my heart's just not in it."

He takes her hand, the tension in his forehead easing a bit. "Thank you for being honest."

"So I guess this is it?" she asks.

He nods and holds up the scroll. "You mind if I give this thing out real fast?"

She stumbles back clumsily and takes her place back on the steps between Addison and Samantha, both of whom look like they've seen a ghost. "Oh, right, of course."

Henry eyes the scroll in his hands. "Well, that was unexpected," he says. "I, um . . ." He closes his eyes and shakes his head. "Addison." His voice cracks on her name. "Will you accept this scroll?"

She lets out a brief squeal before collecting herself and walking coolly down the steps. "Thank you," she says. "I can't wait for a chance to show you who I really am."

"Who she really is?" Stacy whispers.

"Who she really is is actually hiding in plain sight," I say.

Anna, free as a bird, runs down the steps and gives Henry a hug, followed by a dejected Samantha.

Addison eyes me from the other side of the crowd, and I can't help but wonder what happened on her date last night. Not only did she come home early, but she was nearly eliminated too.

Anna rushes over to me and gives me a long hug. "I feel so much better. But I think Mom might kill me—"

"Kill you?" I ask. "That was ratings gold!"

She thinks about that for a moment, straightening into a proud stance. "Yeah, it was! Wasn't it?"

"I love you," I tell her. "You and Drew stay out of trouble—or I don't know, get into trouble." I can't believe I'm going to be alone here now.

Anna's eyes water as she nods eagerly. "Win this shit," she says. "I saw you and Henry up in that boxing ring. There's something there. And that prize money could get you started in a big way."

155

"Samantha, Anna," says Chad, "I'm sorry, but it's time to say goodbye."

The remaining women watch as Samantha and Anna get into the Rolls-Royce and are driven off the property.

We all turn to walk back inside once the car disappears over the horizon, but seemingly out of nowhere, a bright yellow taxicab speeds up the hill and through the gates, honking its horn.

"Henry, I'll let you tell them," Chad says.

"Well, like Chad said, I've got some business to attend to, and I thought, what better way to do it than to take you all with me, so you should all pack your bags. We're going to New York City!"

My whole body immediately eases at the sound of my city's name. My home for the last four years. *New York.*

"Exciting stuff!" Chad says. "You've all got one hour to get ready, and, ladies, we will not be returning to the *Before Midnight* château until the finale. It's time to hit the road."

CHAPTER TWENTY

W e fly out on an Airbus chartered by the network, and we have enough room for each of us to stretch out across a whole aisle, which is definitely much less cramped than my flight here. Henry is kept away from us up front in first class. I understand that the whole purpose of the show is to catch every interaction with Henry on camera and that all of those moments are heavily orchestrated and guarded, but it seems silly to keep us away from him during a six-hour coast-to-coast flight when we're all on the same plane and privacy is impossible. It's a reminder that this isn't about falling in love. It's about entertainment.

I claim the first row of coach just behind Henry in the last row of first class. He stretches back a few times, rustling the curtain between us. We're so close it's maddening. Midway through the flight, when almost everyone else is passed out, a small notebook slides out in between my feet. I reach down to find Henry's notebook.

Written there beside the lipstick kiss I left him a few weeks ago it now reads: *Walkie-talkie date night tonight?*

I dig a pen out of my bag and write back: *Affirmative. Cabbage Patch.*

I reach forward, holding the notebook, and squeeze my hand through the narrow gap between his seat and the window.

His hand catches mine, and he holds on for one, two, three, four, five seconds before taking the notebook and letting go.

When we land at a private airport in Westchester, we're loaded into a few Suburbans. I find myself dozing as we make the drive into the city. Eventually, we stop in front of a hotel near the Battery. When the valet opens the passenger door, I step into a warm flood of light from the hotel sign above that reads THE WAGNER.

We're left to congregate in the hotel lobby while Wes and Beck check us and the whole crew in, like they're our senior trip chaperones.

For the first time all day, Henry is left unguarded, and I'm the only one who seems to notice. Every other woman is either trying to look like an Instagram model for one of the camera guys grabbing some B-roll, or they're crowded around half a copy of yesterday's contraband newspaper someone left out beside the fruit bowl.

Mallory and Zeke, who should be guarding Henry, are bickering over tomorrow's schedule as Henry wanders into the gift shop.

When no one's looking, I follow him inside. I find him shaking a few snow globes and then marveling at them as he sets them back down to watch the snow fall.

"Kind of a different sort of flight than our first one together," I say.

He startles a little at the sound of my voice, but his whole expression eases when he sees me, a smile twitching in his jaw. "Hey there, Cabbage Patch."

"I can't believe it's only been three weeks since we left."

He runs a hand through his hair, pulling on it a little so that it looks nice and rustled. Somehow, he's managed to look disheveled in a sexy way after a six-hour flight. "I think about that day a lot."

I take a step closer to him, so that we're both hidden by a tower of teddy bears in I ♥ NY T-shirts. "Regret getting on that flight?"

He frowns. "It's not the flight I regret." He reaches out to my hand dangling at my side and links his pinkie with mine, and it feels like my whole pounding heart is right there, living in my little finger. And despite my whole body feeling this one small touch, things also seem normal in this moment. Like two people who just randomly met and hit it off standing in a hotel gift shop together surrounded by tacky souvenirs and glittering snow globes.

"I went looking for you today," I tell him. "I was trying to help Anna find you, but then suddenly we had an elimination ceremony going on and . . . well, you know the rest."

He smiles. "I saw her with Zeke last night on my way back to my room. At least someone was getting some action."

"Oh . . . well, you were a good sport."

"What else was I supposed to say? The premise of this whole show is—" He stops and something seems to dawn on him, like the fact that he doesn't really know much about how I feel about this show and what reasons I'm here for.

"It's ridiculous," I say. "You can say it."

"I was going to say ludicrous, actually."

"Henry?" a voice calls. It sounds like Mallory. "We've got you all set up in a suite."

"Shit," he mutters.

I duck around the corner of the display and shoo him forward, and here I am, hiding once again.

He doubles back and bends down, pressing his lips to my forehead and murmuring, "What I wouldn't do for ten minutes alone with you."

My stomach knots into a bow as I wait a few minutes before I slink out of the gift shop, where the annoyed attendant is waiting to roll down the metal grate. "Sorry," I tell the stout old man.

"There she is!" Beck waves me over and shepherds me toward the elevators with the rest of the girls before shoving a key in my hand.

I glance down at the shiny red card. "Who am I bunking with?"

"No one," she tells me. "Don't thank me. Thank the hotel. They messed up on the reservation and comped us a few extra rooms."

I scoop her into a hug and let out an ecstatic yelp. "Oh my God! Are you serious?"

She pulls away from me and steps onto the elevator, rubbing the ear that was closest to the pterodactyl-excitement-screech noise that came out of my mouth. "Yes, I'm serious. In fact, all of you get your own room."

The whole elevator full of women shrieks. I think Sara Claire might actually cry she's so happy.

"And don't get any funny ideas. We're all taking turns monitoring the halls. The televisions have been removed from your rooms. You can order off the room service menu, and if you're the kind of nut who needs to work out all the time, the hotel can bring you an in-room workout kit with weights and yoga something or another."

"Oh my God," someone behind me says—Chloe maybe? "I'm ordering a huge plate of french fries and chocolate ice cream to dip them in."

Addison coughs into her fist. "Heifer."

You! Are! Awful! my brain sings.

Beck rolls her eyes. "I need you all camera ready by ten in the morning. We'll be dropping off group-date envelopes and filming reactions. Other than that . . ." She glances down at the time on her phone. "It's about midnight now, so you're all free until then. Go take a bubble bath or walk around naked or do whatever people do in hotel rooms by themselves."

I walk into my room and go straight for the window without even turning the light on. Pushing the curtains aside, I drink in my view. Across New York Harbor, all lit up on a muggy summer night, is the Statue of Liberty against a deep velvet sky with only the brightest stars in sight. I'm home. Even if it's just for a few nights. I'm home, and it took leaving to know that. No matter what happens, even if I'm still creatively floundering after this show is done, I'm coming back to New York. I'll make sure Erica is comfortable with the new nanny, and I'll sleep on Sierra's bedroom floor if I have to, but I need to come home.

After standing there for a moment with my nose practically pressed against the glass, I turn the lights on and check out the expansive bathroom with a huge walk-in shower, a ginormous jetted tub, and a separate water closet with a phone mounted just above the toilet paper dispenser for when duty calls, I suppose? This whole room is almost twice the size of Sierra's and my entire apartment.

Even the towels are huge, which—as someone who has never been able to wrap a hotel towel around themselves without a massive gap showcasing the goods—is an extravagance. In the closet, I find two oversize robes, and one of them is even big enough to nearly fit me. Just as I'm sliding my arms through the armholes, a bell rings.

"These rooms have doorbells?" I ask myself.

I swing the door open, expecting it to be housekeeping or maybe someone from the front desk, but instead I find Beck in sweatpants rolled at the ankle and two bottles of beer dangling from her fingers. "I thought you might like some company." She holds the beers up. "And a drink."

"No cameras?" I ask with a smile. I want to turn her away, especially since I have a walkie-talkie date waiting for me, but how am I supposed to explain that? I guess I can at least have a drink and then feign exhaustion.

"No cameras."

I offer Beck the other robe, and we post up on my massive king-size bed. I have plenty to ask her about the show, but it occurs to me that I don't really even know Beck, and honestly, she's the only person left here who I feel like I can really confide in.

"You don't strike me as the kind of person who would enjoy working for *Before Midnight*," I say.

161

She takes a swig of beer. "Oh yeah? Gruff workaholic lesbian producing a dating show with misogynistic and antifeminist leanings come as a big surprise?"

"I wouldn't say gruff," I tell her.

She kicks her boots off and stretches out on the bed with her legs crossed. "When Erica found me, I was producing live biweekly wrestling shows. It was a grind. We went from city to city, and I was sleeping for maybe four hours a night. I didn't have an apartment because I was on the road so much, so literally everything I owned could fit in a suitcase and a backpack. Not that my work balance here is what I would describe as healthy, and I wouldn't say this show is in line with my own personal agenda, but Erica is the biggest name in reality television. I grew up watching shows like *The Real World* and *Road Rules* on MTV. I'm sure it sounds ridiculous to say those shows changed my life, but it's true. It was the first time I saw a gay person on television, and it opened me up to a whole world that I didn't see in my little Northern California town."

It's easy for me to think of shows like that as brain-eating time sucks—not that I don't obsessively watch *Teen Mom*—but it never occurred to me that shows like that could be a revelation for someone. "So is this job, like, a stepping-stone on your way to bigger things?"

"One day," she says, "but for now, this show *is* the big thing. I know it seems ridiculous, but there aren't many opportunities out there that guarantee you loyal viewers every week. And the people who are watching this show aren't always the kind of people who would just invite someone like me over for dinner. But they sure as hell watch my show. So I like to think that bit by bit, I'm showing people there's a whole world out there bigger than themselves. I mean, take last season, for example. That was our first interracial couple. Maybe that's not a big deal for a lot of people, but in parts of this country they still look at you like you're an abomination for something like that."

"Wow," I say. "I hadn't thought of it like that."

"Sometimes you gotta sneak people their vegetables. Give 'em the good stuff with a little bit of what they need but aren't ready to digest. And hey, it pays better than wrestling TV. Plus, when we're not filming, I get to go home to my girlfriend and our cat, Horace."

"You have a girlfriend?" I ask. "And a cat?" For some reason, I'd only ever pictured Beck pacing circles in Erica's kitchen and drinking Red Bulls.

"Yes, Cindy, I have a whole life, if you can believe it. I even . . . cook actual meals sometimes."

"Okay, now that's going too far."

She lets out a squawking laugh. "Okay, actually, you're right."

She's right about sneaking people their vegetables, though. People don't want to stand around and talk about how bleak the news was last night or argue about who they're voting for, but they will sit around in the break room talking about what happened on *Before Midnight* the other night. Last season's couple was a big topic of discussion on shows like *Good Morning America* and *The View*.

"Can you keep a secret?" Beck asks.

"No one on this show knows my stepmom is the show runner and brains behind this whole production, so yeah, I'm pretty good with secrets."

"Fair." She takes a deep breath. "Erica's helping me pitch a queer version of *Before Midnight*. We're going to start with a bisexual suitor."

"Oh my God, that's amazing!" That would be huge for a show this big to expand like that. It would definitely send a very clear message. Besides, queer people deserve to have their bad romantic decisions documented for the whole country to consume, too.

Beck tells me all about her vision for the show and how she wants to stage it and what kind of singles she would hope to cast. She's even done some preliminary scouting.

When she's finished her beer, she rolls out of my bed with a groan. "It's late. You need to sleep. *I* need to sleep."

"Can I ask you something? It's okay if you can't answer."

She drops her bottle in the recycling bin under the desk. "Sure."

"Was Henry really going to send Addison home this afternoon?"

She takes her robe off and drapes it over the edge of the bed. "Yes."

"Why? They just went on a date last night. She's so hot. All someone like her has to be to win a competition like this is semi-agreeable."

Beck shakes her head. "I don't know. It was a whole ordeal . . . I can't say much, but it wasn't her time yet and Henry didn't care. He wanted her gone. She said something that didn't sit right with him, I guess."

"You guess?"

She sighs heavily. "You know what I said the other night about Henry's list?"

I nod.

"Well, we have some girls who we just point-blank tell him are off-limits until we hit a certain number of episodes. I know it sounds gross. But they're the kind of girls people tune in for. I might have a total gay agenda, but I didn't say I was a saint."

"And Addison is one of those girls?" I ask.

"Yeah. But Henry fought with us on it. He went head-to-head with Wes and then Erica and then the network. He said either it was him or her. One of them was going home."

"But when Anna volunteered, he chose to send Samantha home and not Addison?"

She shakes her head. "When you can crawl inside that man's head and tell me what's going on, let me know."

I laugh dryly and get to my feet. "You said she said something to him that didn't sit right with him. What did she say?"

She rubs her chin for a moment, thinking. "It was about you, Cindy."

"About *me?* Why would she say something about me?" I ask, confusion wrinkling my brow.

"She's a mean girl, Cin. Addison is a classic mean girl. She knows how flash-in-the-pan fame works, and playing into a stereotype is part of that. She knows the fastest way to get people talking is to do or say something shocking."

I sink down on the edge of the bed, wishing there were a few more sips at the bottom of the bottle. "Was it about me being fat?"

Beck shoves her hands in her pockets and nods.

"And it's going to be in the next episode?"

Again, she nods. "We've got a story to tell."

Erica warned me. She promised me there would be some things she couldn't protect me from.

"I wasn't kidding about people loving you," she tells me. "Some girls out there have never seen someone who looks like them kiss a guy like you did in that boxing ring. Good night, Cindy."

"Night, Beck," I say softly as she lets herself out.

I really like Henry, and of course I want that prize money, but being here, as a plus-size woman, is turning out to be something bigger than I had imagined. It's exciting, but mostly terrifying. I want people to talk about whatever Addison said about me. The morning after this episode airs, people are going to be talking, and it's a conversation that's been a long time coming, if you ask me. I just never hoped to be at the center of it.

CHAPTER TWENTY-ONE

"**H**ello?" I ask into the walkie-talkie as I curl up in bed at nearly two in the morning. "Henry?"

I'm convinced he's already fallen asleep, when finally his crackling voice comes through. "Is that you, Cabbage Patch? Mon petit chou?"

"Mon petite what? I think the last time I could be described as petite, I was still in pull-ups."

"My little cabbage," he tells me. "It's French."

"Oh, fancy boy knows French, does he?"

"How hard would your eyes roll if I told you I went to a boarding school in France for three years?"

"Excuse me," I say, "my eyes are stuck to the back of my head."

He chuckles. "I guess I shouldn't tell you about the two years in Germany and four years in Edinburgh. . . ."

"I used to dream about going to boarding school when I was a kid, and there you were casually living my childhood fantasy."

His laugh is disjointed thanks to the bad connection. "It wasn't so glamorous," he assures me. "School years on my own with a couple hundred strangers and summers spent being my mom's sometimes on-trend, sometimes off-trend seasonal accessory."

I might not have had as much time as I should have with my parents, but they were mine. All mine. Never once did I feel out of place in their lives. The thought of Henry being anyone's accessory makes me wish I could reach over and squeeze his hand. "Are you close with your mother?"

He barks a laugh. "Yes. No. Too close. Not close enough."

"You—you said . . . On that first night, you said you were here for her. . . . What did you mean by that?"

"I am," he says plainly. "I'm here for her. I'm here as a last-ditch effort so her life's work doesn't do a swan dive into a pool of hot, flaming financial ruin."

"I thought . . . LuMac seemed to be doing okay. It doesn't seem so bad from the outside?"

I can hear him shifting, and it sounds like he's sitting up. "She dreamed too big, I think. . . . Cindy, I'm trusting you not to share this with anyone. . . . My mother was diagnosed with rheumatoid arthritis."

My jaw drops, and for the first time, I'm so glad to not be in the same room. Arthritis is an awful thing for anyone to have to deal with . . . but for those of us who very specifically rely on our hands . . . it's a death knell. "That's really awful. I'm so sorry."

"I guess you can understand why it would be bad for business if word got out. We're publicly traded at the moment, so stocks would plummet. Accounts would bail. It would be . . . devastating, and things are already bad. She was diagnosed a few years ago. We thought she could power through and just sort of . . . lead without being so involved, but I guess once a workaholic, always a workaholic."

"Wow, that's so much to deal with," I say with a yawn as the city lights blur in the distance, and I pull the blanket up over my shoulders. "So what does all that mean for the show? No offense, but if things are so bad, shouldn't you be there and not . . . here?"

He coughs out a painful laugh. "You would think, but no, the idea is that the show will drum up support for the brand. Sort of relaunch it for a new generation. Trust me when I say it wasn't my first choice. There's also the potential for future partnerships with the network. . . . It's just . . . I didn't come here expecting to be invested in— Shit, the little red battery light is blinking at me. I think this thing is about to go."

"Oh, uh—okay, well, I guess—"

"I wasted the whole night talking about me, and I didn't even ask you about yourself or how you're doing . . ."

I laugh nervously. "You didn't miss much. There's not a lot worth knowing."

"So says you. I spend a lot of time thinking about all the things I wish I knew about you," he tells me, his voice low and earnest.

My heart jumps into my throat. "Well, I've never been on a walkie-talkie date, but this is the best one I've ever been on."

"We didn't even get to order dessert," he says.

"Blame it on the walkie-talkie curfew."

"Next time I'll take you somewhere that requires shoes."

"Don't tease me. You know how much I love shoes, but I guess this is good night." I don't want to let go of this moment. I'm not ready.

"Or good morning."

"Good morning," I say back to him.

After that, the channel goes dead, and even though it was via walkie-talkie, I think that had to be one of the best dates I've ever been on. All that was missing was the kiss.

CHAPTER TWENTY-TWO

Ladies,
It's a family affair. Actually, a family business affair.
I'll have my people call your people.
Yours Truly,
Henry

A fifteen-passenger van picks us up and takes us to the LuMac showroom in SoHo, a twelve-story corner brick building with huge, beautiful glass windows stretching up the entire length of the building.

As we walk in, we're still buzzing with excitement from spending the night in a hotel room all by ourselves.

"I took a bubble bath," Chloe says dramatically. "I swear that château was giving me dorm room flashbacks and it wasn't good."

Sara Claire shivers with disgust. "No one told me I'd need to bring shower shoes to this show like it was church camp all over again."

Inside, we find ourselves in a long, narrow storefront. All the mannequins and displays have been pushed to the side, and down the center of the room runs a mini runway lined with chairs.

Addison's eyes widen like a hyena preparing to pounce. "Are we walking that runway?"

"Welcome to LuMac," Henry says as he steps out onto the runway, cameras rolling.

Everyone, myself included (ugh, I know), cheers in response. His suit is charcoal with light pinstripes, and considering how perfectly it's tailored, I think it might be custom. He's forgone a tie and undone his top button, and a crystal-blue silk pocket square peeks out of his breast pocket. As Sierra would say, he looks like a snack.

"What better way to introduce you all to the family business than to invite you to the place where it all started. When my mom, Lucy Mackenzie, was starting out, she rented a small office on the sixth floor of this building and shared it with one of her fellow recent fashion school grads. She'd won a small grant at her final student fashion show and had just enough to rent out a small space for a workstation. That student grant allowed her to make the first run of her famous slip dress. And now not only do we occupy the entire sixth floor, but the five below it as well. Today I wanted to give you all a chance to try on some of Mom's most iconic designs and walk the runway before we take you upstairs for a grand tour."

Everyone shrieks with delight, but my stomach drops because I know all about LuMac. The history. The strengths. The weaknesses. But most important of all—the size range. And when it comes to size inclusivity, LuMac is still in the Dark Ages, with a size range that only goes to a twelve and not even in their full collection. The slip dress, as iconic as it is, was always the kind of garment that defined the heroin-chic look on models with protruding hip bones and sunken cheeks.

"Jay?" Henry calls.

A beautiful person with short, perfectly edged lavender hair, a manicured beard to match, razor-sharp eyeliner, and nude lipstick rounds the corner. Jay wears a flirty skirt with a cropped sweater topped with a trench coat and platform sneakers.

"This is Jay," says Henry.

Jay gives us jazz fingers and a curtsy before giving Henry a huge hug. "Our prince has returned from the war," Jay says dramatically.

Henry chuckles and continues. "Jay is the new creative director of LuMac. They are the living embodiment of Mom's vision for the brand, and as my mother continues to take a step back, Jay has pretty much been my other half as we fine-tune the future of LuMac."

"Basically," Jay says. "Henry is Daddy and I'm nonbinary Mommy."

One or two of the girls laugh, a little unsure of what to make of Jay. Despite my uneasiness about what will be available to me for this fashion show, Jay makes me feel settled, like I've found my way back to my fashion-obsessed people.

"Follow me," Jay says as Henry helps them down from the stage. "We've got racks upon racks of goodies for you beauties to choose from."

My whole body is tense with nerves as we're herded into a back room with racks of clothing and makeup and hair touch-up stations. Some girls settle in for hair and makeup, but I know that if I stand any chance of not walking down the runway naked, I need to get first dibs on these clothes.

In a panic, I start shuffling through the items left out for us. I look for the biggest sizes, of course, which is most often an eight or a ten, but I'm also looking for anything with a shapeless or flowy cut to it. Slowly, I begin to amass a pile of clothing in my arms.

Addison clears her throat from the other side of the rack. "Um, you only need one look," she tells me. "That's not really fair to just start taking all the other perfectly good stuff just because you want options. Wes?" she calls. "Are there rules to this? Cindy has, like, a whole damn rack in her arms. Wes?"

I roll my eyes, but otherwise ignore her and continue my efforts even though the other women are also starting to show signs of concern. A storm of anxiety swirls in my chest, and it's the same panic I feel when I attempt to clean out my closet. I'm so used to finding that I have zero options that it's almost impossible for me to part with my clothing. Each piece is something I hunted relentlessly for or customized to my exact taste. I can't exactly walk into a Forever 21 and snag a dress I've personally doctored to be a Badgley Mischka dupe. I hate feeling like I need so many things, but when a chance to buy something in your size is one in a hundred and a chance to buy something *good* in your size is one in a thousand—

"Hey, kid, what exactly is going on here?" Beck swoops to my side.

I turn to her, my teeth gritted. "Did no one consider the fact that LuMac doesn't even make my size?"

Beck grimaces painfully and yells out, "Irina! Get over here!"

Irina stops what she's doing, leaving a half-naked Stacy with a dress bunched up around her waist. She stomps over to Beck with her arms crossed and a safety pin clenched in her teeth. "What?"

"Do we have any *options* for Cindy?"

"What do you mean?" Irina asks incredulously. "She has options coming out the ears." She motions to me. "She looks like a Black Friday sale threw up on her."

"In her size," Beck says as discreetly as she can, like it's something to hide. But it's not. In fact, accommodating me is not that hard. If you want me on your damn show, make it possible for me to be included. That's it. It's that simple.

Irina throws her arms up. "I can only work in the framework of the episode. This is on you and Wes. You two are—"

"Stop," I say firmly. "Stop it. Both of you stop. You're both to blame, but bickering isn't going to fix anything. I need scissors, safety pins, and fabric tape. And maybe a sewing kit."

Beck motions to Irina. "You heard her." Once Irina has disappeared into the chaos, Beck turns back to me. "I'm so sorry. What can I do?"

"Buy me time."

She bites down on her bottom lip, and I'm pretty sure I've just asked for the one thing she can't guarantee. She nods and marches off in the same direction as Irina.

I drop to the floor with all the items I've accrued and immediately begin to put any items back that I definitely can't use. A trench coat. A sweater dress. A neon-yellow slip dress.

My eye lands on a shift dress with huge nude sequins. The fabric is some kind of synthetic satin with stretch. I pull it across the widest part of my hips, and I think it might work.

Irina returns with my requested tools and begrudgingly asks, "Is there anything I can do to help?"

"Yes," I tell her as I stand up and begin to strip down with no mind for privacy. I step into the dress, and even though it's meant to be over-size, it feels immediately too narrow.

"That's a dress," Irina points out.

"Not on me it isn't," I tell her, yanking it up to my waist in what is now a skintight pencil skirt. "I need you to snip out these straps and tape down the freshly cut fabric so it doesn't poke out." I point to something one rack over that's white and billowy in shape. "What's that?"

Irina steps through a gap in the clothing rack beside us and reaches for the item in question, returning with a long white beach cover-up.

"It's a tent!" Irina says gleefully. "This is perfect."

"Helpful," I say, my voice flat as I take the scissors halfway up the front seam and then up the back, leaving only a deep V neck and a dolman sleeve.

I slip it on over my head and find that the fabric is sheer, so my black bra underneath creates a sexy silhouette. Pulling the two panels of fabric I just cut, I tie them in a knot in front of me and let the long pieces hang, creating a nice long line down the center of my body.

"Damn," says Stacy from where she sits in a makeup chair. "I didn't see that on the rack."

"Oh," I say casually. "This was definitely on the rack."

Irina eyes me up and down. "It's good."

After we've sat through hair and makeup, Mallory and Zeke—who still has a job thanks to Anna—line us all up on the other side of the stage.

Jay peeks in from between the curtains with a camera in hand. "Visions! All of you! I come bearing good news. We thought we'd need a third judge to weigh in on this competition, so I am pleased to tell you that *the* Lucy Mackenzie has graced us with her presence on this fine day. Make her proud, people!"

My stomach plummets. As if I wasn't already freaking out enough.

"His mom!" Chloe gasps. "Oh my God. This is a huge deal."

"Uh, yeah, and not just because it's his mom," Addison says.

Sara Claire, in a fuchsia silk wrap dress, looks like she's very nearly turning into a puddle. "Oh Lord. Moms hate me."

Stacy shakes her head. "That can't be true."

"No, it is. A proven fact. My last boyfriend just broke up with me after his mom refused to give him her mother's ring to propose. Said I was a firecracker and not the good kind."

"I don't think Lucy—I mean, Mrs. Mackenzie—would think something like that," I tell her. "And everyone loves firecrackers!"

"Except when they cause forest fires," Stacy points out.

I nod. "True."

Sara Claire takes a heaving breath. "In fourth grade, my first boyfriend was Dylan Timbers and his mama told me that the only way she'd give up her son was if she knew the woman she was handing him over to could be a better mother to him than she could. I. Was. In. The. Fourth. Grade."

I hold up a finger. "Okay, first off—men don't want their partners to be their mothers . . . and if they do, those aren't the men we're looking for."

Stacy holds up her hands and snaps in agreement.

"And second," I add, "gross."

Sara Claire throws herself against Stacy and me. "Hold me. I'm scared of mothers. Even my own. Especially my own."

Stacy and I pat her on the back, and I say, "Well, at least you didn't deconstruct his mother's designs for her own fashion show the way that I did."

Stacy grimaces. "'Deconstruct' is putting it lightly."

The lights dim, and Mallory barks at us to get back in line.

"Ladies," Wes says, "you'll hit the runway one by one. There won't be music, but we're adding it in post, so just pretend you're walking to music."

"What if we're off beat?" Jenny asks.

Wes looks at her briefly but doesn't answer. "After we're done, we'll be lining you up onstage, and Lucy will have the chance to speak to you and ask any questions she might have. Break a leg!"

Luckily, I'm the second one on the runway and have little time to spiral into a panic. When it's my turn to walk out, my hopes that it will be too dark to see Henry, Jay, or Lucy sitting in the audience of employees and random fans is immediately dashed. The lights are low, and the production lights on the runway are intense, but there's still enough natural light bleeding through the floor-to-ceiling windows that the audience is fully visible.

I may have walked in a handful of student runway shows as favors to friends, but this is instantly nausea-making. What do I do with my hands? Do they just hang like limp spaghetti? How do models manage to look cool doing this? Maybe I just need to do the *Zoolander* pout. Tyra Banks's voice telling me *We were rooting for you* rings in my ears.

I begin to walk, and I do my best to make each step nice and elongated while also swishing my hips, but I also think I might just look like one of those dashboard hula dancers. Keeping my eyes straight ahead for the most part, I glance down and risk a quick smile at Henry, which unfortunately means I see Lucy Mackenzie's scowl. *Well, lady, it was either this or walk the runway naked. Maybe start making clothing in my size and I won't have to take a pair of scissors to your work.*

Henry offers me a wink, and I do my best not to beam and to maintain my coolish model swagger.

When I step backstage, Jenny, Chloe, and Sara Claire give me high fives and thumbs-ups while Stacy takes the runway.

My heart pounds in my chest, and I can barely even remember what I just did. It's all a blur, like when you zone out at the wheel and immediately wonder how it is that you even got home.

After we're done, the lights come up, and we're all led out onstage like cattle, where Lucy Mackenzie is waiting for us. Lucy's hair is cut into a sharp, long bob that's so perfect I can practically imagine the painstaking efforts her hairstylist had gone to for it to be so precise. She wears a baggy black linen tunic with matching pants and a chunky neon-yellow necklace. She's the kind of designer who doesn't wear the type of clothing she produces, and it's the kind of disconnect in fashion that I've never quite understood. I can see all the ways she could seem cold and unapproachable, and yet, she's created this empire—albeit crumbling—and that's something I have endless respect for. Even if, after getting to know Henry better, I can't help but wonder what kind of expense her success has cost her.

"You're all such lovely girls," Lucy says as she eyes us discerningly. "Though I think some of you let the clothes wear you." She looks directly at Sara Claire, one beautifully shaped eyebrow raised.

Jay nods knowingly, and I'm trying my best not to be just a little bit annoyed. I love the world of fashion, but the idea that it's this mystical thing only meant for a select few is bullshit. And Lucy Mackenzie—a department-store staple—should know that better than anyone else. Yes, clothes can be art, but they're also a necessity. So many people in this industry act like clothing is for everyone, but fashion is only for a select few. The truth, though, is that clothing *is* fashion and fashion should be for everyone because clothing should be for everyone. And clothing for everyone is a first, small step to equality for everyone. Getting opportunities and access is a whole hell of a lot easier when you look the part.

"But I see one of you has taken liberties with my work," Lucy says. "Step forward—"

I step forward and my stomach bubbles, and I truly hope no one else heard that.

"Cindy," Henry supplies. "Mother, meet Cindy."

"Hi, Lu—Mrs. Mackenzie. I'm a big fan of LuMac," I tell her in a hurry before she can get a word in. "In fact, I'm a Parsons alum too. We have that in common. I just . . . I was so excited to hear we'd be coming here today, but as you can tell, I've got a . . . fuller figure." I want to say *fat*, but I don't think I have the time to also explain that fat isn't a four-letter word. "And when I couldn't find anything on the rack in my size, I decided to . . . reinterpret your work."

She steps onto the stage. "That's a judicious way of saying you had to make do." She touches the fabric of my top and runs her fingers along the edges of the tie dangling along the front. "Jay, is this the Marlena cover-up from the 2019 resort line?"

"Indeed it is," Jay says as Henry watches, obviously a little out of his depth.

"And the skirt?" she asks.

"Holiday collection 2018. The Charlotte shift dress," Jay tells her.

Lucy crosses her arms. "You wear it well, my dear. And I like to see a bit of resourcefulness. The curves . . . suit you."

"Thank you," I say quietly, even though what I really want to say is that I shouldn't have to be resourceful and that it's my body, so of course it suits me.

"I didn't realize this was *Project Runway*," Addison mutters from the other side of Jenny.

I step back into line as Lucy talks to a few other girls, and on-brand for Sara Claire, Lucy seems a little unsure as she asks her, "May I?"

Sara Claire nods and Lucy touches her hair. "Bottle or natural?"

"Uh, a little bit of both?" Sara Claire says.

I'm starting to get the feeling that Lucy Mackenzie was not an easy woman to grow up with.

Once Lucy is done with her inquisition, she steps back down and whispers to Jay, who nods in agreement.

"Ladies"—Jay nods—"you all did a fantastic job here today, but here at LuMac, we always have a soft spot for rule breakers, so the winner of today's runway challenge is Cindy!"

I straighten at the sound of my name as my hand flies up to my chest. "What? Me?" I won something! I've never even won an Instagram contest, and now I've won a *Before Midnight* challenge. I clap giddily while trying not to gloat.

A few of the other women pat me on the back, and sitting beside Lucy, Henry smiles widely as he tilts his chin down to congratulate me. *Good job*, he mouths.

I do a little curtsy in response. (Key word: *little*. This pencil skirt isn't budging.) In this moment it feels so silly to be here with all these ridiculous games and rules when just last night we stood in the gift shop like two completely normal adults who weren't pseudo dating via a reality television competition.

After we share a glass of champagne for the camera—this show will literally toast to anything—we're instructed to get dressed in our own clothes so we can film a tour of the office with Jay and Henry.

We all wave bye to Lucy, none of us brave enough to actually approach her, and when she steps out the back door and into a black SUV, there is a collective sigh of relief from everyone. Even Henry. Especially Henry.

CHAPTER TWENTY-THREE

U pstairs, we're led into a bright and open office with tons of real plants and a huge reception desk in the shape of the blocky LuMac logo with an *LU* running up the side of a very square *M*.

"LuMac is an independent brand, and while many have tried, Lucy has resisted the urge to merge with a larger conglomerate and maintains majority ownership. This independence is what sets LuMac apart, but it also means that every decision counts in a very big way," Jay says as we weave in and out of workspaces.

Henry nods grimly and wraps his knuckles on a door with his name on it. "And this is my office."

Addison lets out a dramatic *Oooooo*. "Genius at work!"

Miraculously, I don't puke. As the group moves on, I hang back and peek my head inside. I don't know what I expected, but this is not it. The office furniture is sleek and minimal with a bright white desk and ergonomic desk chair. A low-sitting midcentury sofa in a soft-looking camel-colored leather sits in front of the window. By the wall is a console with an old record player, and beneath that are crates full of records. It's easy to imagine Henry sitting there on the couch, zoned-out during a conference call as he combs through the records. There are papers covering every surface and file boxes placed haphazardly all over. It's the kind of office someone actually works in. On the desk is one single framed photo: little Henry on his father's shoulders with his mom laughing hysterically as a wave crashes over the three of them.

"I would've cleaned first if I knew you'd be snooping," Henry whispers, his voice tickling my ear.

I jump back a little and find my back pressed against his torso as the rest of the group turns the corner.

Instead of stepping away from him, I lean my head back against his chest and look up, allowing myself this indulgence. "It's nice to know you actually work here and aren't just cashing a check."

His laugh is bitter as he presses his hand to the small of my back and guides me forward so that we can rejoin the group. "Trust me when I say I'm not cashing many checks here."

Before I can manage to ask Henry more, he's swiftly rejoined Jay at the front of the line.

We make our way up a stairwell as Jay explains that each floor is a different micro brand, acquired by Lucy herself, and that with the help of Henry, she's created a mentor program to help each brand establish itself. Henry's eyes light up when Jay explains the program, and I think it's the most excited by LuMac I've ever seen him.

Once we're done filming, Henry is swept away, and all the women congregate downstairs, where a small group of paparazzi and a few *Before Midnight* fans have gathered.

"Does this mean we're famous?" Jenny asks.

Jay laughs as they sit perched on the counter. "Enjoy it while you can."

I detach from the group and make my way over to Jay. "Thanks for the tour," I tell them.

They smirk and hop down before tapping the tip of my nose with their finger. "I like you. Lucy isn't so sure, but I like you."

"Oh really?" I ask, crossing my arms under my chest. "Well, you want to know what I don't like? Her size range."

Their brows pinch together. "I've been telling her this for years. The future isn't exclusive. It's *inclusive*."

180

"See. You get it! I love LuMac," I tell them. "I always have. But I've never been able to wear it. Do you know how many people would flock to this stuff if it were available in their size? This isn't just about politics. It's good business."

They shake their head. "Studies show plus-size consumers don't invest in luxury pieces."

"What the studies don't show is the lack of luxury pieces being offered. Fat people want options. All the luxury pieces out there look like mother-of-the-bride dresses. Lucy has been on the first wave of major fashion moments before. Now isn't the time to be left behind."

"Oooooh," they say, fire in their eyes. "I really do like you. I can see why you're our Henry's favorite."

I fail to hide my annoyance when I say, "Well, maybe one of these days, he'll actually pick me for a date."

Jay smirks. "That boy's a hard read sometimes."

"Ladies!" Zeke calls. "Let's load it up!"

"Thanks again," I tell Jay. "I hope our paths cross again one day."

"I'm betting on it," they say with a wink.

Mallory and Zeke herd us out to the fifteen-passenger van waiting for us as cameras flash and what is now a whole ton of fans scream our names.

"Cindy!" someone yells. "You're my style icon!"

My heart flutters, and I think I might levitate at any moment. "Thank you!" I call back into the crowd.

"Cindy!" another—almost familiar—voice calls. "Cindy!"

A hand reaches past Zeke, who is literally standing between me and fifty *Before Midnight*–obsessed fans. A head bobs over his shoulder and it's—

"Sierra!" I shriek.

My best friend wriggles past Zeke and gives me a tight hug. "Holy crap! What is your life? What is even happening?"

"Cindy, we gotta move," Zeke says with a warning in his voice.

I look up to him. "Should I remind you who's keeping whose secret?"

His lips press into a thin line as he lets me squeeze under his arm while he continues to help the remaining women into the van.

Sierra is wearing a ribbed black maxi dress with huge red sunglasses and bright yellow platform Tevas.

"I wish I could stay and talk," I tell her, suddenly feeling like I might be on the verge of tears. "And PS, you look delicious. Did you get the gig with Opening Ceremony?"

"Yes, and it's all I've wanted to talk to you about! I mean, besides all this." Her mouth wrinkles into a pout, and I can see tears welling in her eyes.

"Don't cry," I beg her. "If you cry, I'll cry."

She nods furiously. "There's just so much happening, and there's so much I want to talk to you about and— I've seen you on TV, but it feels like I'm having a one-way conversation and I just—"

"Cindy," Zeke says.

I take both Sierra's hands in mine and squeeze tight. "I gotta go, but I'm so proud of you for landing that gig. I miss you so much it hurts," I tell her. "I love you, and I promise we're going to have a major catch-up sesh when this is all over. I promise-promise."

She gives me another hug and slides something into the pocket of my jeans.

"Smooth operator," I whisper.

"You know it, baby!" she says, swallowing back tears.

CHAPTER TWENTY-FOUR

B ack at the hotel, the valet helps us out of the van and the concierge is waiting for us with camera people also in full swing.

The concierge, a round man with an olive complexion, thick silver hair, and a matching mustache, says, "I have a note for a Ms. Cindy."

I gasp and push forward to the front of the crowd. "I'm Cindy! That's me!"

He smiles with a chuckle and hands me the note, which I quickly tear open.

Dear Cindy,
I always wanted to fall in love in New York. Join
me for an evening in the city that never sleeps. They want
a show? How about a show they'll never forget?
Love,
Henry

"Is it a date?" Sara Claire asks, peering over my shoulder.

"Of course it is." Addison pushes through all of us and storms off into the hotel lobby.

Stacy rolls her eyes. "Forget her. She has the temperament of a thirteen-year-old." She shakes her head. "Actually, scratch that. My thirteen-year-old niece would never."

I croak out a laugh, but I can't get to my room fast enough. A solo date. Henry and me. And about fifteen crew members. I didn't expect to be this anxious, but my nerves are more frayed than a Canadian tuxedo.

Upstairs, I have a few hours to myself, so I pace the length of my room until all I can do is crash face-first into the freshly made bed. There's nothing I can do to prepare for this. No homework or studying. All I can do is the hardest and most terrifying thing of all. Be myself.

I didn't expect to be invested in this. I wasn't prepared for this guy to be someone I can't get out of my head.

I'm full of jittery energy, and I've got to do something to occupy myself or else I'm going to be bouncing off the walls by the time I go on my date. I reach into my suitcase for my pencil bag and sketch pad. Lying down on my stomach with the view of the city spread out before me, I open my pad and just let myself doodle. Everything from flowers to patterns to just signing my name over and over again. The last few times I've attempted sketching, this insurmountable pressure hung over my head, but today I decide to just let my pencil lead me. This morning at LuMac when I had no other option but to act felt freeing in a way. My choice was to innovate or walk down the runway naked. Backed into a corner and left with no other alternative, I created . . . something. Something that, it turns out, I was quite proud of. And for the first time in a very long time, I'm sitting down to sketch. Not because I have to, but because I want to.

An hour before my date, Irina, Ash, and Ginger descend upon my room armed with everything they need to turn me into a princess, and I'm still sketching. I hide my sketch pad away with my nearly dead walkie-talkie and let them groom me. After this morning's near catastrophe, Irina even scoured the city for size-eighteen-and-up options.

Even still, I scroll through the rack of dresses she's rolled in, fully expecting to have to wear the backup dress I ironed just moments ago. I appreciate her efforts, but nothing on the rack is what I would call *striking*.

"I bring you every dress in the city and still nothing to your liking?" she asks incredulously.

"It's not that," I say. "And don't give me that 'every dress in the city' crap. Surely you can at least admit that the options out there in my—"

There are three quick knocks on my door, and Ash rushes over to answer it.

Beck is standing there sweaty and short of breath. "I got it," she tells Irina.

Irina gives a sly grin as she takes the dress bag from Beck.

"What is it?" I ask anxiously.

Irina's only answer is to hang up the dress and unzip the garment bag for me to see.

"Wow" is all I can manage to say. My fingers brush against the most luxe silk I've ever felt in my life. I pull the dress fully out of the bag to find a dramatic high-low gown in ice blue.

"Ahh," says Irina with satisfaction. "The Dolce and Gabbana."

I eye the tag. A D&G dress is guaranteed to run small, even though it's probably part of their recent extended sizes. It's still a European-based designer who is more interested in dressing "plus-size" starlets who are just a size ten with big boobs than in dressing actual human beings with normal lives.

Beck shakes her head. "Irina had me clear across the city in the middle of rush hour, trying to get these people to let us borrow it for the night." She turns to Irina. "Which, by the way, is definitely the job of an assistant or a junior producer."

"But, Beck, you are so convincing. Never send a child in to do the job of a professional."

Beck shrugs. "It did require all the network television wooing I could muster. Apparently this thing is a sample for next season."

"It's not even available for purchase yet?" I ask. "Will it even fit me?"

Irina tilts her chin as she pulls the dress from the rack. "It could work."

I shrug, trying to sound nonchalant like I'm not completely in love with this one-of-a-kind find. "Can't hurt to try."

After sitting for Ash and Ginger to do my hair and makeup, I take the dress into the bathroom as Irina retreads the floor I'd paced just hours ago.

As I'm shimmying out of my jeans, a piece of paper falls to the ground. Sierra. After getting the date today with Henry, I completely forgot that not only did I see my best friend today, but she shoved a note into the pocket of my jeans. I'm struck with the absolute bizarreness of my current life. One day this will all feel like a surreal dream.

I open the letter with my name scribbled across the top in Sierra's curling handwriting.

Cin,

I have about a thousand and one questions and since this is a letter instead of a text thread and you can't give me the gratification of an immediate response, I'll just tell you what I think you need to hear and save my questions for later.

I don't know how or why you landed on this show—I mean, Erica, obvi, but you know what I mean. However, I do know this: If you're going to be there, you have to let yourself stand in the spotlight. Don't be meek or shy. You tried that sophomore year and it didn't work out so well. Remember? Julian and Elise took all the credit for your big group project. Be the Cindy I know, and stop doing this halfway. Be a showstopper. I can see your little brain going into overdrive every time you're on camera. It's the overthinking tailspin I know and love. But you've gotta trust yourself. It's what I've been telling you all year. You've made it this far in one piece, right? You're there for a reason . . .

I love you.

xoS

PS: I definitely added "My BFF is Cindy on Before Midnight" *to my Twitter bio.*

The roller-coaster ride my stomach has been on all afternoon settles as I hear her voice in my head. *You're there for a reason . . .* That's not something I can easily wrap my head around, and yet it does feel like there is some sort of unknown purpose for me being here. Whether it's Henry or getting my name out there or maybe even getting back into some kind of creative groove. I don't know. . . .

Trust yourself. I can practically hear Sierra's voice in my head. I look into the mirror and find my face totally made up and my hair swept into a bun with soft tendrils hanging down and a thin black choker adding just a touch of edge to the look. *Let's do this.*

After getting fully undressed and putting on a strapless bra and an undergarment to save my thighs from chub rub, I slip the dress over my head. So far so good.

"Irina? Beck? Someone?" I call. "Zip me up?"

Beck lets herself into the bathroom, and I hold my arm up so she can access the side zip. "Irina's coming to help too. I'm sort of scared to even touch the thing, if I'm being honest."

I laugh. "Try wearing it."

Irina shoulders her way past Beck and goes right for the zipper.

I nearly hold my breath, but you wanna know what? Screw it. If I have to literally stop breathing to get into this Dolce & Gabbana dress, then D&G doesn't have the good fortune of gracing my body. I have no intention of suffocating all night.

"These damn zippers," Irina grunts. She mutters something in Russian that I'm pretty sure equates to some kind of curse, but either I block it out, or the sound of the zipper sliding up distracts me.

"Am I in?" I ask. "Does it fit?"

Irina lets out a low whistle. "Like it was made for you."

I take a quick look in the mirror. This fat girl looks like a damn princess.

"One final touch," says Irina as she rushes back to the bedroom and returns with a white shoe box, JIMMY CHOO embossed across the top in gold. She opens the box to reveal the most decadent shoes I've ever seen. "On. Loan," she says emphatically.

The pointy-toe stilettos are encrusted with Swarovski crystals that cluster together at the toe to create an incredible burst of crystals. They are glass slippers in the truest sense. These are the shoes of my dreams, and if I can only wear them for one night, I better make it count.

CHAPTER TWENTY-FIVE

W ell, I've never been on a date with three hair/makeup/ wardrobe people, a sound engineer, and a few producers, but I guess there's a first time for everything.

While we're waiting outside the hotel for the car, it's pouring.

"I need an ETA on the car!" Beck barks into the phone. "I don't care about the rain or how gridlocked Forty-Fifth Street is. I need our— You know what? Never mind."

"Uh, we're not walking in this, are we?"

"Taxi!" Beck shouts. "I need a taxi!"

The valet dutifully runs out to the curb and calls over the next cab waiting in line for hotel guests. A bright orange minivan with an ad for Olive Garden on the roof pulls up.

"Your chariot, ladies!" the valet says as he escorts us to the car under the protection of his umbrella.

"Is that *orange*?" asks Beck. "Sorry about the lack of luxury, kid," she says to me. "We'll get you in the fancy black car on the way home, but for now it's this."

"Why does it matter?"

Beck shakes her head. "It's all about the shot. Black car service dropping you off for your fairy-tale date is romantic. A yellow cab is iconic to the location. A neon-orange minivan . . . is a neon-orange minivan."

I shrug. "It's better than walking twenty-plus blocks in these heels."

When we pull up to Z Café in our neon-orange minivan, it's still pouring—a short and sudden summer shower that fills me with nostalgia. Humid steam rises from the grates on the sidewalk, and commuters dash into the subway entrance on the corner with newspapers held over their heads and the occasional umbrella.

I turn to Beck. "This is a lunch place."

"Exactly," she says. "Perfect for nighttime filming."

Zeke holds an umbrella out for me as I step out of the orange cab. "But what about all those people and the waitstaff?" I ask as I peer in through the window to find the restaurant bustling.

"Actors," Beck says simply. "Hasn't anyone ever told you reality television isn't real?"

While we're standing under the canopy, a sound tech checks my mic, and I get a glimpse of Henry sitting at a table in the middle of the restaurant. His dark brows pull together as he pops his knuckles and takes a deep breath. He's the kind of good-looking that doesn't even feel real.

"He looks nervous," Beck says to Wes just far enough away that I'm pretty sure she thinks I can't hear.

"He's been wound up since this afternoon. Mommy issues. You know how it goes with these guys. Seeing family stirs shit up."

When I walk in, Henry stands to greet me with a hug and a kiss on the cheek. He grips my elbow before I can pull away and whispers, "You look stunning."

The cameras are close on us, and I can't help but look up every time a crew member moves.

"Is this how you do all your dates?" I ask.

He chuckles. "Yeah, first my date meets my mom and then the camera crew acts as our chaperone for the night."

My mouth splits into a grin. "Your mom was . . ."

He reaches under the table and takes my hand. "Intimidating."

"You said it. Not me." I smile, my brows raising. "She's an icon."

"To me, she's just Mom. Your turn," he says, quick to change the subject. "Tell me what your dad was like. And I want to hear about your mom too."

My face falls at the mention of them. Instinctively, my hand sweeps over the locket around my neck, but I keep forgetting that I swapped it for a black choker. Just for one night.

"You don't have to," he adds quickly.

I shake my head. "No, no, it's—people don't usually just ask like that. They're usually scared to bring it up . . . or that I might cry." I laugh, but it sounds more nervous than I mean it to. "You just caught me off guard is all. My mom—well, my stepmom is great. She's driven and career-focused . . . Actually, she reminds me a lot of Lucy—your mom, I mean. My mom was a little wild. Dad would always say he didn't know where she got it from, because her parents were, like, die-hard country club people. She grew up going to all-girls schools. She and my dad met in high school when she was trying to steal a tape from the Blockbuster where he worked."

Henry gasps through a laugh. "No! What movie? Did she get away with it?"

I smile, and I know that it is scientifically impossible, but I wish I could have been there. I've heard the story so many times, but I'll never know what the store looked like or if Mom was wearing cherry lip balm or if Dad's uniform shirt was tucked in. I want to know every small, little detail. The meaningless ones that died with them. I swallow back the tears I can feel building. "*Pretty Woman*, and sort of," I say. "He bought her a copy and wrote his number on the back of the receipt."

"Whoa. Your dad had some moves."

"He did," I say. "He really did. He, uh, died when I was a senior in high school."

He bites down on his lip, like there's more he might say if it weren't for the cameras. "Again, I'm— Do you hate when people say they're sorry? I'm sorry."

I shake my head. "I feel bad for people mostly. No one ever knows what to say or how to talk to me. It's like dropping a bomb on any conversation. The ultimate mood killer." I laugh a little. "I wonder if my dad would just love to know that even though I'm twenty-two years old, he's still crashing my dates from the grave." I dated very rarely in high school, and Dad was never the type to be overbearing, but he did always ask for the license and registration of every car I got in whether it be friend or a date.

At that, he laughs and I can feel the tension deflating a little. "Well, if he's anything like you, I'm sure he was great."

My throat closes a little at the memory of him. "He was so kind. Always stopping to help people on the side of the road even though he didn't know anything about cars. And he loved building stuff, but he was awful at it. He spent, like, ten years making me a tree house in the backyard, and even then, it was only a shoddy platform that couldn't support both our weights at once. He always let me order pizza from his least favorite place because he knew I had a crush on the delivery driver, even though I couldn't bear to say so out loud. But he was a great cook too, and he loved his job—managing a small chain of bargain basement stores. He loved the people he worked with, and he always told me that he was just thankful to have a job that could provide for us and—" I take a breath. "I . . . He was my favorite person." It's all I can manage to say without letting myself cry, which I have no intention of doing.

"He sounds like the kind of guy I'd like to know," Henry says softly.

Beside me, a crew member moves, and I'm reminded that this is no normal date. I feel myself clamming up a little as I say, "You would have loved him. He would have been unsure about you and all your fancy suits, but he'd see past all that soon enough."

"To be honest, the fancy suits aren't all they're cracked up to be." He leans toward me. "Now, tell me more about this pizza delivery driver. Should I be worried?"

My lips spread into a toothy grin. "Very."

The mood lightens some, and we talk for a while longer. Wes asks us for a few specific shots, including a *Lady and the Tramp* spaghetti moment over a bowl of spaghetti and meatballs while Irina has an absolute fit over the possibility of marinara sauce in a ten-foot radius of this dress on loan. And just like that I can feel our night slowly slipping away from us, like it was never ours to begin with.

"What's next?" I ask.

"Well, I thought we could take a stroll and maybe catch a show," Henry says.

As we stand to leave, Beck says, "We just want some B-roll of you two walking around the city, so we'll follow at a distance, but your mics won't pick anything up. We'll come grab you after a few blocks and then drive over to the theater."

I nearly tell her thank you for the brief privacy but think better of it.

Outside, the two of us crowd under an umbrella and step out into the drizzling rain.

"New York smells the most like New York after a fresh rain," Henry says.

I can't help but laugh. "You say that like it's a good thing. What kind of New Yorker are you? Do you even take the subway?"

He scoffs. "I've been known to take a subway or two."

"How cultured of you," I tell him. "Do you think they really can't hear us?"

"I don't know. But I don't really care either." He holds his hand outside the protection of the umbrella. "Rain stopped." He closes the umbrella and drops it in a souvenir store umbrella stand for someone else to find. "Besides, I've been waiting to do this." In one swift motion, he takes my hand and holds it to his mouth, inhaling deeply before kissing my open palm.

My breath hitches at the touch of his warm lips against my skin and the unexpectedness of it. My brain feels foggy at first, but if he's going to catch me off guard, I'm going to do the same to him. "Is this real for you?"

He glances over his shoulder. "Coming in with the big-gun questions, eh?" He thinks for a moment before saying in a very matter-of-fact way, "It wasn't, but now it is. At first it was a joke, sort of. I was newly single when the producers approached me. What better way to rebound?"

"Newly single?" I ask. I only have vague memories of him in a few local gossip mags with a thin model on his arm.

"Sabrina," he says, his voice low.

"Sabrina Allen?" I ask. "You were dating Sabrina Allen? She's, like . . . huge now. She's a household name."

"Not when I first met her." He takes a deep breath. "We met at a Labor Day party." He laughs. "It was a white party and she showed up in red. Mom loved her immediately. It got serious fast. She closed out Mom's next show. Featured in print ads. And I loved her . . . or at least I loved that my mom loved her." He shakes his head. "Wow, that sounds awful. I promise I only have the normally allotted amount of mommy issues."

I snort at that, wishing I could tell him about my own real-life step-mommy issues.

"My mom and . . . We don't share a lot in common. Sabrina was something we could share. God, just saying it now, I see how messed up it was." He sighs. "I proposed. In Paris. She said no, and the next day she'd signed a one-year exclusive contract with Victoria's Secret. When I told my mom that Sabrina didn't say yes, I quickly realized she was more upset about losing her ingénue and muse than she was about my heart being broken. So I took a step back from the business. From Mom."

"If you took a step back, how did you end up on a dating show trying to drum up excitement about the brand?" I ask, trying to fill in the gaps.

"I was bumbling around out in LA for a few months when I met Beck. She tried getting me to meet with her boss, and I kept saying no, but she was relentless. Then one day, my dad called, and he basically said, 'Your mother's arthritis is debilitating and the only thing she can do to slow it down is to step back from LuMac. Either you come home and run it, or we sell it for parts.' When I got back to the city and teamed up with Jay, I found out that the brand was in bigger trouble than I thought. We were past the normal measures you could take for a failing business. We needed something wild. Something viral. I called Beck, and next thing I knew, I was the next suitor on *Before Midnight.*"

We briefly stop at a crosswalk like good New Yorkers, and I look up to him. "But what about when we first met? You said you had missed your first flight because you couldn't decide if you wanted to go to LA?"

His jaw twitches. "I didn't say this whole thing didn't freak me out. I've seen dozens of people I grew up with open themselves up to fame. It doesn't usually end well. The internet has a way of digging up your past or—"

"Are there things to dig up?" I ask. "In your past?"

"Oh, you know," he says. "Just the standard skeletons. Family drama. A few questionable drunk pictures, but . . . I never wanted to be a public person. I wasn't some child star or something, but to a degree, our lives were always public property anyway. Going on this show sort of feels like giving up what privacy I had left."

"You could have always gone on *Shark Tank,*" I say.

The crosswalk signal turns white, and he tugs my hand, pulling me through the throng of people. "Yeah, Mark Cuban would be all over an aging formerly relevant fashion brand. I guess you could have always gone on *Project Runway*."

"Make it work," I say, mimicking Tim Gunn. I glance over my shoulder. "I can't see the crew behind us anymore. Do you think we should wait for them?"

"Definitely not," he says, his voice giddy. "You think you can run in those things?"

I glance down at my sparkling shoes. They're art, but run in them? I'm not so sure. "I'm not much of a runner to begin with, but I'm willing to attempt a light jog," I tell him, the thrill of losing the crew sending adrenaline rushing through my body.

"Let's go."

CHAPTER TWENTY-SIX

There's a wild expression on Henry's face. It's the most carefree I've seen him since . . . ever.

We take off down the street, our feet slapping against the pavement as we turn the corner. My dress ripples behind me, and it feels like we're playing a wild game of tag. With Henry by my side, what would the crew even do to us if they caught us? Send us both home? I think not.

I shriek as I trip forward, my heel catching in a missing chunk of sidewalk. As I stumble out of my shoe, my fingers slip from Henry's.

"Shit," I mutter, catching myself with one hand on the pavement.

"Are you okay?" he asks, doubling back to pull me up and steady me.

"I'm fine." I hold my bare foot up, balancing on one heel now. "It's the shoes. They're on loan. They're worth more money than I have to my name."

He grabs a glittering stiletto, inspecting it closely. "Not a scratch." He quickly pops down to one knee as he guides my foot back into the shoe, his fingers wrapped around my ankle as I balance myself on his shoulder.

He looks up at me, his eyes heavy-lidded as the city spins around us, streetlights flickering on as the sky turns to a misty dusk. "You sure you're okay?" he asks.

I nod wordlessly at the sight of him on his knees before me as a simmering heat spreads through my abdomen.

He stands and takes my hand again as he pulls me off the ground into Bryant Park.

"Are you trying to woo me?" I ask.

His eyes search mine.

"Bryant Park," I say. "The Cathedral of Fashion."

"I should lie and say this was totally on purpose, but I'm just trying really hard to lose our wardens." Clear from view of the street, we slow to a stroll.

Sierra and I spent the last four years lurking around Bryant Park like it was some hallowed space. It might not be the home of Fashion Week any longer, but we couldn't help but feel like we might catch a glimpse of one of our idols just strolling around, reliving their Bryant Park glory days. But today the park is just a park full of normal people doing normal things.

Constantly looking over our shoulders for signs of the crew, we walk right into a ballroom class for senior citizens.

"Come on," says Henry, pulling me farther into the class run by a petite middle-aged couple using nothing but their iPhone and a plastic cup to amplify the music.

"It's a class," I say as I kick off my shoes and let them dangle from my fingers to stop my heels from continuously sinking into the grass. "We're not students."

"I don't think they'll mind." He leads me to the back of the group and pulls me to him, his hand spread across the base of my spine.

I lean my head against his chest and let myself be held.

"Let's pretend for just a moment," he says.

And he doesn't have to be any more specific than that. I know just what he means. Let's pretend we're two normal people on a normal date taking a normal stroll in a normal park that I haven't been dreaming of since I was old enough to know what Fashion Week was.

Looking around, there are all sorts of couples. Some spry and others who are a little slower these days. Some men with men and women with women.

"Sometimes," I whisper, "I look at older people and wonder what my parents would have looked like at their age."

He rests his chin atop my head and pulls my hand to his lips, kissing each one of my knuckles. We sway quietly to music we can barely hear, but that's okay, because this city is our soundtrack. Honking horns, conversations about little things and big things, flocks of birds descending, and the sounds all slightly dulled by the trees surrounding us.

"Do you think Beck and Wes are losing their minds yet?"

"They've probably already hired private detectives to find us." His chin moves from its perch on my head. "But I think the instructors have found us out." He takes my other hand. "Excuse us," he calls as we weave through the rest of the class and exit back out the way we came. Currents of electricity flow between us, and I think I'm catching feelings for him. The kind that burn.

Dutifully, we walk in the direction of Times Square, like a couple of kids preparing themselves to face the music. Our whole history thus far is just a series of these bite-size moments, and I wonder what we could even become with time that was our own. It excites me and frightens me in equal measure. But instead, we're constantly racing against the clock. Always running out of time. In the distance, I spot Mallory spinning in circles, hands waving as she talks into her Bluetooth headphones, not yet noticing us.

"There's Mallory," I say. "And she doesn't look happy."

Henry groans. "I'm not ready."

I shake my head. "Me neither."

"Follow me."

My heart pounds as Henry pulls me across the street, dodging in out and of cars, and into a two-story souvenir store that stretches an entire block.

The clerk barely even looks up from their book as we rush to the back of the store. Henry's chest is heaving as he curls an arm around my waist. "The cameras can't follow us in here. Private property."

I press a hand to his chest and throw my head back in a breathless laugh. "You're going to get me kicked off this show."

He leans down and presses his lips to my throat, and I gasp softly. Goose bumps trail up my arms as he wraps another arm up my back, pressing our bodies as close as two bodies can be while still fully clothed.

I don't even have time to think about how sweaty I feel or if I need deodorant after our little run. All I can manage to think about is his arms around me and his lips on my neck and all the things we might do if we weren't standing in the middle of a dusty Times Square souvenir shop.

His hand finds the back of my neck, and my fingers run up his arms to his shoulders as he tilts his head up to meet my lips.

"Hi," I whisper.

"Hi," he says, studying my lips.

I feel intoxicated with want as we both dance around this moment for a second longer, his nose grazing mine until finally—finally!—he presses his lips against mine, like I'm the only oxygen he can breathe.

My lips part against his tongue, and it's these moments of just the two of us that trick my brain into thinking that we're just a couple of lovesick nobodies slowly falling for each other.

Someone loudly clears their throat, and it takes two more times before we manage to disentangle ourselves.

I peer over Henry's shoulder to find Mallory standing there with her hands on her hips. Just behind her is Beck, outside with her inhaler in her mouth and the crew fuming beside her.

"I think we're in big trouble," I whisper.

"It was worth it," he tells me with a quiet growl to his voice.

We walk outside like two defiant teenagers with Henry's hand cradling my hip. After our little runaway situation, we're loaded into a black SUV and driven just a few blocks to the Minskoff Theatre for a showing of *The Lion King*, where we're seated in a private box that is not at all that private if you count our entourage.

As we're sitting in our plush chairs away from the horde of tourists, waiting for the show to start, Henry leans over and says, "If you haven't guessed, they don't actually let me plan the dates."

"Mr. Henry Mackenzie, do you mean to tell me that you're not a fan of *The Lion King*?"

"Listen, I've got no beef with Simba, but if I were going to take you to a show, it wouldn't be at an overstuffed Broadway theater."

"Oooo, now that's some New Yorker shade. Well, I, for one, am truly enjoying the ideal my-grandmother-is-in-town date. All that's missing is a trip to Serendipity for frozen hot chocolate. This date sponsored by the New York City Board of Tourism."

"You're ruining the surprise!" The lights around us lower, but I can still see the brightness of his smile as he says, "One day I'll show you my New York."

I lean my head against his shoulder. "I'll show you mine if you show me yours."

And even though we briefly pretend we're both a little immune to the touristy parts of this city that out-of-towners so often flock to, the show is incredible and we're both taken with a little boy about the age of the triplets sitting below us who stands in his seat to sing along with Timon and Pumbaa.

In the middle of the show, Henry stands and returns with his suit jacket, which he'd hung up just outside of our box. He drapes it over my shoulders to protect me from the icy air conditioner, and while I'm not drowning in it in that annoying way where girls think it's so cute to flop around in oversize suit jackets or their boyfriends' boxers, I still appreciate the gesture.

"Thanks," I whisper. "I think we might actually wear the same size."

He shrugs. "Looks better on you than it does on me."

"Well, I don't know if you've heard, but I'm sort of, like, a big-deal model now."

He clutches his heart. "Too soon."

I gasp. "No, I meant this afternoon. Not Sabr—"

In the next box over, someone shushes me.

Henry reaches into my lap and takes my hand. "I know."

We hold hands like that for the rest of the show, and afterward, we're taken backstage to film a segment with a few members of the cast. I gush over their incredible talents and costumes, and once we're done, we're loaded into another SUV. This time, Henry and I sit as close together as two people can, and I find myself praying for a traffic jam—anything to slow us down. But on this sticky summer night with the clouds rolling back behind the bridges into the boroughs, we hit every green light and there's not a single reason to slow down. Not even a honking cabdriver. It's a New York City miracle.

At the hotel, we walk as slow as we can to the elevator with Henry's arm wrapped around my waist, his hand again resting comfortably on my hip.

With a cameraman close on our heels, Beck announces, "Time to say good night, lovebirds."

I turn in to Henry, and I want to kiss him, of course, but with the cameras on us—

"Oh," says Wes, "so you two are okay with getting hot and heavy in the back of a souvenir store, but you can't give us a little kiss good night?" He throws up his hands and leaves Beck on her own.

"Ignore him," she says. "And us," she adds quickly. "But I gotta be in bed before midnight. We got an early morning, and I'm fading."

"Don't want you to turn into a pumpkin on us, Beck." Henry shrugs. "I guess we should give the people what they want."

I nod and close my eyes as my lips melt into his for a long but chaste kiss that leaves me wishing for more.

His hands wrap around me in a tight hug, holding me close to his chest, and I can hear the thumping beat of his heart. It might be my new favorite sound. One of his fingers traces a pattern into my bare back over and over again.

My head is foggy, so it takes me a moment to realize he's telling me something. He's giving me a message. His finger continues to trace over and over again until he pulls away with an innocent, barely there smile on his face.

I can still feel his finger dragging across my skin in a familiar way, leaving a trace of heat, and I hope to God I got exactly what it was that he was trying to say.

CHAPTER TWENTY-SEVEN

E ight. Two. Six. Eight. Two. Six. Eight. Two. Six. Eight. Two. Six. Eight. Two. Six.

Three numbers that could only mean one thing. Henry's hotel room.

As soon as I walk through the door of my room, Irina is waiting for me. I let out a yelp. "What are you doing here?"

She holds a hand out. "The dress," she says simply, not looking up from the game on her cell phone.

I hold my arm up. "The least you could do is unzip it."

She unzips and gets a whiff of my armpit. "Ugh, I've got to get this thing dry-cleaned. It smells like a sports bra. A sad lost-and-found sports bra at the YMCA. Not even the nice YMCA. The kind with a drained pool and one of those jiggle machines from—"

"I get the point," I tell her as I step out of the dress and into a pair of leggings and an oversize men's undershirt I cut into a crop top. "The shoes too?" I ask, the memory of Henry kneeling before me sending a chill up my spine.

"The shoes especially," she says.

I pick up the Jimmy Choos from the floor and give them a quick kiss on the side of the toe. "Goodbye, beauty."

Irina sighs. "They are very, very good shoes."

I nod. "They were good to me."

She takes them from my hands, and for the first time, I think Irina and I have found common ground. At least the woman can appreciate good taste in shoes.

"You might be smelly," she says, "but you were really something tonight. I perhaps have to put money on you."

"I'm not a racehorse," I tell her as she slinks out of the room with the garment bag over her shoulder.

"Tell that to Wes. He won the pot last year and went on a two-week trip to Bali."

"What?" I ask, but she's already gone. "What pot?"

Well, that's just great. Not only am I dating a man who's dating seven other women, but I guess the crew is betting on us too. Delightful. I sit down at the desk by my window with my sketch pad, the Statue of Liberty glowing through the nighttime haze, and I write his room number over and over again. Eight twenty-six. Eight twenty-six. Eight twenty-six. Eight twenty-six. Eight twenty-six. Eight twenty-six. Eight twenty-six. Eight twenty-six. Eight twenty-six. Until eventually, it doesn't look like numbers at all. Just an abstract pattern.

I don't even have to look to know that Mallory or Zeke is outside guarding the hallway. There's no way I'm getting out of this room and making it all the way to Henry's without getting stopped. After our disappearance tonight, I'm sure we're being even more heavily guarded than usual.

With his walkie-talkie dead and mine very nearly, I'm left with no way to contact Henry. I wish they hadn't taken the phones out of this room. Surely that's some kind of insurance liability. If I had my phone, I would curl up in bed and call him and we would talk all night until our breathing became heavy and we just fell asleep to the sound of one another.

I try washing my face. Eight twenty-six. I try pulling my hair into a ponytail. Eight twenty-six. I braid it. Eight twenty-six. It doesn't look good. Eight twenty-six. I settle for a sloppy bun instead. I try a Korean face mask. Eight twenty-six. I lie in bed. Eight twenty-six. But none of it works. Eight twenty-six.

I can't do this. I can't stop thinking about him, and I can't stop thinking about the chance to spend a whole night with him without a camera in sight.

That's it. I jump out of bed and put on my gold glitter Kate Spade Keds and a hoodie. Slowly, I creak my door open to peer out into the hallway and find Zeke sitting a few doors down, slumped against the wall, dead asleep. I was fully prepared to blackmail him again just so I could make it to the elevators, but Lady Liberty must be watching over me. If I had a cell phone, I'd snap a picture to send to Anna so she could see how dopey he looks.

With the coast clear, I step out into the hallway, closing my door slowly to stop it from slamming, and tiptoe past him to the elevator. Just as I'm about to hit the button to go five flights up, I stop myself. The dinging sound. It could wake Sleeping Beauty back there, so I opt for the stairs.

As I lean over the rail and take a nice long look at the never-ending staircase, I remind myself that just a few weeks ago, I lived in a third-floor walk-up. By the time I make it to the eighth floor, though, I'm a little sweatier than I was, but I'm relieved to find no producers guarding this floor. I feel like I'm in a video game trying to dodge zombies, when really all I'm trying to do is hang out with a guy I like. Somehow, this show has mentally reverted me to sixteen and I'm scared of being caught inside a boy's room.

After one knock, the door of room 826 opens to reveal Henry, barefoot with his shirt partially unbuttoned and his tie dangling between his fingers. He smirks. "For a minute there, I was worried you might just assume I was very specifically obsessed with one part of your back."

He reaches for my hand and pulls me inside.

As the door closes behind me, I slide the tie from his other hand and run my fingers over the shadowed stripes. The silk melts beneath my touch, and I flip the tie over to find the label. "Fancy. Hermès."

"It was a gift," he says.

"From your mom?" I ask.

He tilts his head to the side. "Sabrina."

"Oh, that's nice," I tell him, "wearing a tie from your ex on a date with your new—person."

He takes a step closer to me. "Not a fan of labels?"

"Well, I wouldn't exactly call myself your girlfriend," I tell him. As I'm talking, he takes another step toward me and dips his head down so that my lips brush his on that last word.

"This feels pretty serious to me," he says, his voice husky as his fingers dig into my waist.

"I don't know," I say, breathless from his touch. "Feels a little crowded."

He leans his temple against my shoulder so that his breath is hot on my neck. "I want to make so many promises to you right now. Almost as badly as the things I want to do to you."

I feel like I know two versions of him. On-Screen Henry and Private Henry, but it's as though the two versions can't even talk to each other or share information. On-Screen Henry is sweet and flirtatious, but I never fully know where I stand with him. Private Henry is a little rougher around the edges, but he never leaves me wondering.

I know what I should do. I should ask him where I stand. I should ask him if he feels just as strongly for Addison or Sara Claire or one of the other women and if this is all just some dance we have to get over with and if in the end, we're going to give this a real shot. But for once, I want to stop worrying. I want to let go of all the things I can't control and just be here in this moment with Henry.

I wrap my arms around his waist. "How would you have made it different?" I ask.

He picks his head up, his deep brown eyes lingering on my lips. "What do you mean?"

"You said tonight wasn't the date you would have planned for me. What would you have done differently?"

He checks the sleek black watch on his wrist. "We can still find out."

CHAPTER TWENTY-EIGHT

"**B**ingo starts in ten," the waitress says as she slaps our bingo sheets on the table alongside a chubby-looking marker. "Dot markers are extra. Food will be out soon."

"I think we just ordered enough dim sum for a party of six," I say.

"I could put away enough dim sum to feed this whole place. I'm so tired of TV food," Henry moans.

"TV food?" I ask.

He shakes his head. "Didn't you notice how tasteless the food was tonight? They take me to closed restaurants for these dates and basically feed me cold spaghetti. I miss real food. It's like eating airplane food every night."

"I think that might be my own personal hell. Airplane food for eternity."

"Oh, I think my actual personal hell is a party that I can't seem to leave. Like every door I go through is just a door that takes me back to the same party and no matter how hard I try I can't get out."

"So I guess a surprise birthday party is your worst nightmare?"

He shakes his head. "I hate them. My mom threw me one for my thirteenth birthday, and it was mostly adults who came."

"Didn't she invite your friends from school?"

"Well, yeah, but I had four or five friends. Not nearly enough for the kind of party Lucy Mackenzie intended to throw. There were waiters on roller skates. And ice sculptures."

"Ice sculptures?" I ask.

"Of me."

My jaw hits the floor. "I'm sorry. Did you just say ice sculptures? Of you?"

"Make fun of me all you want, but we were competing with bar mitzvahs so intense that TLC filmed a pilot for a guy in our building called *My Ballin' Bar Mitzvah.*"

"Whoa. My thirteenth birthday party was at the neighborhood pool. We rented a picnic table and ate nachos from the snack bar."

"That's the kind of party I would gladly attend."

I laugh at the image of Henry at my dingy old neighborhood pool with all the teenage lifeguards who I thought were so hot but in reality had bacne just like me. "See, parties aren't all that bad. And hey, you met Sabrina at a party. Aren't parties sort of a way of life in the circles you run in?" Of course I wish our relationship wasn't playing out on this TV show, but even if all this was stripped away, our lives are still worlds apart. The elite NYC parties Henry grew up attending are just one example of that. Maybe I should be more thankful for our little reality television bubble.

"Exactly why I hate them," he says. "And I met Sabrina because I'm always looking for the person who can help me escape the party. The person who wants to take a walk or—"

"Go back to your place?" I ask playfully, but fully serious.

The corner of his mouth turns upward devilishly. "I guess that too . . . Back when I had time to meet people and I wasn't trying to dig my family's company out of the Mariana Trench."

"Nice. A marine biology reference."

"Cape Cod Marine Biology camp. Third grade through sixth grade."

"Sleepaway camp?" I ask. "First boarding school. Now sleepaway camp. That's rich-kid shit."

"Well, you gotta dump your kid somewhere while you're trekking across the globe bouncing from one ayahuasca retreat to the next."

"Whoa. I didn't realize Lucy went that hard."

"Yeah, she's real hip until the camp nurse is calling because her son broke his arm trying to dive out of a tree because he thinks if he just believes hard enough that he's an astronaut, gravity will cease to exist. The only adult sober enough to talk was my mom's assistant's assistant, and he thought my name was Carson."

"Okay, I have a lot of questions, but how does anyone get Carson from Henry?" I wish so hard that I still had my dad in my life, but at least when he was alive, he was the kind of dad that Father's Day was made for. "What about your dad?" I ask. "He's still around, right?" I remember seeing the picture of the three of them in his office, and it felt so far off and distant that I almost wondered if he was even still in Henry's life.

He nods. "Roger Mackenzie is Lucy Mackenzie's number-one fan. He hates clothing, and to this day, she sets an outfit out for him every morning. His parents died when he was young and still living in Edinburgh, so he took what inheritance they'd left him and moved to New York. He fell in love with my mom on the subway before he'd even made it to his hotel. They haven't spent a night apart since. Neither of them really had family, so they were and are everything for each other."

"That's a good love story," I say.

"It's no Blockbuster meet-cute."

I smile.

"I think usually when people have kids, they prepare for their lives to change. Sometimes they leave the city or give up going to the bar on weeknights, but my parents had no such intentions. They just kept on . . . living. And brought me along when they could and then shipped me off for boarding school when I was old enough. The first one was just outside of London. No one really knew what to make of the half-Scottish, quarter–Puerto Rican kid from America. Anyway, if it's possible to be the third wheel with your own parents, that's me."

"That's not fair," I say. "It's like . . . the one place you should always belong."

He shakes his head. "I don't think I've ever said this out loud, but sometimes I think I proposed to Sabrina just to say I'd found my person. I'd found my family without them. . . . But now suddenly, they need me. And how do you say no? I couldn't. I guess I need them too in a way."

I reach across the table and take his hand, offering him the comfort of shared silence.

"I bet you have shitty-parent stories too," he says, watching our linked hands.

Not really. Even though I could think of a few, they would all involve my teenage angst over Erica trying to assert herself as my mother. That was a rocky transition, to say the least, but guilt twinges in my stomach as I remember all the things I've kept from him. He knows my parents are dead, but after all he's shared, I feel so wrong lying about Erica. "My stepmom is . . . She's there for me when I need her. Not perfect, but she tries. And my mom and dad . . . It's not that I think dying made them some kind of saints, but I miss them. Especially Dad . . . even when he was at his worst . . . which was rare."

He swallows and bites down on his lip, thinking for a moment. "I think that's love. The real stuff. When you love someone at their worst. When you believe they can be better."

"Is that . . . Is that how you feel about your mom?"

He sighs. "She's better now. Calmer. She doesn't treat me like as much of a set piece as she used to, but sometimes I wonder if that's her actively changing or if it's just age wearing her down. Or maybe, in the end, with the show and me taking over the company . . . maybe I'm more her set piece than ever before."

"That's not what I see," I tell him. "I see a person who's there for his family in their hour of need, even when they might not deserve it. And despite your parents' best efforts, I think you turned out pretty great."

"So says my therapist and Jay."

"I like Jay," I tell him.

"Oh, they really like you too. I've got the text messages to prove it."

My eyes turn into saucers. "You have a cell phone? You've been holding out on me this whole time!"

He snorts and fishes it out of his pocket for me to see. "Oh, it's definitely one of those old-people ladybug phones. This thing doesn't even have a color screen. I'm actually a little embarrassed to be holding it in public, but Jay would just tell me that's my toxic masculinity talking, or ageism or something."

"Jay would be right," I say, taking it from his hand. And sure enough, the phone is a little red walkie-talkie-looking thing with two tiny antennas you can actually pull out for better reception. "This thing looks like a relic."

"You should see how long it takes me to text on that thing. It's honestly not even worth it, but I told them that if they wanted me to do the show, I had to be able to get in touch with work." He takes the phone back from me and puts it back in his pocket. "This was Beck's idea of a compromise."

"Hey, it's more communication with the outside world than I'm getting." I want to ask him what he knows about how the show is being received or if it's making any difference for the brand, but I also don't want to spend our precious private time together talking about this show. "Can I ask you something?"

"I think so," he says playfully.

"If you could do anything with LuMac, what would it be?"

He nods, and I know he already has a very clear answer to this question. "There's this program that we've got going for up-and-coming brands. We foster them and help them release a micro line. They pay back their loan to us slowly over time, but we just don't have the resources to really dig in and do it up big. I would love to see us launch exclusive collaborative items as part of their lines and vice versa. I mean, we have the future of fashion just sitting right there in our offices. We should be doing so much more. Making connections. Building relationships. We just don't have the money or the people to make it happen. At least, not yet. Mom calls it my pet project, but I think it's the path forward."

"I can't even begin to tell you what an opportunity like that would mean to a fresh-out-of-fashion-school newbie. I love fashion. I love this industry. But sometimes it feels like the only way to succeed is to know someone."

"Well, if your wardrobe is any indication, I'm positive you're deeply talented, Cindy."

"Can I get that in writing?" I joke.

Without a word, the waitress places our tower of dim sum steamer baskets on the table and takes two sets of chopsticks from her apron for us. "Bingo's starting in just a minute."

"Are we doing this?" Henry asks from the other side of the dim sum.

"The food or the bingo?"

"Both," he says.

"Oh, it's on," I tell him.

"How do you feel about sitting on the same side of the booth?" he asks, seemingly out of the blue.

"What do you mean?"

"Are you one of those people who looks at people sitting on the same side of the booth together and thinks they're ridiculous? Or are you pro-same-side-of-the-booth?"

My brow furrows, and the smell of the dim sum is so good it's almost hard to concentrate. "I think . . . I think I used to see people do that and feel like they just had something to prove. Like, they had to show the world that they were so in love and couldn't even stand sitting that far from each other . . . but now—"

"Me too," he says. "I used to think that too. But I think I've found someone who I want to share a booth seat with."

"Henry Mackenzie, are you asking me to sit next to you?"

"Mainly so I can cheat off your bingo card," he says, "but yes."

I slide out of the booth and squeeze in next to him. The booths are old and tiny with a few tears in the cushions, and my butt sinks in so deep that my feet barely even touch the ground.

Henry opens the first layer of the steamer, and we both tear open our chopsticks.

With my bingo dotter in one hand and chopsticks in the other, I pick up a perfectly made dumpling.

"Cindy?" he asks.

I look up to him, fully prepared to chastise him for blocking the one-way dumpling ticket to my mouth, but he tilts his head down and his nose brushes mine. And I just let myself sit in this moment. Our chopsticks and dumpling and bingo cards and dotting markers, and the low-hanging red lamp hovering above our table casting a spotlight on our food while we are just barely cloaked in darkness.

"I was lying about cheating off you," he says. "I just wanted to be close enough to do this."

His lips touch mine as the waitress begins to call off bingo numbers, and there aren't many things I'd choose over dumplings, but this kiss would be it.

CHAPTER TWENTY-NINE

The next morning, we have an elimination on the runway of the Westchester private airport in front of a small luxury jet that we won't actually be flying anywhere because not even a quarter of the crew would fit.

Henry and I walked around the city until the sun began to slowly crawl up the horizon. We got two bagels on our way back. I couldn't decide between smoked salmon, cream cheese, and dill, or rainbow bagel with Nutella, so Henry insisted we get both and split them, which is basically my exact love language. Sierra says I'm indecisive, but I like to think I can make any meal tapas, so whatever person is willing to tolerate that might be my soul mate.

When we got back to the hotel, Henry snuck the doorman and the front desk clerk each a twenty and asked them not to mention to anyone that they saw us coming or going. We took the elevator to my floor, and I wish that we could have put a spell on the rest of the world to freeze time and anchor the moon in place. Everyone would just wake up a little more rested, and Henry and I would win more time together. Time. It's the one thing he and I can't seem to get enough of.

We held hands, walking as slowly as we could until just a few paces ahead of us, a door clicked, opening. Henry snaked an arm around my waist and pulled me across the hallway into a small room with an ice machine and a vending machine.

I ducked into the space between the ice machine and the wall, my hips just barely fitting, and Henry stepped in just after me. He hovered over me, tucking his head down and blocking out the light.

A person stepped into the little room, and the ice machine began to rumble to life. Henry arced backward for just a moment, and mouthed, *Wes.*

"Shit," I said.

Henry's hand swept up, pressing his finger to my lips.

I took his wrist and pulled his hand down, stretching up on my toes so that our lips were within grazing distance.

His fingers dug into my waist, and he sank even closer to me somehow, my back pressed flat against the wall.

Our mouths hovered, breath hot, as Henry's hands drifted upward, grazing the band of my lace bralette. I gasped at the feeling of his touch so close and his lips crashed into mine, silencing me.

His mouth was urgent and tasted like hazelnut. All I wanted was to drag him into my room and then to wake up beside him and ask him all the questions my brain can't stop asking.

And now, just hours later, standing on this runway, I can still feel the weight of his body against me and his hands traveling up my torso.

After I went back to my room, I slept for an hour and a half and woke up with my heart racing. Something happened last night between us, and suddenly, when I picture my future, I picture Henry there with me.

I can imagine *us.* Sleeping in late on Saturday mornings. Eating ramen together in the wee hours of the night. Going to little run-down hotels just so we can stay as close to the beach as possible. All I want is time with him. Just a little more time.

Henry calls my name, and then Sara Claire, and before long Gretchen and Valerie are the last girls standing, both of whom are sent home. Gretchen gives the producers the ugly-cry departure they've been waiting for while Valerie is stoic and doesn't attempt to give Henry a hug goodbye.

Once they're gone, Chad claps Henry on the back. "Should we tell them?" he asks.

Henry smiles, the wrinkles around his eyes revealing the little bit of concealer Ash must have put on him when he showed up this morning with bags under his eyes from a sleepless night. "Jenny, Addison, Sara Claire, Stacy, Chloe, and Cindy." His voice hitches a little on my name, and my stomach explodes into a chorus of butterflies. "I think it's time we take this international. I hope you've got your passports, because we're going to the villas."

Like the helicopter landing pad at the château, the villas in Punta Mita, Mexico, are a *Before Midnight* staple. Despite the fact that we all know it's coming, it's no effort to let out a shriek of surprise. A few years back, I remember Erica trying to drop the villas for a luxury train trip through Europe, but the logistics and cost were a nightmare. And as incredible as that sounds, I think that's the kind of experience I want to save for after all this is said and done and it's just Henry and me. And hopefully a hundred grand in cash.

Like in our last flight, there's plenty of room to spread out and Henry is kept in first class. But as I board the plane, I hold my hand out slightly, hoping that he might catch it when I walk past. Playing coy, Henry doesn't even flinch, but just ahead of me Zeke drops a bag of equipment as he's trying to wedge it into an overhead bin and causes a traffic jam just long enough for Henry to hook his pinkie around mine and kiss it gently.

I pull my hand away as discreetly as possible, and as I glance over my shoulder, Addison is frowning right at me.

CHAPTER THIRTY

When we land in Puerto Vallarta, we're rushed through customs and split into a caravan of vans and SUVs, which take us along the coast to Punta Mita. The sprawling skyscraper resorts of Puerto Vallarta begin to fall away in favor of dense jungle that sometimes gives way to the sparkling blue ocean. The only time I've ever gone to a place like this was when Erica took all of us to Cabo for our first Christmas without Dad. Erica spent the whole week sleeping on the beach while the three of us skipped around the resort until Anna and Drew ran off with some older boys they'd been flirting with. I ended up rejoining Erica, who felt a little bad for me and ordered me enough margarita swirls that soon enough I was asleep on the beach too.

The villas are a chic and modern cluster of efficiency apartments grouped along the beach with one main house at the center and an infinity pool that stretches the entire length of the property.

The smiling staff dressed in all white greets us with fresh cucumber-and-lime water.

"I could get used to this," Sara Claire says.

Stacy chuckles quietly. "Yeah, eliminate me all you want, Henry, but I plan on haunting this place from now into eternity."

I swat at her. "He's not eliminating you." Even though, actually, I do hope he does.

"I haven't had a one-on-one yet. I'm just here for background noise at this point."

Sara Claire and I look at each other, waiting for the other to comfort Stacy, but we both know that nothing about that would be genuine.

In New York, it felt like the crew was racing against the inevitable as they tried to hide any and all technology and media from us. But here, everyone is so relaxed—even Wes seems at ease—and with how secluded we are, I can see why. Of course, the televisions have been removed from our rooms, but in these gorgeous villas they don't seem to leave a gaping hole like they did in our NYC hotel.

Each room has an enclosed outdoor shower, soaking tub, and intricate macramé hammock. Inside, the bed is fitted with white linens and set into a low, dark wood platform frame with a huge canopy overhead and a sheer white fabric draped over the top. Honestly, it feels like we're all on a polyamorous honeymoon.

Inside my room, I push the huge glass doors aside and the sound of the waves crashing against the rocks is a lullaby so potent that I nearly fall asleep on my feet. A ways down in front of the main house, a huge outdoor dining table stretches across the deck nestled in front of a peaceful sandy alcove leading into the translucent blue water.

"Hi, neighbor!" Sara Claire calls, waving a card in her hand. "Guess I'm first up for the solo dates!"

"Knock 'em dead!" I call back, uncertainty spiked with jealousy gnawing at my insides. "Not all the way dead, though. Just, like, temporarily unconscious."

That night, Sara Claire and Henry are swept off somewhere for a private romantic dinner with Wes and a bare-bones crew. I get the feeling that this is an attempt from the production staff to make the villa dates as intimate as possible.

This morning, after bagels and the vending machine make-out

session, when Henry and I said goodbye, I nearly just blurted out, *Choose me*. We could go along with this whole charade and I would be a good contestant and wait it out until the very end if he could just tell me here and now that, in the end, he would choose me. But I couldn't seem to get the words out. I couldn't manage to expose that much of myself and risk him rejecting me. But most of all, I didn't want to spoil the absolute gift that last night turned out to be. I wanted to freeze that moment like one of the hotel souvenir shop snow globes so that anytime I was feeling sad or unsure, I could just shake the globe and see us squeezed into that booth with our dim sum and bingo cards.

Stacy, Addison, Chloe, Beck, the rest of the crew, and I all gather on the deck of the main house for an epic buffet. It's the best food we've had since the start of the show—tamales, flautas, gorditas, street tacos, every veggie you can imagine from fresh pico to grilled cactus, and rows of fresh fruit carved in the shape of flowers.

"Trust me," Beck whispers, "we're eating way better than those two."

Despite Addison's permanent scowl, the evening is delightful. The crew takes turns telling stories about former contestants, and there's everything from the woman who pooped her pants skydiving to the man who was scared of worms. Some mention Erica and how she used to live on set in the early days. They tease her in the way you can only tease someone who you simultaneously fear and admire. Even though I can't let on how true all their stories and memories ring, I still feel a twinge of pride at simply knowing her.

After dinner, Stacy and I each take a mango on a stick and kick our sandals off before settling onto a beach bed.

Behind us, the drunken crew sets up a karaoke machine, and their songs and laughter bounce off the water like skipping stones. I have to think that the villas are a sort of celebration for them after slogging through the rest of the season.

"Can you keep a secret?" Stacy asks the moment we're settled.

"My five favorite words," I tell her.

She downs the rest of her margarita and plants the cup in the sand before leaning back onto the beach bed. "My ex has been watching the show."

"How do you know he's been watching?" Though what I'm really thinking is that I'm pretty sure everyone's exes are watching.

"She."

"Oh, sorry, I just assumed," I say, feeling incredibly foolish.

She leans her head toward me and takes a bite out of her mango. "I like who I like, and just FYI, if you weren't totally in love with Henry, you'd totally be my type."

"Wait, wait, wait, I have so many questions, but first off, I think if I were in love with Henry, I'd know."

She gives me a look that says she's not willing to contest her point.

"Fine," I say, "we can hash that out later, but first, can we go back to how exactly you know that your ex is watching the show? Do you have secret ties to the outside world that you're keeping from me?"

She laughs wildly. "I wish my life was that scandalous."

I cringe a little. If she only knew.

"No, she got wind from some gossip blog that we were headed to New York for filming, and she took the overnight train from Chicago to New York and showed up at our hotel the morning of the fashion show challenge."

"Ho-ly sh—"

"I know. I was a little bit freaked out but also weirdly endeared by the whole thing. Who doesn't love a grand gesture?"

"How did she even find you in the city?"

"Her brother is a concierge at the St. Regis. There is not a New York City question he can't answer or find the answer to. Admittedly, as a librarian I find concierge back channels deeply sexy."

"That is so very specific."

"Mmmm." She moans dramatically. "That sexy, sexy information."

I nearly choke on a chunk of mango as I snort out a laugh. "Okay, so what exactly did your ex say?"

"She said she'll be waiting."

"That's it?"

"Well, when we left this morning, she was still in my bed." She bites down on her bottom lip.

I gasp and shoot up right to my feet so I'm hovering above her, standing on the beach bed. "Stacy! You naughty, naughty librarian!"

She hides her face in her hands, and her squeal of excitement turns into a groan.

I sink back down to my knees. "Are you freaking out?"

She nods wordlessly.

"Does it feel like your insides are screaming?" I ask like a doctor listing off possible symptoms.

"God, yes. And the thing is, I haven't gone on a solo date yet. Chloe hasn't either. We're definitely the next to go. Top three is without a doubt you, Sara Claire, and Addison. But I just didn't want to be the girl who left because of her ex. The internet would slut shame me the same way they are doing with Anna."

"Oh no," I say. "Did your ex say if it was bad?"

She nods. "Taylor said the Twitter buzz was harsh."

Selfishly, I nearly ask her what she's heard about me. The bits of information I've received from Beck have only made me hungry for more, but Stacy is a woman in crisis.

"Anyway," she says, "back to you and Henry. It's pretty obvious that you two are all moony for each other."

I make a scoffing noise. Nothing here is obvious. Trying to decipher who has genuine feelings and who doesn't is harder than scoping out a fake pair of Louboutins from two blocks away. Even Addison, who is absolutely batshit, might be acting the way she is because she's lovesick. There's no way to know for sure.

"Did you hear Sara Claire on the way here?" she asks. "She sat there the whole time making a pros-and-cons list, trying to talk herself into falling for Henry. He's not even her type!"

"How do you know her type?" I ask. "Her type could be Stanley Tucci for all we know."

"Actually," Stacy says, "Stanley Tucci is everyone's type."

I nod in solidarity. "Amen."

"But really, Sara Claire's type is a guy who grills. And wants to take care of a pool and wears cowboy boots with tuxedos."

"Henry probably owns a grill," I say.

She arches a single brow. "But does he introduce himself as the grill master to guests? Important distinction."

I shake my head. "No, definitely not."

"You two make sense."

Thrill pulses through me at that. Henry and I could make sense. Someone else sees it.

"It's, like, the most fashionable happily-ever-after. TV gold and IRL gold. But that's not what's important. Do *you* like him? It really seems like it."

I lie back on my side and face her with my hands tucked under my cheek. "I . . . sometimes I feel like I don't even know him, and other times I feel so in sync with him that I could predict the next word out of his mouth. But when we're . . ." I hesitate for a moment before deciding not to tell her we've been alone together. I know I can trust Stacy, but being on this show has me feeling like I can never be sure of my footing. "When we're simpatico, it's like when you meet someone new and you should be freaked out by how much you like them, but you're too in it to care."

"What would you do if he proposed at the end of all this?"

It's a possibility. And happens more often than not during the finale. I can't imagine saying no, but I can't see myself saying yes either. Everything around me seems to be shifting. I graduated. I moved. Erica moved. I was creatively blocked for so long, and I can feel something in my brain becoming slowly unstuck. Like all this frenetic movement has forced something loose. And now this new possible future with Henry and a real chance for us to get to know each other in the real world.

But despite all that, there's some kind of hesitation in the pit of my stomach. A shadow of guilt for moving on to this next phase of my life without Mom and Dad. In many ways, college felt like an extension of high school, but that's gone now, and I'm not a child anymore.

I shake my head finally. "I don't know. All I know is I don't want it to end."

"Oof." She laughs.

"Oof is right."

CHAPTER THIRTY-ONE

After Stacy has a few more drinks and accidentally tries to go into Addison's villa instead of her own, I decide to walk her to her door and say good night.

As I'm walking back, I see the camera crew clustering around two silhouettes on the beach in the distance.

Deep down, I know what Stacy said about Sara Claire having a type isn't completely true. She could have said all that just to make me feel better. Still, I feel more confident, like maybe this attraction is shared and not just one-sided. Even now, seeing Henry and Sara Claire on their romantic date from afar doesn't give me the gut-churning feeling I expect it to.

Back at my villa, I find my duvet turned down with a piece of dark chocolate waiting for me on my bed. Definitely beats the barely two-bedroom apartment Sierra and I shared for two years.

I try getting ready for bed, but I'm too restless to sleep, so I start the water in my outdoor tub and order a drink from room service.

I find a lavender bath bomb and throw a T-shirt on to answer the door. I sit perched on the edge of my bed, waiting for my room service to arrive, but a few minutes turns into fifteen and then twenty. The bath is full, and since I'd hate for it to get cold, I leave a note wedged into the door that reads *In the tub, please leave drink here.* This moonlight bath is more luxury than I've experienced in a very long time, so I think I can handle skipping the fruity drink.

Outside, even though the outdoor shower and tub have a large vine-covered partition protecting me from unwanted onlookers, it's still a shock to my senses when I strip out of my underwear and T-shirt. I know that no one can see me, but that doesn't stop me from undressing and hopping into the tub and under the milky bath-bomb-infused water as quickly as I can.

I scoop my hair into a loose ponytail and lean back to take in the starry view. The quiet is so deeply comforting. I let the heaviness of it sink into my bones as I try to find some kind of peace in all this uncertainty.

My thoughts circle back over and over again to my conversation with Stacy. If Henry asked, would I say yes? I don't know. I don't know for lots of reasons, but maybe one of them is Dad. After he died, I kept brushing aside the future, only preparing for as far as my headlights out in front of me could see. The thought of meeting someone—someone who I could imagine myself being with for a long time—felt so distant and impossible. I couldn't see that happening without my parents, but especially Dad, there to witness it all.

But that's not reality. The realization snuck up on me at high school graduation and then again last summer when Erica asked me to sort through his belongings and then last month when I graduated from Parsons. Mom and Dad are gone. It makes me feel awful to even think it, but they are. And I wonder if all the language around grief and your loved one being there with you always makes it that much harder to deal with their deaths.

Sometimes I can't fall asleep at night, because I'm scared that when I wake up some detail or memory will be fuzzier than it was the day before and eventually I'll forget them. But it can't all be woo-woo feelings or morbid reality. When I was in elementary school and Mom died, and then again in high school when Dad died, my everyday life was almost the same. I still went to school and took the bus home. But this adult version of my life? It's my second act—my sophomore collection—and neither of my parents will ever be in the audience. I have to find a way to move through all these new experiences without forgetting them. And I have to find a way to create again. All the pieces are there inside me. They've just been lying dormant for the last year.

"Hello?" a voice calls, interrupting my thoughts.

"Yes!" I say. "You can leave it on the doorstep. Thank you!"

"You don't want it to melt, do you?" There's no mistaking that voice.

My heart skips and my limbs splash as I frantically sink down lower into the bath. "Henry? Don't come in here! I'm naked!"

He chuckles. "Was that supposed to be a deterrent?"

"Yes," I say with uncertainty. "Did it work?"

"Sadly, yes. Don't worry," he says. "I'm staying right where I am. . . . I just . . . I guess I just wanted to see you."

"Well, I guess you'll have to settle for talking." It's been less than twenty-four hours since our steamy make-out session in the early hours of the morning, and somehow it feels like years ago.

"You mind if I eat the cherry out of your drink?" he asks.

I pretend to gag. "Please. I hate those things."

"Excuse me?" he says, his voice steeped in shock. "You hate cherries? How does anyone hate cherries?"

"In fact," I tell him from the other side of the partition, "just take the whole drink. It's been cherry tainted."

"Wow. Okay, well, now that I know where you stand on cherries, I might as well take myself and my cherry-infested drink back to my room for a quiet night in."

"Noooo." I laugh softly. "Don't go."

Silence hangs in the air for a moment as I hold my breath.

"Okay," he finally says.

I can hear the sound of his back sliding down the wall as he sits down in the grass. "Making yourself comfortable?" I ask.

"Well, I'm not open-air-tub-in-a-Mexican-villa comfortable, but this isn't so bad either."

"How was your big date?" I ask, even though I know I shouldn't.

He groans.

"That bad or that off-limits?"

"You know it's just part of being here, right? This isn't real."

"It's not?" I ask, and I know it's too big of a question for either of us to answer, so I quickly change course. "Olives too," I tell him. "Can't stand 'em."

"Okay, well, you've left me with no choice. I choose Zeke."

"Oh, I'm pretty sure someone's already called dibs on Zeke." I clap my hand over my mouth, then remember that he saw them in the pool that night.

"Yeah, he and Anna make a pretty cute pairing. Neither of them is very good at sneaking around, though."

If he only knew. I open my mouth to tell him about all the times Erica caught Anna sneaking out but quickly stop myself.

"Anyone who hooks up in a pool behind a house full of women isn't keeping any secrets," he says.

I don't know how to talk to him about Anna without also telling him that she's my sister, so I return to a proven tactic. "It's not that I don't like olives and cherries. But they have to be fresh. Like, with the pits in them. None of that canned or jarred stuff. Though, on my twenty-first birthday, I ate twenty-one moonshine cherries."

He coughs, choking on his drink a little. "Did you say moonshine cherries? Are you from some kind of Appalachian dynasty? Is that what you're not telling me?"

I fight back a chill as my bath begins to cool. "No Appalachian blood. Just happened to meet some guy from Queens who brewed moonshine in his bathtub." My twenty-first birthday was epic, thanks to Sierra. She has this belief that seminal birthdays should be a quest, so we went on a multiborough hunt for the best baklava money could buy and ended up in some guy's bathroom eating moonshine-soaked cherries.

"I . . . have so many questions, but first: How did he shower?"

"Huh. I hadn't thought of that . . . and I think I don't really want to."

His laugh fades into the quiet darkness, and for a moment it's just the sounds of bugs and breathing.

"Henry?" I ask.

"Cindy."

"Do you regret coming on this show?"

He's quiet at first. "I think . . . I think going back to real life and constantly wondering if people actually take me seriously or if I'll just always be that guy who went on a reality TV show and then let his mother's company flop . . . And when I was on my way here, I thought I was already regretting this whole thing. But now, no matter what happens, I don't think I'll ever regret this. That flight. You being here. I wonder if maybe it's all fate."

"You don't actually believe in fate, do you?"

"I don't know. I think I just might. What else do you call being on the same flight and then the same television show?"

"Coincidence," I offer.

"Oh, come on," he says.

"It's . . . hard for me to believe that something is orchestrating all of these specific moments so that our lives end up just as they were always meant to. I can't help but think that if the universe is playing by the rules of fate, my parents died for a reason. And ovarian cancer . . . a car accident. There's no sense in things like that." I pause, thinking about what he said. "But . . . I don't know. Something about this whole experience does sort of feel . . . meant to be. Then again I don't even know what we are, so maybe this was all just for nothing." There. I said it. The impossible thing. The one thing I don't know.

"Cindy—"

"I have to tell you something," I say. "I need you to know."

"Cindy, whatever it is, it's okay. I want to be the person you need me to be, but I just—I can't promise you anything. Not right now. I know that's not fair, and I wish—"

"I'm here for the money," I blurt. "Or I *was* here for the money. And the exposure for my career. I mean, I won't lie. Winning the money would still be nice, but I—I didn't come here looking for *this*. I didn't come here expecting to find you."

"I guess we both surprised each other, then, didn't we?"

"And you hate surprises," I remind him.

"This one wasn't all bad. Cindy—"

"Shoot," I whisper under my breath.

"What?" he asks, just a hint of worry in his voice.

"It's nothing. I just left my towel on my bed."

"I can get it," he answers quickly.

I can already hear him standing. "Oh—okay."

"No peeking," he promises.

I nod, even though he can't see me. "Okay."

As I listen to him walk around to the front of my villa, I sink down even lower into the tub so that my chin is dipping below the water.

The glass door slides open. "Eyes closed, I swear. What I was trying to say is—" He steps forward and immediately trips on the lip of the door.

"Oh, be careful," I tell him.

Tonight, he wears dark navy shorts with a fitted, purposefully rumpled–looking white Oxford with the sleeves rolled up and brown leather sandals. His eyes squeeze shut as he swallows a curse.

"You okay?"

231

He nods. "Maybe less talking while I'm walking with my eyes shut."

"Okay, one step forward, and then one step down," I tell him.

He follows my instructions cautiously.

"And then two steps forward. Follow my voice."

"Gladly," he says, and suddenly he's looming over me, eyes still shut, with a fluffy towel spread out for me.

"I don't want to get you wet," I say.

His voice is gravelly. "I won't melt."

I hoist myself out of the tub carefully, feeling deeply vulnerable as I stand completely naked before him.

"I'm not looking," he reminds me as though he can read my thoughts.

I wrap the towel around me, and of course, it barely covers anything, and suddenly I'm wishing for the very large, very luxurious towels at our New York hotel.

But my thudding heart begins to slow, and the queasiness in my stomach isn't a result of being so nearly naked with him only inches away, but instead at the thought of him leaving.

"You can open your eyes," I whisper.

He does so, and there's something immediately heavy about his deep brown eyes as they linger on my wet, bare shoulder and then down the length of my body. "Hi."

"Hi."

"Would it be completely crude of me to say that I love your outfit?" he asks.

I lick my lower lip before biting down on it as heat spreads down my chest and into my abdomen.

He holds a hand out for me as I step out of the tub, but the drop down is higher than I expect and I stumble forward.

In a second decision, I decide to hold my towel rather than break my fall.

"Whoa, there," Henry says as he catches me by the elbow. "We can't have two clumsy people in one relationship."

I let out a breathless laugh. "With a shoe collection like mine, I can't afford to be clumsy, so I'll leave that title to you."

"I'd walk into a brick wall for you," he tells me. "Fall into a manhole. My accidental tendencies are at your service."

I look up to him, his broad hands still bracing my forearms. "Was that a pledge of allegiance?" I ask.

He tilts his head farther down as his arms snake around my waist.

I stand on my toes, my towel thankfully staying in place as I wrap my arms around his neck and playfully nip at his lip.

He groans into my mouth, and my entire body melts into his.

"Stay," I plead.

He devours me with a kiss as he slides one hand down the length of my hip and pulls my thigh up, hooking it around his.

An urgency I have no intention of saying no to consumes me, as I pull Henry back inside my villa, the door shutting softly behind us, sealing us in our own private bubble. Neither of us is in the position to promise each other much of anything, but we have tonight.

CHAPTER THIRTY-TWO

The next morning, I wake up in a half-made bed with a pink hibiscus on the pillow next to me and a note written on a scrap of paper in scraggly handwriting that definitely does not match all the various notes we received from Henry at the château.

Couldn't bear to wake you. See you soon. xH.

Last night, I fell asleep to the sight of his chest rising and falling as he slept soundly beside me with his arm pulling me to his side. I was scared to fall asleep, because I knew in the morning, he would be gone. Unless we wanted our secret hookup on national television.

Today is my villa date. One last chance for Henry and me to have "alone" time before I leave for home the moment our date is through. I'll be sent back to LA to wait and find out if I'm in the final three. If so, I'll be invited back to the château for the season finale.

I'm thankful to be going on the second date night, because even though this place is a slice of heaven, I don't think I'd survive watching Henry go out with a new girl every night. I walk outside to find the cleaning crew descending on Sara Claire's room, and my chest twinges with regret as I realize she's gone and I didn't even get to say bye.

After a late lunch, Ash, Irina, and Gretchen get to work, and for the first time I don't micromanage Irina to death as she attempts to dress me. I let them primp and buff and moisturize me until my hair is tossed into loose beach waves and Irina is buckling the strap of my wedge, an espadrille with baby-blue bows over the toe. The dress she's picked out is a sleeveless swiss-dot white sundress. It's the exact thing you'd wear after lounging on the beach all day.

The only thing I semifought them on was the spray tan, but Ash insisted. "You haven't been here long enough to get a glowy tan, and the sun will kill you anyway."

So by the time Mallory arrives at my door in a little golf cart, I look like I'm in full-on vacation mode even if I don't entirely feel it.

As Zeke drives, Mallory sits on the backward-facing second row and looks over her clipboard. "We're looking for lots of moony shots tonight. Lots of staring into each other's eyes and maybe some kisses."

"Wow," I deadpan. "That sounds so romantic."

She waves me off just as we hit a massive bump, the three of us popping up into the air.

"Sorry!" Zeke says, even though he doesn't sound like it and I'm pretty sure he's having a little too much fun manning the golf cart.

"It'll be like we're not even there," Mallory tells me.

"Oh, you mean I've been filming a TV show this whole time? I hardly noticed."

Zeke makes a hard left, and Mallory slides across her bench seat. "This is not *The Fast and the Furious*. You are not Vin Diesel."

Zeke chortles into his fist.

We wind around the property until we pull up to a small private dock where a massive sailboat full of camera crew is waiting. There are actual boat crew too in white shorts and white polos, but my eyes immediately search out Henry, who is watching me despite Beck talking directly to him.

I give him a little wave, and he winks.

"Was that some off-camera action I spied?" asks Zeke.

Immediately, my brain goes into middle-school mode, and I'm

scared I'm in trouble. "What? No. I mean, maybe. We're supposed to like each other, aren't we? Isn't that the whole point?"

"Chill," says Zeke with a laugh.

"Maybe don't tell women to chill," Mallory says as she storms off down the ramp.

"You think she likes me?" he asks once the coast is clear.

I look at him with utter disgust. "Did you really just ask me that?"

"It was a joke," he calls after me, but I've already filed it away in my sister vault. "Don't tell Anna!"

Beck runs up to meet me and takes a quick look at Ash, Irina, and Gretchen's work. "In the immortal words of Jim Carrey, *smoking*!"

I heave in a deep breath. "Thanks, I think."

"You ready for this?" she asks. "You'll be miked up, but it's going to be pretty loud out there, so really we just want some—"

"Moony shots," I finish for her. "Mallory already told me."

She claps a hand on my shoulder. "You're a pro."

"I'm not acting," I mumble as she turns to lead me down the ramp, already a few steps ahead of me.

Henry is waiting for me with a life jacket in hand. He gives me a long hug and whispers, "Good morning."

Chills run up my spine. "Is that a floatation device or are you just happy to see me?"

His laugh tickles my neck. "I've been told we have to go over safety procedures, and then we'll be rewarded with cheap champagne."

"Cheap champagne is key."

He steps back and holds the life jacket open for me. "Ahoy, matey."

"I take safety very seriously," I inform him. "You joke now, but when this ship goes down, you're going to wish you'd paid attention. I'm going to be backstroking to shore with my life jacket on."

"This is taking a serious *Titanic* turn," he says, and cups his hands together. "Bloop."

"Bloop?" I ask. "What is bloop?"

"You know, bloop, there goes the heart-of-the-ocean-necklace thing. That's, like, the ultimate *Titanic* reference."

"Uh, I think not," I tell him defiantly. "Maybe Kate Winslet's hand on the steamy window. Or 'Draw me like one of your French girls, Jack.' Or the band playing as the ship goes down! Or even the door that Jack makes Rose float on. But not bloop. That is not high on the list of *Titanic* pop-culture references."

"I feel like there's a need for more nuance in this conversation than you're willing to allow."

"Quiet, people! Listen to Captain Jorge," Beck shouts.

Henry leans over, and in a loud whisper says, "For the record, there was definitely room for two on that door. Jack died in vain, and I stand by my case, Your Honor."

I gasp. "Oh my God, yes! Justice for Jack! Justice for Leo!" I shout.

Everyone around us is completely quiet as Captain Jorge clears his throat at the sound of my interruption.

"Sorry," I screech as I try for an apologetic smile.

"Oooooo," Henry says just loud enough for me to hear.

"No room on my door for you," I tell him.

After the safety procedures, Beck and Mallory lead us to the front of the boat, where a blanket, chocolate-dipped fruit, and a bucket of champagne are waiting for us.

"Told you there was a bottle of cheap champagne at the end of the safety-briefing rainbow," Henry whispers into my ear.

For a while, the boat crashes against waves until we settle out at sea without any land in sight. We are posed like dolls with a lavender-and-orange-sherbet sunset at our backs, and Gretchen curses under her breath at my hair's unwillingness to obey. Henry and I have nothing left to say in this moment with the cameras rolling, so we say nothing at all.

He leans back with his arms braced behind him, and I lean against his chest as the boat rocks gently back and forth and the sun dips slowly down the horizon.

We share a soft, chaste kiss or two, but for the most part, our silence is comforting and lived-in. I resist yelling over to Beck to ask if we're moony enough for her. She must be happy with whatever footage she's getting, because she doesn't interrupt us or give us any direction at all.

My eyes flutter shut for a few moments, and even though I can't distance myself enough from the cameras and crew and boat staff to actually fall asleep here against Henry's chest, I'm able to let my mind drift just enough that for a few brief seconds I can trick myself into thinking it's just the two of us floating on the *Titanic* door. Because there was definitely room for two.

And maybe—just maybe—fate isn't a total crock. Maybe the fairy tales aren't all wrong.

CHAPTER THIRTY-THREE

The crew follows us as we walk back to my villa, our fingers intertwined as ours hands swing between us.

"Was that awful?" Henry asks.

I shake my head. "For a TV date, it was decidedly not awful."

In the distance, the waves crash and there's enough noise for me to feel comfortable asking, "I'll see you soon, right?" It's the closest I can bring myself to asking him if I'll see him back at the château next week.

He brings my knuckles up to his lips. "Not soon enough."

In front of my door, he wraps his arms around me and kisses me. It's not a television kiss. It's a private kiss, the kind that makes me sure that his decision is made. Henry has picked me. And I've picked him.

"All right, you two," Beck says as we begin to pull apart. "Mallory, escort Henry back to his villa. And, Cin, it's time to go home."

Home. Home. I can't even fathom what real life will feel like. Cell phones and television and the triplets and my stepsisters and my stepmom and Sierra and tabloids and internet. Just the thought of it all makes me feel like I'm drowning.

"Soon," I whisper to Henry.

He links his little finger with mine in a secret pinkie promise.

Inside, my bags are packed except for the leggings, Vans, and cropped sweatshirt I left out.

When I walk back outside with my dress draped over my arm and the baby-blue espadrilles dangling from my fingers, I find Mallory smacking on a piece of gum and waiting for me.

"Where's Beck?" I ask.

She shrugs. "We gotta go. You're on the last flight out, and if you don't make it, you're stuck here until tomorrow."

I hand her the dress and shoes. "Irina wants you to keep the shoes," she says. "And honestly, you could just take the dress too."

"Oh, okay," I say. My complicated feelings about Irina are slowly growing into a soft spot, and I'd like to think she feels the same way about me.

"Will I get to say goodbye to everyone?"

She looks at me, her brow pinched together. "That's not really how this works."

I nod and follow her to the entrance with my two suitcases, my most faithful companions, rolling along on either side.

A black limousine is waiting for me, and the driver hauls my suitcases into the trunk as I stuff the dress and shoes in my carry-on.

"Well," I say to Mallory, and hold my arms out for a hug.

She doesn't move and just eyes me uncomfortably.

"I guess this isn't a hugging situation?"

She laughs a little and shakes her head, before taking pity on me and giving me a quick side hug.

I realize that for the crew, this whole experience is a constant cycle of people going home, but I'm feeling a little more emotional than I expected; I imagined this moment would be bigger, but instead, I'm quietly heading back home to sit by my door and wait for an invitation to the final ball.

I settle into the seat, and we begin to drive toward the gates.

Leaning my head back against the leather seat, I feel a resistance growing in my chest. I don't want to go home. I don't want to go back to the real world. I also don't want to compete with other women for

Henry's attention, but I'm not ready for whatever comes next. There were times in the last few weeks when I couldn't even imagine this moment finally arriving. But it's here and gone. And now so am I.

Behind us I hear a muffled rumbling and a faint scream.

"Sir?" I ask the driver. "Do you hear that?"

The driver looks over his shoulder quickly, but I can tell from his expression that we have a language barrier to contend with.

I roll down the window and stick my head out.

Sure enough, a golf cart is chugging toward us. "Cindy! Wait!" Beck screams. "Wait!"

"Stop," I tell the driver, and he seems to know what I mean, because he slams on the breaks.

I swing my door open and begin to scoot out of the car, but Beck jogs up to the door, leaving Zeke in the golf cart.

"Scoot over," she says. "I'm going with you."

"To LA?" I ask incredulously.

"No, no, the airport. Hurry," she says, motioning again for me to scoot.

She settles in and gives the driver a thumbs-up to continue on. "Privacidad por favor," she says.

He nods once, and the privacy screen separating us from him slowly rises.

I lean over and give Beck a suffocatingly tight hug. "You wanted to say goodbye!"

She croaks a little. "No."

"Oh." I pull back from her.

"Well, yes, I wanted to say bye, but I'm going to see you in a couple days, so not really. I really just needed to talk to you. Privately."

"Is everything okay?" I ask, panic ratcheting my voice higher. "Is it something back home?"

"Everyone is fine. Erica is going a little batty not being here to helicopter-stepmom produce you, but other than that, everyone is fine."

"Okay. So what's going on?"

She turns to me and grips my shoulder. "I have huge news for you. It's the execs. They love you. They weren't sure at first, but seeing the response to you—and our ratings . . . let's just say their love language is numbers and you've got them."

"Well, that's . . . nice."

Beck's face is red and her eyes wide with excitement, like she could burst. "Cindy, they want *you* to be the female suitor next season."

"What?" I'm so confused. I can't quite piece together words. "I thought . . . the show . . . it's not over. I can't be the suitor if—I . . ."

Beck shakes her head. "We've had wifey on lock since the very beginning. That's how it's always worked. Surely you knew that. Besides, that's not the real prize, anyway. Cin, I'm talking a show—a whole show with you as the star. You're already America's sweetheart. Now it's your turn to find *your* sweetheart. Oh my God. I need to write that down. I just gave myself chills."

"Wifey?" Dread begins to settle in my bones like cement, and I feel completely disconnected from this present moment. "What do you mean, wifey?" They don't think I can win? They don't think Henry will pick me?

"Wifey . . . it's just a dumb thing we call the girl who's the sure thing. We agreed on it from the beginning. Even Henry knew. God, probably right after goat yoga. He's agreed to pick Sara Claire. The network execs really love her for the finale. They're pitching a wedding special to Henry right now. They want to tie it all into some LuMac-sponsored thing or something . . . I don't know. I just work with what they give me, and this season it was Sara Claire."

"Does she . . . Surely Sara Claire has no idea."

Beck shakes her head. "Oh God no. At least, I don't think so. Honestly, it doesn't really matter. We're just glad the network decided so early on and that Henry agreed. Really helps us frame our narrative for the season and kind of warm viewers up to—" She stops abruptly as she realizes she's getting into territory I have no interest in. "None of that matters, okay? So listen, go back home and chill for a bit. After this season wraps, we'll bring you in for some meetings. You'll want to get an agent. And . . . pocket money . . . I could probably expense you some pocket money until we settle on a deal for—"

"But what about the finale?" I can feel my eyes begin to water and my breath hitch, like I might start hyperventilating if I don't concentrate on breathing in and out.

"Oh, Cin," she says, her voice fully of pity. "Okay, this was a lot to just drop on you." She nods. "I know that. And I'm sorry. But we can't have you at the finale. We need you to be only slightly hurt, so the audience doesn't think you're rebounding too quickly. And don't worry. We'll coach Henry through his interviews so it'll sound like a really tough decision. After the finale airs, we'll set up a few interviews. You can shed a few tears. Say something like yada, yada, yada, if it couldn't be me, I'm glad it's my friend Sara Claire. You lie low for a few weeks and then boom! Big splashy announcement. Oooo, maybe we could do an exclusive with *People* or *US Weekly*. We could even have Sara Claire come back as a special guest next season. . . . We could do a girl-chat segment . . ." She begins to lose herself and me as she spews idea after idea.

The car stops, and Beck checks her phone. "Oh shit, you gotta catch this flight. Erica's driver will be waiting for you at LAX." She reaches into her back pocket and digs out a twenty and two fives. Using her mouth, she uncaps the pen she slid from her front pocket and scribbles a phone number on one of the fives. "Here," she says and hands me the wad of cash. "Call if anything happens or your flight gets canceled. We've got Mallory watching the airline schedules, though, so if anything happens, we'll send a car."

"I . . . I don't have a phone" is all I can manage to say.

"Ask the airline clerk or, I don't know, but you're going to miss this flight if you don't go now." This time it's her who hugs me. "You're a star, Cindy. America loves you. And I really like you too. I'm proud to call you a friend."

I nod into her shoulder, unable to bring myself to say anything for fear I might burst into tears if I so much as open my mouth. Normally, I'd find the declaration of friendship so charming and endearing, especially coming from her, but I barely even hear what she's telling me.

My door opens, and the driver helps me out. I wheel my bags inside as the car drives off, and wordlessly check in at the counter, showing my ID and going through the motions.

America loves you, I hear her say over and over again in my head.

America might love me, but Henry does not.

CHAPTER THIRTY-FOUR

The hardest part about Dad dying was not being able to say good-bye. The last time I saw him was just like any other time. At least with Mom, despite my age, I knew things were serious and that every time I saw her could be the last. But with Dad, I barely even remember it, honestly. He dropped me off for school. I probably mumbled *I love you too* as I stared blankly into my phone, and that was it.

And now I've missed my chance to really say goodbye again. Henry and I said bye, of course, but that was when I thought I'd be seeing him again in a few days, and that when I did, he'd be picking me. But suddenly it's over, and I'm numb with shock.

Filming up until this point has not been what I would describe as a peaceful or even quiet process. And yet my senses are overwhelmed from the moment I walk into the airport. Cell phones ringing. Crying children up past their bedtime. News reports in English and Spanish. Security guards snapping and pointing at my dazed expression. It's the first time in weeks I haven't been led by the hand to exactly where I'm supposed to be.

On the plane, I'm seated in international business class, where men in golf shorts and their bejeweled arm-candy wives look at me like I'm diminishing the value of their airfare. If my brain wasn't so cluttered and if I had a phone, I'd be furiously texting Sierra. Our imaginary conversation would likely play out like this:

Sierra:
Do they even know who you are? Are they even aware whose
presence they're in?

Cindy:
You mean a recent fashion school grad with no job prospects
and only a brief stint on a cringy reality television show?

And then Sierra would say something inspirational and I would
send her a series of poop emojis.

But I don't have my phone and I don't have the mental energy to
stew over what my fellow passengers think of me, so I plop down in my
seat, drink a cup of tea, and pass out.

Just like when I flew in from New York after graduation, Bruce is
waiting for me. But he's not the only one. A few photographers are circling the security exit like vultures, waiting for any semifamous person
catching a late flight in. But Bruce is a pro. He swoops in, shielding me
with his body from the constant clicking of the cameras.

"Cindy, what can you tell us about the villa?"

"Will we see you back at the château for the live finale?"

"Who do you think your biggest competition is?"

"What do you have to say about Addison?"

"No comment," Bruce barks at them as a staff-only door swings
open just outside baggage claim and Bruce shuffles me inside. "It pays
to know the custodial staff. I'll be right back."

"Awww, come on, man," I hear a paparazzo say as the door shuts,
leaving me in a musty broom closet. Normally I'd have some pithy
LAX joke to make, but tonight I'm just thankful for this gross little
bubble of quiet.

"No dice," Bruce tells him as he goes, I assume, to retrieve my bags.

Even in this broom closet, the world is so much louder than I remember, but I'm grateful to Bruce for helping me ease in. The silence is just as deafening, though, because then I'm just left with my thoughts and the memory that Henry and I are over.

When I get home, Erica is pacing in her kitchen. Her face is bare, and her normally effortless silk robe has been replaced with one of Dad's old T-shirts and running shorts.

The moment she sees me, she rushes to me and pulls me in for a crushing hug. "Oh God, I wanted to fly down and escort you home myself. Beck just barely talked me out of it." She steps back to take me in and sweeps her fingers down the side of my face before smoothing my hair behind my ear. "She said the last date went well. It went well, didn't it?"

I nod. "It was . . . good."

"God," she says, "the network loves you. The higher-ups haven't stopped talking about my hidden gem. Did Beck tell you . . . about the next season? That they're looking at you for—"

I nod. "I . . . think my reality television career might be a one-hit-wonder sort of thing."

She nods slowly. "We can talk in the morning," she says carefully.

And I can't help but wonder what discussions Erica's had and what promises she's made on my behalf.

"Uh—" My voice cracks. "I better go to my room. I need to call Sierra."

She runs a hand up along her slender neck. "I . . . actually locked your phone in the safe . . . I saw you left it in the kitchen drawer."

"You locked up my phone?" I ask.

"Just for the night. I . . . There's a lot to digest, and I wanted you to get just one good night of sleep."

Not gonna happen, I nearly blurt. If my cell phone isn't going to keep me up, my thoughts will. But then I remember how overwhelming just walking through the two airports was, and I think I can manage to last just one more night without my handheld information highway. I finally nod in defeat. "The triplets?" I ask.

"Asleep," she confirms with a soft smile. "Though Gus fought until the very last yawn. I'm sure you'll have them crowded around your bed earlier than you'd like."

"I missed them," I tell her.

"They missed you. And your grilled cheeses."

That gets a smile out of me. I take my bags and head for the expansive sliding glass door leading out into the backyard and the pool house.

"I filled your mini fridge with mineral water and fruit leather," she says. "Do you need anything before bed? A late-night avocado toast? Jana picked up some Ezekiel bread at the store."

"I'm good. I ate on the plane," I lie. I don't know why, but now that I'm with someone from the outside world—even if it's just Erica—all I want is to be alone.

"Oh God, don't even get me started on plane food. It's just dehydrated astronaut—"

"Erica, did you know?" The question is eating away at me. "Surely you knew."

Her brow furrows with confusion.

"Did you know the network was going to have him choose Sara Claire all along?"

She crosses her arms over her chest and leans her hip against the counter. "I . . . did, but, Cindy, you yourself made it very clear you weren't going into this expecting to find anything. This was about visibility for you from the get-go."

"Yeah," I say, my voice flat. "I guess that changed."

"Cindy." The way she says my name is so gentle, just like the night she told me Dad died. It stings, still. "Was it . . . real for you?"

"I'm pretty sure nothing on that cheap ratings-grab excuse of a television show is real. It's trash. The whole thing is trash, and so is everyone who has anything to do with it." The second the words have left my mouth, I regret it. "I gotta go to bed."

Erica masks the hurt on her face by pursing her lips in a thin smile. "Don't forget that you chose this, Cindy. Good night."

The next morning, it's not the triplets who are waiting for me. Instead, Anna and Drew stand hovering over me with multiple cell phones and devices in their hands.

"We can't let her sleep any longer. These requests are rolling in and I can't keep track," I hear Drew say through my foggy, partially asleep state.

"I'm up," I grumble. "I'm up."

"She's up!" Anna echoes.

Drew holds three lattes hugged to her chest. "Oh my God, finally. Have you been online? Talked to anyone? Anything?"

I shake my head, unable to string together many words so soon after waking up.

"We got your phone out of Mom's safe," Anna says as Drew hands me a coffee. "The lock combo was—get this—90210. Is Mom old? Do we need to teach her about how to make good passwords or whatever?"

"Extra whip," Drew says as she plops down on the bed beside me. "I can't believe you're back."

Anna cozies up on my other side. "And that we're all three together again."

They both lean their heads against my shoulder as I take a nice long sip. After a few blinks and a yawn, I manage to say, "I'm so glad to see you both. I am. But did someone say something about my phone?"

Anna fishes a phone out of her sports bra and hands it over. "For safekeeping," she explains.

"I've already sorted your in-box," Drew tells me. "Interview requests, old friends trying to creep in on your newfound fame, job offers, famous or semifamous people reaching out to say hi—apparently, James Van Der Beek is a *Before Midnight* stan; who knew?—and managers and agents looking to pitch themselves to you."

"Wait, how did you know my passcode?"

She coughs up a laugh. "All of that and you want to know about your passcode?" She shrugs. "Your old apartment number was my sixth guess. Speaking of apartments, Sierra called dibs on being the first friend you talk to."

"Noted." I take another swig of coffee and can feel the light board of my brain start to slowly come to life. "Go back a sec. Did you say something about job offers?"

"Yeah, there are a handful. The media interview folder is bursting at the seams, honestly, and I think we should really be strategic about who we give access to."

My thumb begins to scroll through the endless emails. There are so many my hand starts to cramp, and Anna must see the horror on my face, because she softly pats my thigh. "Turns out Drew's calling is publicity. When I got home, everyone wanted to interview me about leaving the show. I guess I caused some waves in the *Before Midnight* universe. Drew was basically my own personal and really well-dressed bouncer but politer and with an email address."

"I feel like I've found my calling," Drew says as she leans back against the headboard and crosses her legs.

"Well," I tell her, "I officially dub you my publicist and agent and manager and whatever else you want."

"Oh, good," Drew says. "Honestly, I wasn't really waiting for you to offer."

"What are you gonna do before the last ball?" Drew asks as she bounces up from the bed. "Go shopping? Get your hair done? Go to the beach? Get a spray tan?"

"I'm not getting an invitation." I look up from my phone to find them both awaiting further explanation. "Beck said so on the way to the airport. I guess Henry knows what he wants, and it's not me. And all I really want to do is just veg out and watch old movies."

"He's dead to me," Drew says, like a switch has flipped in her brain. "Scorched earth. Dead to me."

Anna nods. "His pulse is nonexistent. The doctor is pronouncing the time of death as now o'clock. They're calling the morgue. He's dead." She sighs lightly. "You get dressed . . . not really dressed. Just, like, daytime-pajamas dressed. And Drew and I are on snack duty. Meet you in the main house in five?"

"Deal," I say.

Drew presses a soft kiss to the top of my head, and they both meander to the door as I down the rest of my latte and slither out of bed.

"Oh," I say, stopping them just before they walk out into the backyard. "Thank you both. For being here first thing this morning." I hold my phone up. "And for dealing with this."

"Of course," Drew says, like there's no other place they could possibly be.

CHAPTER THIRTY-FIVE

Anna knows the way to my heart is through peel-and-eat cherry Twizzlers and *The Lizzie McGuire Movie*. (Closely followed by the High School Musical franchise.)

My in-box is . . . daunting. And I can't imagine how much worse it was before Drew got ahold of it. The interview requests range from podcasts with twenty listeners to *Entertainment Tonight* and even a few late-night shows. The messages from old friends and acquaintances are interesting, to say the least. There's even an ex or two and a few elementary school teachers, all of whom I cringe to think have now seen me make out on network television.

Some people I haven't heard from since Dad died. Most are nice and encouraging, but a few are a little passive-aggressive and some are just . . . aggressive. A handful want to know how they can get on the show, and my most recent ex, Jared, emailed just to let me know he's now engaged and that he unfriended me on Facebook because his fiancée was less than pleased to know he had watched a few episodes without telling her.

My thumb hovers over the folder titled Job Prospects (6). This is why I chose to come on the show, isn't it? I wanted to jump-start my career. To get some visibility. Maybe even get that spark back. I've got no boyfriend and no cash prize, but maybe this could be my silver lining. But why do I feel so awful at the thought of landing a job because of the show? I never expected to fall in love.

And there it is. I fell in love. I'm in love with Henry Mackenzie. I always assumed I would have a difficult time knowing if I was in love. What if I didn't recognize the signs? Or what if it wasn't as intoxicating as the whole world has built it up to be? But, for me, it feels very simple. It's the kind of thing I know with just as much assurance as my birthday. It's not something I feel lost in or confused by. It's a truth, and some truths hurt more than others.

I read the email at least twenty-eight times before taking a breath.

Dear Cindy,

My name is Reneé Johnson, and my firm scouts out creatives and helps place them in positions that perfectly match their skill set.

Since I'm sure you're being inundated with offers and requests, I'll be brief and concise.

My client, Crowley Vincent, president of Gossamer, is looking to expand his brand and move into women's footwear. To make that happen, he is in search of a team of fresh, new talent. I'll be honest, you first caught my eye when I was watching over my daughter's shoulder as she was catching up on *Before Midnight,* but after speaking with your advisers and faculty at Parsons, I'm nearly positive that my instincts are spot-on. We would like to bring you to New York for a meeting with Mr. Vincent. This is a time-sensitive offer, so please reach out to me immediately if you are interested. We would need you in New York by Friday, July 16.

Your fan, Renée

Gossamer. GOSSAMER. Holy . . . Gossamer has been around longer than Chanel. They're a men's footwear dynasty, and their designs range from sensible and everyday to extravagant and avant-garde. And with Crowley Vincent at the helm, they've been breaking rules left and right. Last season they included two pairs of heels in their men's line and moved into outerwear.

"What day is it?" I ask over the sound of Hilary Duff absolutely belting it out to a concert of thousands as she pretends to be an Italian popstar.

"Sunday funday," Gus calls from the floor, where he lies on his tummy with his iPad pressed to his face.

"No, like the date," I say.

Drew glances at her phone. "July eleventh."

I have five days to get to New York.

After reading my response aloud over and over again to Sierra over Facetime, I email Renée back, and her assistant immediately books me a red-eye into JFK for Thursday night.

I pack and repack my bag at least six times over the next few days. What do you wear to a meeting that could likely change your life?

I spend the week at home—not leaving once. Anna, Drew, and the triplets keep me distracted enough to avoid the news and social media. I catch up with Sierra, and after I give her the scoop on the show, she does her best to distract me with gossip about random people from school. I barely see Erica, as she's busy working on the two-part finale this week. On Thursday night, the three-hour villa episode will air, followed by a live finale on Friday night. Neither of which I plan on watching.

On Wednesday night, after helping put the twins down for bed, I go back to the pool house and lock the door behind me. It's time to do something I've been putting off for a very long time.

I reach under my bed and pull out the box of Mom and Dad's stuff. After placing it on my bed, I get situated and take a deep breath, looking up to the ceiling for . . . something. A sign. Anything.

"Here we go."

Inside, I find T-shirts of Dad's with my elementary school mascot, the Panthers. There are Mom's favorite slippers. A scrunchie of hers. A well-worn Clive Cussler paperback of Dad's. A folder full of paperwork. Their marriage license, birth certificates, social security cards . . . All the things you forget exist even after a person dies.

At the bottom of the box is a small velvet box. I open it to find three rings tied together with a thin blue ribbon. Their wedding bands and Mom's engagement ring. Tears begin to spill as I imagine the moment Dad tied them all together like this. Surely sometime around when he started dating Erica. He must have taken his ring off then, but I guess I just never noticed.

I slide Mom's rings onto my fingers, despite them being a little too small. I don't care if they stay on my fingers forever. And even though it's big, I wear Dad's ring on my thumb. I'll do something with them tomorrow. Put them away for safekeeping until I find a necklace to wear them on or a special place to keep them.

Underneath the small jewelry box is a small envelope with my name in delicate letters written on it. The handwriting is too soft to belong to Dad, and I immediately recognize it from the birthday cards I'd saved as a child. Mom. A letter from Mom.

The envelope is sealed, and I'm very careful to open it so that I can preserve it as much as possible. Inside is a note card.

My dear Cindy,

I told your father to give you this note on a special day. On a day when he thinks you might need it most. So maybe today is your graduation. Or your wedding day. Or the first day at a new job. Whatever day it is, I wish I were there to witness it.

I could fill pages with all my wishes, but instead I'll just say to you, my lionhearted girl, that you are my wildest dreams come true. And if I had to choose from a full, long life without you and only seven sweet years with you, I'd choose you every time. My greatest hope for you, my love, is that you choose yourself as well. Choose what makes you happy. Things, places, people. Only choose the ones that bring that delight to you. Don't be a hostage to duty or obligation. I didn't carry you and birth you and raise you to waste your precious life on anything except unbridled joy. Choose joy. As I lie here, I can tell you my only regrets are the times I did not choose myself.

Maybe joy isn't always a choice. Maybe things aren't that simple. But then . . . maybe they are.

I love you, my dear girl. I love you.

Watching over you always,

Mom

PS: Cut your dad a little slack. And be nice to the new stepmom. Whoever she is. It can't be an easy job.

I wipe away tear after tear with my thumb before any can drop onto the note card. It's hard to remember my mom sometimes, but her voice is fresh in my head now. Her words whisper in my ear. *Choose yourself.* I hear it over and over again as I fall asleep with her letter clutched to my chest and my parents' rings on my fingers. *Choose joy.*

As I'm splashing around with the triplets one last time on Thursday morning, I hear my text message alert from where my phone sits on one of the loungers with my towel and water bottle.

When I told Erica I was going to New York, I didn't tell her what for. I don't know why. Maybe I didn't want to disappoint her and ruin her plans for next season, or maybe I was scared that I'd go all the way there and not get the job offer. Or maybe I was just still feeling a little bit bad about calling her life's work trash. Either way, Erica seemed a little distant and unbothered, only asking if I needed some pocket money and when I would be home. I lied on both accounts. No, I didn't need any pocket money. (Yes, I very much did.) And I would be home next week. (Despite only having a one-way ticket booked at the moment. Renée insisted we see how things go and assured me that a return flight could be booked at any point.)

Again, my phone chirps. "Okay," I say to the kids, "you three stay in the shallow end while I check my phone."

Mary, who has turned into a cannonball daredevil over the summer, despite her inability to tread water for longer than four seconds, lets out a loud *hmmph.*

After drying my hands off, I sit down on the edge of the chair and pull up my messages.

Erica:
Are you home?

Beck:
Back in LA. Coming by. Get pretty!

After shooting off a quick message to Erica, I flip back over to Beck and my lips curve into a soft smile. Beck might be one of the best things I got out of the whole experience. I've been trying to think of how to break the news to her that I'm not interested in my own season, and if she's coming by today, I'll be happy to get it over with before I leave town.

All dolled up over here, I respond, with an upside-down smiley face.

After another hour of pool time, I herd the triplets inside and send them to get changed while I whip up some goodbye grilled cheeses. I asked Erica to give Jana the day off so I could spend one perfect day with the kids, which was much needed after the reaction I got when I told them I was leaving again. (Gus cried. Mary called me a traitor. And Jack asked if I was leaving again because he'd wet his bed. In terms of guilting, they're all three very gifted.)

I toss one sandwich in the pan while I turn around to prep the other three, and the doorbell rings.

"Great," I say, looking down at my ensemble. Still in my damp swimsuit and a Dora the Explorer towel that doesn't actually wrap around my whole body. "Coming!" I call. "At least it's only Beck," I mutter as I swing the front door open. "You want a grilled chee—"

"Good afternoon, Cindy," says Chad Winkle in his signature tux with an entire camera crew at his back.

Beside me, a man dressed as a herald blows into a trumpet with a flag embroidered with the *Before Midnight* logo.

"I told you to look pretty," Beck barks from behind him. "Let's reset," she calls. "Keep rolling in case we get anything. Hair, makeup, give her that no-makeup-just-out-of-the-pool look. Can we get her a real towel? Irina?"

258

"I don't think towels constitute wardrobe," I hear Irina's voice say from somewhere.

"This is a real towel" is all I manage to say. "And I sent you an upside-down smiley face. Wait. What are you doing here? What are you all doing here?"

"What does an upside-down smiley face even mean?" asks Beck. "That's just a smiley face, but upside down."

"It's like the eye roll of smiley faces," I tell her as I cross my arms over my chest.

Beside her, Mallory sighs. "Do you only answer doors in a towel?"

"A lot of people answer the door while they're wearing a towel," I say defensively.

Bruce's car pulls into the half-circle driveway, and Erica is stepping out before he can put the thing in park. "Did they tell you?" she asks, and then turns to Beck. "Did you tell her?" She looks back to me. "I thought you told her to look pretty."

I throw my arms up and my towel falls down, revealing my mismatched bikini. Roses on top and stripes on the bottoms. "Why do I need to look pretty? What does that even mean?"

Beck turns to me. "If someone in television tells you to look pretty, it means you're going to be on camera."

"Just say I'm going to be on camera," I say, the frustration raising my voice an octave.

"That ruins the surprise," Beck says.

"Being on camera should never be a surprise!"

Chad checks his watch. "Uh, Beck, I've got a thing across town that I need to—"

"Just give it to her," she blurts. "Forget hair and makeup," she calls over her shoulder, and Mallory runs off to relay the message.

Chad stretches his mouth in that way very serious actors do and clears his throat before plastering a sparkling smile across his face.

"Cindy," he says in a debonair voice, "it is with great pleasure that, on behalf of Henry Mackenzie, I invite you to the final ball. Please join us at the château tomorrow morning, where we will be filming the live finale later that night with a live audience. You've made a lasting impression on our suitor, but will it be enough to win his heart?"

My jaw drops as he holds a scroll out for me.

When I don't move, he reaches for my wrist at my side and awkwardly places the scroll in my hand.

"Does it smell like burnt grilled cheese?" the herald asks.

I blink over and over again, waiting for someone to tell me this is a joke.

Behind Beck, Erica nods. This isn't a joke. This is very, very real.

As real as the red-eye to New York I'm booked on tonight.

CHAPTER THIRTY-SIX

E rica shuts the door behind the last of the crew members. "Well, that was exciting," she says.

I don't even know what to say. "I thought—"

She shrugs. "Beck says he was adamant about you being at the finale. Text Beck and tell her to have Mallory call my travel agent. She'll deal with the airline ticket you booked."

I open my mouth to say why that's not possible, but she beats me to it.

"We can fly Sierra out here when filming wraps if you like. A girls' weekend. Or maybe we could rent you two a place in Malibu for a few days. . . ." She pouts a little and touches her fingers to her temples. "I've got a migraine. I'm going to lie down for a bit. One of the execs is hosting a get-together tonight in honor of the villa episode, and I've got Jana coming in to do bedtime with the kids so you can get packed up for the finale. Bruce will pick you up at eleven tomorrow morning."

Still partially wrapped in my Dora the Explorer towel, I make my way back to the pool house, where my fully packed suitcase sits on my bed alongside the dead-parents box. I plop down in my armchair and scroll through my messages—thankful that Drew deleted every single social media app before I could get my hands on this thing.

I want to call someone. Sierra. Beck. Anna. Drew. Even Sara Claire or Stacy. Just someone so that the burden of this decision isn't entirely my own. I need some sort of nudge so that whatever decision I make, and whatever the outcome, I'll be able to look back, and in some far corner of my mind, not take full responsibility.

I know that if what Henry and I share is real, then we are bigger than some silly television show, but I also know that ditching him on live TV to jump across the country for a job interview sends a very clear message.

All he needed to say was *I choose you. You win. We'll still play their little game, but you win.* In some quiet, stolen moment. Just a whisper would've sufficed.

But no matter how many times I dreamed that he would, Henry never said that. He never chose me. After putting my life on hold since graduation, I don't think I can put it off any longer if all that's waiting for me is a maybe.

I sit in the backyard by the pool with my suitcase beside me. Inside, Jana is helping Mary with her bath while the boys unwind with some reading time. My phone lights up, alerting me that Georgie, my Lyft driver, is here. No going back now. At least not without jeopardizing my passenger rating.

I sneak away through the kitchen, holding my breath as the sliding glass door squeaks shut.

After snagging a green juice, I make my escape for the front door, and just as I'm about to step outside, a small voice says, "Cindy?"

I turn around to see my sweet Gus in one of my old T-shirts from high school that I'd made for spirit week that says GO TEAM in black permanent marker.

"Hey, Gus-Gus," I whisper. "What are you doing out of bed?"

He sighs. "I wanted some water. What I really wanted was some ginger ale, but Ms. Jana said water."

I leave my bag in the partially open doorway and rush over to the kitchen. After taking a fresh cup from the dishwasher, I pour a splash of ginger ale in. "Shhh," I tell him. "Our secret."

He drinks it all in one gulp and immediately lets out a quiet burp.

I stifle a giggle and take the cup from him, rinsing it out and filling it with water.

As he's taking a drink and wisely holding the cup with both hands, I squat to get on his level and smooth back his soft curls. "Don't forget to go to the bathroom," I remind him.

He nods dutifully. "Where are you going?"

"I'm going on a trip," I whisper.

He leans in, and his bright blue eyes widen into saucers. "Is it a secret?"

I nod. "Can I trust you?"

"Oh yes," he says without pause. "But do you have to go?"

And that's the question, isn't it? The big question pounding in my head and in my heart. "Yes," I tell him with a firm smile. "I do."

He pouts briefly before putting on a brave face, shoulders pinned back. "I love you, Cin-Cin."

"I love you, Gus-Gus."

"Tell the pilot to do a good job," he says as he turns to walk back down the hallway to his room.

"I'll let him know you said so."

CHAPTER THIRTY-SEVEN

My meeting with Crowley Vincent is at a restaurant so fancy I didn't even realize it existed after living in this city for four years. Le Bernardin is situated in Midtown on West Fifty-First Street, just a block from Radio City Music Hall. When I arrive at noon—9:00 a.m. back in LA—I'm escorted to a private dining room large enough to seat at least eighty people.

I check my phone once more before putting it on silent and out of sight in my camel-colored Madewell tote. The villa episode aired last night, and between sneaking out and catching my flight, I managed to miss it completely, which is just as well. I don't think I could handle seeing Henry and me together for the last time. Just joking on that boat, like I had no idea what was coming.

Inside the private dining room, the tables are bare save for one large round one, which has two settings opposite one another. Crowley Vincent sits with his long legs crossed and dangling at the side of the table. His pointed white crocodile loafers are exquisite and look like they've never seen a walking surface rougher than shag carpet. He wears a white mesh tank top tucked into a pair of tailored green velvet trousers, and hanging like a cigarette between his lips is a felt-tip pen.

He clears his throat and stands, plucking the pen from his lips with two fingers. "You must be Cindy," he says in a severe British accent.

"I am. It's so wonderful to meet you, Mr. Vincent."

"Call me Crow," he insists, pronouncing it like it rhymes with *wow*.

He makes little flighty wings with his hands before motioning for me to sit down. "I'd like to actually eat lunch if that's okay with you."

"Of course," I say, unable to hide the confusion in my voice.

"You'd be surprised to know that no one ever eats lunch at lunch meetings."

"Oh." I laugh. "Well, I pregamed the menu before I got here."

"Oh, do tell," he gushes.

"I think I'm going to take a chance on the halibut."

"Brava," he says. "The pickled beets are a revelation. Did you catch that?" he calls over my shoulder.

I glance behind me to find a sharply dressed woman lurking a few tables behind us. She nods.

"I'll have the salmon," he says.

"Thank you so much for meeting with me today," I tell him. "I'm trying to act as professional as I can . . . but I'm . . . just a really big fan."

"I like people who aren't scared to like things."

That sets me slightly at ease.

"So Renée tells me you're straight off a television show." He says the word *television* like it's a foreign word he's only just trying out for the first time.

"I am. I . . . hope that's not a problem. . . ."

He nods and puffs on his pen, and I get the feeling he's recently kicked a smoking habit. "I saw a highlight reel of sorts. You've got good taste."

"Thank you," I say, trying not to pump my fist in the air.

"In fashion and men."

My cheeks warm with blush, and even though I try to keep my expression neutral, I can't help but think of Henry and where he might be right this moment. A sinking feeling settles in my chest. He's probably at the château on the verge of finding out I've ghosted him.

"Sore subject?" Crow asks. "I guess nothing on television is real, but you had me fooled." He clears his throat. "I assume you've brought your portfolio?"

I reach into my bag to see my phone buzzing incessantly. Streams of messages. Beck. Erica. Missed calls. Drew. Anna. Even Sierra—who knows I'm here and is probably fielding calls from everyone else. I flip my phone over and reach for my iPad and the large portfolio resting against my chair. "Digital or hard copy?"

"Oh Lord," he says, "I do love a woman prepared. Give it to me old-fashioned."

I pass the leather portfolio across the table. "Those are a little rougher than my digital versions."

"I like rough." He taps his pen against his lips. "I've heard good things about you from a contact of mine."

"From Parsons? I really loved my adviser, Jill. She—"

"No, no, a little birdie by the name of Jay."

"Jay? LuMac Jay?"

"Watch out, there," Crow says. "Before they were LuMac Jay, they were Gossamer Jay, and I'm a Scorpio, so once I claim you, that's it. I tried to poach them for this new . . . venture. But they're too good. Too loyal."

As he's perusing my portfolio, I feel like after coming all this way, I owe him some honesty. "Uh, Mr. Vin—Crow, I should tell you . . . I've had a hard year, and my portfolio isn't as up-to-date as I'd like it to be. I just . . . I spent the last year just trying to survive and it didn't leave a lot of brain space for creating. But I think I'm ready to dive back in. I think it's time."

Without looking up, he says. "Use it," he says. "Whatever it is that had you hung up. An ex, a death, or just plain old depression. The best part about crossing any bridge is the chance to look back and be able to fully understand where you came from. You're not a machine. You're

266

not a computer. You're an artist, and any good artist knows life feeds into art and art feeds into life."

I clear my throat. My mind knows he just said smart things that will undoubtedly sink in over the coming days, but my heart and my body are in total overdrive from just being in the same room with such an icon. "I—I really appreciate you taking the time to share that with me."

He snaps the portfolio shut, and my heart drops to my gut. He didn't like it. No one can tell anything about a designer with that brief of a glance at their portfolio. "I, uh, have some other things I could show you if—"

"Renée will reach out soon." He stands and pulls an olive-colored bomber off the back of his chair before tossing it over his arm. "Darla? Darla?"

I nearly tell him my name isn't Darla, but then the woman who took our orders appears behind him, as though she materialized at the sound of her name.

"I'll be in the car. Please have my meal wrapped up to-go for me."

"Uh, I think they just plated—" She stops short. "I'll meet you down at the car."

"De-lightful." Crow turns back to me. "You're interesting. I like interesting. Is your passport up-to-date?"

"Uh, yes," I say, sounding more unsure than someone who was just in another country with a legal passport should.

He's gone before I can say anything else.

I throw my hands up, not entirely certain of what exactly just happened. "What was that?" I mutter to myself.

"He let you order lunch, didn't he?" a voice asks.

I turn around, and Darla is standing there with a brown bag in her hand and her nose in her phone.

"Um, yes," I say. "I can pay for that if I—"

"That means it went well," she says without looking up. "Did they put you in the St. Regis? The late-night room service menu is surprisingly good. Try the sweet potato fries and ask for a side of vanilla glaze."

"Got it . . ." It takes a minute for what she just said to really sink in. She's nearly gone when I say, "I'm—I'm sorry, did you just say this went *well?*"

She slides her cat-eye sunglasses on and glances over her shoulder. "And it so rarely does. Stay and finish your lunch. We have the room for another hour."

As I sit back down in my seat, a waiter brings out my first course. I don't actually know what it is, but it's orange and I'm starving, so I scarf it down in one bite. The only time my lunch has had multiple courses is when I've gone back for a second grilled cheese.

I scoop my cell phone out of my bag to face the music. Normally, in a restaurant like this, I'd be embarrassed to even reach for my phone, but considering I have a whole banquet hall to myself, my etiquette is flexible.

My finger hovers between Erica and Beck in my missed call list. Both of them are going to kill me, but I just can't decide whose wrath will be less.

It doesn't matter, though, because right that moment, my phone vibrates, choosing for me.

"Hi," I say after the second ring.

"Well, I'm glad you're alive," Beck says. "But could you please explain to me why I'm standing here with an empty limousine."

In the background, I can hear people asking her questions. "I've got her," Beck calls out. "She finally answered."

A distinct voice definitely belonging to Erica barks, "For Christ's sake, where is she? Is she okay?"

"Where are you?" Beck asks me, her voice slightly nicer than Erica's. "I'm sending a car."

"I don't think it would get here in time . . ." I say quietly.

"The helicopter, then. Whatever. We're live in five hours."

Honestly, I couldn't even get there by plane if I wanted to. "I'm in New York," I finally blurt.

"As in the state on the exact opposite side of the country?"

"The one and only."

"You're kidding. This is a joke. Ha-ha, Cindy. So funny."

"I'm not. I'm sorry."

"I need you to get your ass to the airport. Pronto. We'll stall. I'll helicopter you in from LAX. It'll be great. The drama of it—"

"Beck, no. I'm not coming. I'm done."

"But you— But what about Henry?"

"He got his wifey," I say, my voice more venomous than I wish. "You said yourself that he wasn't picking me. Why should I show up just to come in second place?"

"Cindy," she says quietly.

"Beck, I have to go. I'm sorry I let you down. Tell Erica that I love her and I'm sorry. I'll explain everything later."

I hang up before she has a chance to say anything else. Guilt racks me completely. I knew this would hurt. I knew giving up the possibility of Henry would be excruciating, but I wasn't prepared for what it would do to Beck and Erica.

CHAPTER THIRTY-EIGHT

"We don't have to watch this," Sierra tells me for the fifty-seventh time.

"If I don't watch it now, I'll just watch it later. And if I'm going to watch it at all, I'd rather it be with you."

"Aw, babe," she says, rocking back against the leather headboard as she touches a hand to her chest. "I'm honored to witness your pain."

After crying through one of most delicious meals I've ever eaten, I showed up on Sierra's doorstep with six pieces of pie and my lucky baby-blue Louboutins that Erica gave me for my high school graduation dangling from my fingers. It takes a certain kind of desperate to walk through a New York City apartment building barefoot, but I did not need to add climbing four flights of stairs in the tallest heels I own to my growing list of struggles today.

After we devoured the pie and I had given Sierra every awful and wonderful juicy detail about my meeting, I explained I had a room booked at the St. Regis for one more night. (I had yet to tell her I would be crashing with her in her bedroom after tonight until further notice, but surely that was implied . . . right?)

Sierra quickly packed an overnight bag and we splurged on a cab to take us back uptown. I don't, by any means, consider myself to be famous, but after the brief airport run-in with the paparazzi and the live finale airing tonight, I didn't want to take my chances with public transit.

At eight o'clock on the dot, the opening credits begin to play, and I see Chad's familiar face. "Tonight is a very exciting night for our *Before Midnight* family," he says with that fake charm. "Tonight we learn which of these lucky ladies will have won Henry's heart . . . and a hundred thousand dollars. But first, let's get a recap of the villa dates to see who sank and who swam."

"Is this, like, the weirdest thing ever?" Sierra asks as a montage of Henry on different dates with each of us begins to roll.

It's so bizarre to see him with Addison and Sara Claire and even Stacy, but then I see Henry and me, the wind gusting on that sailboat, and my heart stops. My wild hair ripples behind me as I laugh, tossing my head back against his chest. That was just last week, and somehow, it feels like a distant memory that I can barely hold on to.

"It feels like I'm at my own funeral, honestly."

Sierra snorts. "For what it's worth, I can't imagine that Addison chick at your funeral."

"Oh, you don't even know. She'd be there with her fake tears and telling everyone we were best friends."

"Ugh, what a leech."

"Yes, thank you!" I loop my arm through hers, and if nothing else, I'm glad I get to endure this with my best friend at my side.

After a commercial break, Chad returns with Henry as they both stand on the steps of the château. Henry wears a deep navy three-piece suit with a matte black tie and matching wing tips. Somehow, television doesn't do him justice, which is probably some sort of crime against nature, because who looks better in real life than they do on camera?

"Was he a good kisser?" Sierra asks. "He's, like, daytime-soap hot."

I frown. "Yeah. Yeah, he was."

She squeezes my hand. "There will be other tongues in the sea."

I smile at her. "Gross, but thank you."

On the screen, a Rolls-Royce pulls up, and after a dramatic pause, Chad opens the door as Sara Claire emerges.

"How are they going to play this?" Sierra asks.

"I hadn't thought that far."

Henry greets Sara Claire with a kiss on the cheek and a long hug. "Is this hug unusually long?" I ask.

Sierra pours a Pixy Stix down her throat. "Do we hate her?"

I sigh. "That would make things much easier. But she's actually really great."

"Boo. Hiss."

Chad congratulates Sara Claire on making it this far and directs her to the house. "Now I think it's time we let the audience see who's in our second car. What do you say, Henry?"

Henry nods as another Rolls-Royce pulls up the hill. This time it's Addison. She slinks out of the car in a black gown with strategically placed cutouts so that she's showing just a hint of under-boob.

Sierra twists her head to the side. "Is that, like, a swimsuit evening gown? Like, a *Sports Illustrated* evening gown? And do you ever wonder how God decided whose bodies would require bras and whose wouldn't?"

"I don't think God had anything to do with those boobs," I say.

She nods. "Fair."

The final car pulls up. My Rolls-Royce—the one that should be carrying me. I wonder if they went with one of the other girls from Mexico or if they scrambled and brought in a previously eliminated girl. Maybe even Drew or Anna.

The driver stops and Chad steps forward to open the door.

But nothing. No one. Dramatic music plays as the camera lingers on the empty back seat.

Confusion knits Henry's brows as he leans down to look inside the limo. "Wha-what's going on? Where is she?"

Chad turns to Henry, a solemn expression on his face. "Henry, I'm

272

sorry to break the news to you like this, but Cindy isn't here. When we invited her to this evening's ball . . . she declined."

Confusion slowly turns to pain as Henry pieces the words together. "Why would she— Where is she? I just need to talk to her. I just—just us— I . . ."

Chad claps a hand to Henry's shoulder. "Everything happens for a reason, Henry. And I think one of those reasons might be waiting inside for you."

I hate seeing this unguarded version of Henry exposed on television. All I want is to shield him from the pain, but he's there and I'm here. I chose to be here. I chose this.

"That was intensely agonizing to watch," Sierra says. "Are you okay?"

"Why would they do that to him?" My chest tightens and tears begin to well. "They knew since this morning. They didn't have to tell him on live TV."

"Talk about brutal."

After the commercial break, Chad returns. He sits in an armchair in the middle of the courtyard with Sara Claire and Addison sitting across from him.

"We're back with Sara Claire to talk about her emotional and deeply meaningful time with Henry at the villa last week. But first, Sara Claire, I'm sure you've now heard about Cindy standing Henry up this evening."

Sara Claire gives a measured nod, and I can see that she's trying her best not to look too excited. She wears a beautiful ivory gown that has just a touch of a train to it. It's very sexy while also very clearly saying *Marry me.* "Poor Henry."

I bristle at that, even if I do share the sentiment. *Breathe in. Breathe out.* Sara Claire is a perfectly good option for Henry, and she's supposed to be the one he chooses anyway. I chose to be here. I chose myself. They'll be happy together, and all I'll have to do is ignore all pop culture news for the next year—maybe two so that I don't have to see any evidence of their love ever again. That's all. Simple, right?

Chad and Sara Claire talk for a while, reminiscing over the villa and her first big date earlier in the season.

"Are you okay?" Sierra asks. "You look like you're way in your head. Like you could be in a Stephen King novel kind of in-your-head moment."

"I'm fine," I tell her.

"Famous last words."

"Well, before we bring Henry back out," Chad says, "let's check in with Addison."

Addison preens and sits up, pushing her shoulders back and her chest out.

"Addison," Chad says. "How are you?"

She flips her long hair over her shoulder as she lets out a soft sigh. "I'm just so heartbroken for Henry. I know that he's got some healing to do, and that he and I have had our share of trials and tribulations, but true love is worth fighting for. So I'm here, Chad, and I'm fighting. I'm fighting a hell of a lot harder than Cindy ever did, because she was never here for Henry to begin with. We all know it. All Cindy cared about was getting her name out there. But I'm not here for fame, Chad. I'm here for Henry."

"Turn it off," I say as I jump out of bed, scrambling to search for the remote. Red-hot anger pulses through my veins. How dare she say that? "I can't afford to replace this TV if I break it. We have to turn it off."

"I'm on it! I'm on it!" Sierra springs to action and runs right for the outlet, pulling the plug completely. "It's off," she says, holding the plug up in her fist.

I let out a shaky sigh. "Okay, okay, I'm fine."

We both fling ourselves back onto the bed. "What now?" I ask.

"Room service?" Sierra offers.

"I hear the sweet potato fries are good. And ask for a side of vanilla glaze."

She rolls over and reaches for the phone on the nightstand. "You got it."

As I'm lying there, listening to Sierra place her very detailed and extensive order, my phone rings.

I let it go to voicemail. I can't right now.

Sierra hangs up and in her most serious voice says, "I really hope you don't have to pay for all the food I just ordered."

"Gossamer is footing the bill. It can't be more than the most expensive private lunch of all time I had earlier today."

"Is that a challenge?" she asks.

My phone begins to ring again, and this time I sit up to answer. Maybe it's an emergency. "Everyone I know is watching this show—"

"Could be about the job," Sierra says.

"Yeah, at ten o'clock at night."

"Fashion never sleeps."

I look down to see Beck's name lighting up my screen. "Hello?" I ask into the phone. "Beck?"

"Where is he?" she asks. "Do you know where he is? Has he tried to call you?"

"Has who? What's going on?"

"Are you literally the only American not watching this damn show right now? Henry is gone. He's MIA. The suitor is missing. I repeat: The suitor is missing."

I gasp. "Oh my God."

"What?" Sierra asks.

"Turn on the TV. Turn on the TV!"

"Ugh, first you want it off. Then you want it on." She forces herself

275

out of bed and begins to fidget with the plug and then the remote. The TV screen is static, and clearly, we've somehow reset it after ripping the plug from the wall.

"I don't know where he is," I tell Beck, but the line is already dead.

"Ho-ly shit," Sierra says as the TV comes back to life.

On the television, Sara Claire is sobbing with her back to the camera, and Addison is on an absolute tirade, demanding to know where Henry is. Chad is arguing with Beck, and the whole thing is being televised.

Chad crosses his arms. "So you're telling me you don't know where this guy is? Literally one of the most heavily guarded reality television stars, and he just up and disappears?"

"Should I remind you that we're live?" Beck asks.

"We're back from commercial," Mallory snaps.

Beck gives Chad a *do something* look.

Chad turns to the camera, a crazed look in his eyes and hair disheveled. "Well, folks, it appears we've got a missing person to report. Anyone want to put an AMBER Alert out on Henry Mackenzie?"

"Maybe it's not the best time to make jokes about abducted children," Sara Claire says through her tears.

"Does this mean no one wins the money?" Addison asks.

Chad looks to Beck, and she shrugs and nods.

"What a crock," Addison says before storming off past the camera.

Chad begins to laugh maniacally, going from American dad to American psycho in record time.

Sierra turns to me. "I think you just broke Chad Winkle."

THREE
WEEKS
LATER

CHAPTER THIRTY-NINE

At first, Henry was on every tabloid and gossip website. #MIAsuitor was trending for three days with one particularly memorable Twitter account posed as a fake tip-line, tweeting Henry spottings everywhere from Mount Rushmore to a Sbarro's in Iowa.

Part of me thought he would turn up at the hotel or that I'd see him on the street somewhere, but every night when I go to bed, my hope that I might see him again diminishes a little bit more.

I'm on a first-name basis with most of the staff at the St. Regis. Sierra offered to let me stay in her room with her, but as part of my Gossamer contract, Erica insisted that I push for them to cover moving expenses and housing for the first six weeks. When I haven't been at work or apartment hunting, Sierra and I spend most nights at the pool or in the hot tub. Luckily, last week I found the perfect place in Park Slope. When I told Sierra I wouldn't be in Manhattan, she acted like I'd just cut off one of her fingers, but she quickly decided that this just meant she had a place to crash in Brooklyn.

I do a quick lap around my hotel room to make sure I haven't forgotten anything. Earlier, I found a shoe stashed under the bathroom sink, so there's no telling what I've left behind. I touch my hand to my neck once more to make sure my necklace is still there. I found a heavy-duty corded gold chain to hold my parents' rings. I wear both their wedding bands around my neck every day on a long chain along with my locket, and I left my mother's engagement ring back at Erica's for safekeeping.

"All clear," I mutter to myself as I pull out the bedside drawer. Whatever I might have left behind belongs to the St. Regis now, as far as I'm concerned.

After work today, I'm leaving for a two-week seminar in Italy with the new women's footwear team, some of whom are industry giants and others who are just as green as I am. It's all a little intimidating, but I've already made a few work friends, which Sierra is very impressed by. (Of the two of us, she was the only one who ever attempted to expand our friend group.)

As I step into the elevator, my phone vibrates. "Hello?"

"Oh, Cindy, I wasn't expecting you to answer. I was just going to leave a voicemail," Erica says in a hurry.

"I'm just now leaving for work. What's up? Isn't it, like, five thirty in the morning there?"

"I'm trying a new hot-yoga class with Drew, and the only time we could get in was the six fifteen class. Anyway, I'm in the car, so apologies for the road noise, but what was the apartment number again?"

"One thirty-four," I tell her.

"Oh, darn, I could have sworn it was eleven thirty-four. I'll have my assistant call and fix it. I've got a delivery company all set to deliver your wardrobe when you return home from Italy. I'm planning on coming out that weekend so we can go furniture shopping?"

"Erica, you really don't have to do that. Sierra and I can take her uncle's truck out to an IKEA."

Erica clicks her tongue. "I'll not have you furnishing your first adult apartment with Scandinavian particleboard, thank you very much."

I sigh into the receiver. "You know you can just come visit. You don't have to use furniture shopping as an excuse."

The day after the finale, I called Erica to apologize, and slowly over the last few weeks she's warmed back up to me. It doesn't hurt that the show has been the talk of the town since that night, but we're still trying to find out how our relationship functions post *Before Midnight*. She was also impressed to know that I'd run away from home for the sake of a job interview.

Erica is silent for a moment. "Thank you. Noted."

"How is—"

"Have you heard from him?" she asks, interrupting me.

"No," I say glumly as I step out of the elevator. "Any word on your end?"

"Only from his lawyers," she says matter-of-factly.

"Is the network really that upset about him disappearing that they need to involve legal? It's probably some of the best ratings they've ever seen."

"You're not wrong," she whispers as though someone is spying on her in her own car. "To be honest, it's the highest finale numbers we've seen since the first season."

"How's Beck recovering from her prime-time debut?" I ask.

"Well, Mallory taught me how to send GIFs over text message, and apparently Twitter deemed the death stare Beck gave Chad highly GIFable, so I've found a great deal of pleasure in communicating via GIF only."

"I'm sure Beck is really enjoying that. Hey, I've got to check out. Can I call you when I get to the airport later tonight?" I ask.

"Yes, please. The kids are dying to talk."

"It's a date," I say.

After we hang up, I head to the reception desk, and Lydia, the manager, comes around to give me a hug and wish me good luck. She'd watched the show and even asked me to sign her eleven-year-old daughter's autograph book.

There have been a few moments like that. Getting recognized on the subway or in line for coffee or in the hotel lobby. But for the most part, New York is a good place to disappear. Recent fashion school grad turned reality television star is just another square on someone's NYC bingo card.

On my way to Gossamer, I make a quick stop. Unlike the first time I visited LuMac, there are no paparazzi or producers or film crew. The storefront has been converted back from a runway to its usual flagship layout.

When I knock on the glass door, the tall, slender salesclerk who definitely overslept this morning ignores me. I try again, rapping my fist a little harder. This time, she looks up and rolls her eyes before marching to the door and pointing at the store hours.

I glance at my phone. It's only nine o'clock, and they don't open until ten, but there's no way I'll be able to make it across town on my lunch hour.

"I need to speak with Jay!" I yell through the glass. "I'm a friend." Then more quietly, I add, "Sort of."

The girl points to her ear and mouths, *I can't hear you*, even though she so obviously can.

"I said"—yelling even louder and feeling like an absolute lunatic— "I'm a friend of Jay's."

She holds her hands up and shrugs before walking away.

"Hello, friend."

I spin on my heel. "Jay!"

"I hear we're friends," Jay says playfully. Today they wear a blue-and-white seersucker romper with a pair of Gucci sneakers. It's the perfect summer-in-NYC outfit.

"I think I scared your store manager."

They shiver. "Nothing could scare that troll. You know she once told Lucy herself that she couldn't take more than six pieces into the fitting room."

My eyes widen. "And she still works here?"

"Would you believe that Lucy thought she was kidding and gave her a bonus for her dry sense of humor?"

"That's a thing people give bonuses for?"

Jay smirks. "Not on my watch. I'm guessing you're not here to give me all the latest Gossamer gossip."

"I could?" I offer.

Jay reaches for my hand and cuts right to the bone. "He still hasn't been back to the office."

"You'll let me know when he has?"

Jay's smile droops.

"I guess it makes sense that he'd get you in the divorce," I say.

"Honey, I belong to no one. But you've got to understand, Henry's spent most of his life playing second fiddle to someone's career."

"So he knows, then? He knows why I wasn't there?"

Jay narrows their gaze. "You're a real sneaky one, aren't you?"

"Hey, you can't blame a girl for trying to read between the lines." I push my sunglasses up into my hair so that they can see my eyes and, somehow, I can hypnotize them into delivering this message for me. "Listen, I'm leaving tonight for Italy . . . I don't expect to see him before then, but can you just tell him that I'll be back . . . and at the very least, I'd like to talk about what happened. To apologize."

They nod pointedly. "I can't promise anything, but have a safe trip. Think of me wasting away at the Olive Garden in Times Square while you feast on fresh pasta."

"Hey, when you're there, you're family. And yes, I'll clean every plate," I tell them. "Just for you."

***

The Gossamer offices remind me of my classrooms at Parsons. I have my own work desk complete with all the technology I could ever need and my own personal cobbler station so that I can craft prototypes before sending them off to our manufacturer for official samples.

Beside me is Freja, a Danish designer fresh out of school in London. We've been practicing a few Italian phrases every day at lunch, and she's convinced that I'm going to meet a great European rebound guy in Italy. Multiple rebound guys if she gets her way.

"Buongiorno, Cindy!" she calls over her shoulder. "I'm running home to get my suitcase at lunch, so maybe we can get to the airport a little early. Get a little vino to kick off the trip?"

"You know this is a work trip, right?" I remind her.

"You Americans are such prunes," she says.

I let out a snort.

"What? Did I say it wrong?"

"I think you were going for *prudes*." I sit down at my desk and pull out the shoe I've been pecking away at for the last few weeks. Even though most of us have been in the office for a little while now, our team doesn't officially assemble until the trip to Italy, so when we're not doing HR trainings, we've all been encouraged to just . . . play.

My phone chimes, and I find a text on my group thread with Sara Claire and Stacy.

Stacy:
What if I told you I was already moving back in with my ex?

Sara Claire:
RED ALERT TOO SOON

Cindy:
Meh. Life is short.

I got their numbers from Beck a few days after the finale. That night, the three of us talked over a video call for almost five hours. I told them everything. Meeting Henry on the plane. Erica. My parents. Anna and Drew. And it turned out Sara Claire and Stacy had secrets of their own. Sara Claire's father had bribed someone on the craft service's team to give her a cell phone, and of course Stacy spilled all the details about her ex crashing our hotel room.

Sara Claire was upset at the finale, of course, but has fully embraced her status as America's new favorite meme. Since I've bowed out of the next season, it looks like Sara Claire is being eyed for my position. She's already made it very clear that the only person choosing the winner will be her. And Stacy is happy to be back to life as normal, though Beck has already reached out to say she'd love to have her on her queer take on *Before Midnight*, which was just greenlit, should Stacy's girlfriend ever once again become her ex.

Since that marathon video chat, the three of us have stayed in constant touch, and Sara Claire is already demanding we rendezvous in Austin for a girls' weekend.

I drop my phone back in my bag and return my focus to my workstation. In school I never really did much menswear, but in my free time over the last few weeks, I've been challenging myself to try. After rolling my suitcase under my desk, I open my sketch pad to the page I've revisited over and over again the last few days.

At the top in a soft script, I've titled my design *The Henry*. Below that is my sketch and fabric sample. A deep blue suede loafer with a slightly pointed toe and a super-soft brushed finish with a tassel on top. They're more extravagant than my Henry might wear, but the details remind me of him. Refined and polished and bold without being too loud or taking themselves too seriously.

Crow was right. Crossing one bridge had allowed me to look back and see all that I had been through, and when I sat down to sketch a few days after the finale, things started to feel more and more natural. I was designing again. Really designing. Some of it was bad. Some of it was okay. And some of it was even great. But I was thankful for it all. Most importantly, I was relieved to have the thing that brings me so much joy back in my life. I think for a while there, I began to wonder if I'd made it all up, and that the inkling of talent that had gotten me through the first three years of fashion school was just a fluke.

"Did you find that tassel I dug up for you?" Freja asks.

"No." I turn around in my chair to see a soft navy tassel next to my keyboard. The tassels are thick—not too delicate—and remind me of the ropes from the sailboat that last night. "This is perfect," I tell her.

I pull the shoe out from the cubby beside my desk where we can keep our current works in progress. It looks like an old card catalog, except the drawers have been replaced with shoes.

The shoe I've been working on is rough-looking to the naked eye. Exposed seams. Obvious shoe nail tacks. But I can see what it's supposed to be. I can see the potential, and this tassel is the crowning finish.

CHAPTER FORTY

At the end of the day, as Freja and I are walking down the street with our suitcases to catch a cab, she begins to frantically pat down her pockets and dig through her bag. "I forgot it. Damn it. I can't believe I did this. Or I left it at the office."

"Forgot what?" I ask. "Whatever it is, we can just buy it when we get to the airport."

"Unless you know a guy who's selling Danish passports out of JFK, I need to run home."

"Honestly, that's not such a far-fetched business idea," I tell her.

My joke doesn't ease the panic in her eyes.

"Okay, you run home," I say in my most soothing voice. "You're just a few blocks away. I'll run up to the office and check there. Leave me with the bags, and I'll make sure we have a car waiting for us when you get back. Airport vino can wait."

She nods and sprints off down the street.

I roll both of our suitcases back into the lobby and take the elevator up to the forty-fourth floor. I walk through the waiting room and wave to Carlos, the receptionist, as I pass his desk. He's on the phone but gives me a puzzled look. "Freja forgot something," I whisper.

The whole floor is empty, except for one desk—my desk.

My work lamp is turned on, illuminating him so that I can't miss him—not that I ever would.

"Henry," I say, his name sucking the air right from my lungs.

He looks up with a sad smile spread across his lips, and the constant five o'clock shadow I left him with has turned into a slight beard. "I—I thought you'd gone."

"I had . . . I am . . . I just— My friend forgot something, so I . . ."

"Do you permanently live out of suitcases?" he asks. "Or do you just like to keep a collection of shoes on your person at all times?"

"Still a smartass," I say.

"Turns out reality TV didn't bleed my whole personality dry."

"Lucky me." I take a few steps closer, hesitantly. I feel like I've trapped a wild animal, and I don't want to run the risk of spooking him. "Did Jay tell you where to find me?"

"Among other things. Honestly, I was just hoping to leave you something for when you got back." He sits down on my stool. "Congrats, by the way. Gossamer is a pretty big deal. They're lucky to have you."

"Thanks." My pulse quickens the closer I get to him, and I wonder if he feels it too—that electric excitement that comes when it's just the two of us, like we still have a whole production crew and house full of women to hide from.

He holds up a glossy white shopping bag with *Jimmy Choo* spelled out across the front in delicate gold letters. "I thought I'd bring you a peace offering. I've got to get back to work eventually, and it turns out fashion is a small business, so what better way to clear the air than with shoes?"

"You're speaking my language," I say, tiptoeing closer so that we're only a foot apart.

"Erica is my stepmom," I tell him. "I wanted to tell you the whole time."

He nods. "Beck told me."

"What?"

"Yeah, I, uh . . . When I wasn't working on the show or putting out fires at work, I was duking it out with the network execs over 'wifey.' God, is that just the worst word of all time or what?"

"*Moist*," I say. "But after that, yes, *wifey*. But you wanted to choose me? Why didn't you just tell me?"

"I didn't want to promise you anything I couldn't deliver on," he says. "Contracts had been signed. They wanted me to propose. To Sara Claire? Can you imagine? I barely even know her. I said yes at first, because, yeah, I liked you, but I went on the show to save LuMac. They promised me things that . . . well, things that could have saved the business overnight. Featuring LuMac in all their programming and productions. Runway sponsorship. Prime-time commercial spots. But, uh, I pretty much ruined all that."

"What now?" I ask. "What happens to LuMac?"

"The show gave us a boost. That's for sure," he says. "It's not the big splashy deal the network offered. But we're out of the SOS zone, and we've bought ourselves enough time to figure out how to move LuMac into the future. And we get to do it without selling out to Hollywood, which makes Mom happy."

"You and Jay are a force," I tell him.

He runs a hand through his disheveled hair, long overdue for a cut. His jeans are worn, and his white T-shirt is likely nothing more than an undershirt. I wonder if all the suits were Irina at work, and if this is the real Henry. Threadbare jeans, T-shirts, and Converse. This is much closer to the version of Henry I met on the plane. "Well, I thought my peace offering was splashy, but I guess you one-upped me." He motions to my open sketch pad, where my Henry-inspired design is on full display.

My cheeks flush with mild embarrassment at the thought of him seeing my work and the fact that it's so heavily inspired by him. I reach past him for the prototype, and a vein in his neck jumps as my waist grazes the side of his arm. "This isn't even a sample," I say. "Just something I've been fooling around with, but, Henry, meet . . . the Henry."

He takes the shoe in his hand, running his thumb along the

289

material so that he can feel both the rough and smooth sides of the suede. "Do you mind?" he asks, looking down at his own feet. "They look to be about the right size. And then I could say I'd tried on a Cindy original."

"I'd be honored," I tell him as I take the shoe from him and drop to one knee. Carefully, I untie the laces of his well-loved all-white Converse. Looking up to him, with my shoe in hand, I ask, "Ready?"

He nods as he slides his foot in, his heel popping perfectly into place.

"It fits," he says, a lilt in his voice.

"It looks perfect on you," I say, trying not to sound as sad as I feel. "Henry?"

"Yeah?"

"I'm so sorry. I'm so sorry I wasn't there. I just . . . I didn't think you would pick me, and I couldn't risk missing out"—I motion around to this beautiful space—"on all of this."

"Don't you be sorry," he says with force, pulling me to my feet so that we're only a breath apart. "I'm the one who's sorry. I was trying to save LuMac and play my cards just right when I should have just been up front with you all along. Cindy, it was always you. It was you from the moment we met outside of our gate at JFK."

"But—but then why did you agree to choose Sara Claire to begin with?"

He shakes his head. "I didn't think it could be that simple. Surely, I wouldn't just meet the girl of my dreams on a flight and then that would be it. I just . . . wanted to be the son who saved the day. But I can't be that for them. For some twisted reason, I thought that if I couldn't save LuMac for my mom, then I didn't deserve you. But if I'm going to save LuMac, it has to be because of my own vision. Not my mother's." He reaches up and pushes a loose hair back behind my ear. "I just didn't see you coming. I didn't know someone like you could exist. Cindy, being with you makes me feel like I can come up for air."

"Are you sure you're not in love with Addison?" I ask.

He scoffs and rolls his eyes.

"Well, you didn't kick her off when you had the chance."

"Oh," he says, "I swear the network—your stepmother included—was about to behead me if I didn't keep her. Then Anna fessed up, and I figured, what the hell? I'll give them this one thing to make them happy."

He gathers my hands in his, and I look up to meet his gaze and lose myself in his deep brown eyes.

"But the real question is, are you sure you can get romantically involved with your competitor? That won't be a conflict of interest?" I ask.

He leans into me, nipping at my bottom lip. "I think I can handle the pressure, but I can always check with HR real quick." He holds his phone up to his ear, not moving an inch from me. "Hello? HR? This is your boss. I've got a hot new girlfriend, and she works for a competing brand. Oh? What's that? You don't care. Okay, good."

"I'm less concerned about HR and more concerned about your mother," I tell him.

"She and I have had some time over the last few weeks to talk through a lot. She's a bigger fan of yours than you think," he says, and parts my lips against his as his arms coil around me. "Are you really leaving?" he asks into my mouth. "Right now?"

I nod. "I'm running late, actually."

"I'm very good at missing flights . . . and disappearing. I'm good at that too."

"You feel like disappearing this weekend and meeting me in Italy?" I ask, my lips brushing against his as we kiss with every syllable.

"My disappearing act has been known to go on the road."

"I'll be back in two weeks," I tell him. "But I guess we'll have to see if you make it past the first elimination."

"The competition stands no chance," he says as he pulls me tightly against him.

"Oh, and I'm moving to Brooklyn."

"Well, that's it," he says with a playful smile. "We're over."

I still don't know if I believe in fate and if everything happens for a reason, but I do know that the best thing I can do is find purpose in everything, as well as joy, like Mom wrote all those years ago. Whether it's living as fully as I can to honor my parents or if it's just being thankful for the friends and connections I found on a silly reality television show. Anything can have a purpose. Anything can have a meaning if you make the choice to give it one.

I grin into his lips. "Henry?"

"Mon petit chou?"

"What's in the shoe box?"

"Shoes, of course. A very memorable pair of shoes."

"And they're really for me?"

"If the shoe fits," he whispers.

ACKNOWLEDGMENTS

I'm still pinching myself over the fact that I got to write this book. As a child, I spent so much time obsessing over Disney princesses, but especially Cinderella. The slippers, the dress, the carriage, the music, the Fairy Godmother. It was all so magical. Having the opportunity to reimagine this iconic tale with a modern-day twist, and with a heroine like Cindy who is plus size (and much closer in size to the average American woman than the original Cinderella) and navigating grief while finding her purpose and even falling in love has been a dream come true for me. Just like the original says, "A dream is a wish your heart makes," and this dream wouldn't have come true without some truly amazing people.

Thank you so much to my editors, Jocelyn Davies and Brittany Rubiano. Jocelyn, thank you so much for having faith in my vision for this modern fairy tale and for imparting endless *Bachelor* wisdom to me. Thanks to you, I've upgraded from casual observer to an involved citizen of Bachelor Nation. Brittany, I'm so grateful for your kindness and patience, especially as I tried to figure out how the heck to write a book during a global pandemic. (Lots of homemade bread, Zoom, and old seasons of *The Bachelor*.)

To my agent, John Cusick, thank you for always being my partner in crime and for wearing any hat I need you to on any given day. (Though I shouldn't be surprised. You have excellent fashion taste.)

The whole team at Disney has been so warm and welcoming. Your enthusiasm for me and this book has been absolutely overwhelming. Thank you especially to Tonya Agurto, Kieran Viola, Jennifer Levesque,

Cassidy Leyendecker, Seale Ballenger, Lyssa Hurvitz, Dina Sherman, Elke Villa, Holly Nagel, Tim Retzlaff, Danielle DiMartino, Monique Diman and the rest of the Sales team, Sara Liebling, Guy Cunningham, Jody Corbett, Jacqueline Hornberger, David Jaffe, Dan Kaufman, and Ariela Rudy Zaltzman.

I am in love with the cover for this book and the great deal of attention spent on bringing Cindy and Henry to life. Thank you to Marci Senders for your vision and to Stephanie Singleton for your art.

I wrote this book in 2020, and no one could have prepared me for the type of year we would have. My friends and family are such a support system for me, and we had to all find creative ways to be there for one another. Even though we've spent much of the year apart, I feel closer and more supported by you than ever. Thank you to Bethany Hagen, Natalie C. Parker, Tessa Gratton, Ashely Meredith, Ashley Lindemann, Luke and Lauren Brewer, and Kristin Treviño.

Mom and Dad, thank you so much for buying me the Disney storybook-cartoon VHS tapes that were such an important part of my childhood. I'll never forget the magic of watching *Cinderella* for the very first time at Nanny's house while I sat on the floor far too close to the television. Thank you for always letting me believe I could be the princess and the hero.

Thank you to my extended family—Bob, Liz, Emma, Roger, Vivienne, and Aurelia. I wrote this book for lots of reason, and one of them was definitely so that my nieces could have bragging rights, so live it up, girls! Auntie Julie loves you.

Dexter, my dog and the best boy, and Rufus and Opie, my mischievous kitties, I love you three so much.

Ian, thank you for always being my biggest inspiration. If I had to be quarantined with anyone, I'm glad it was you.